FROM WHENCE IT CAME
D.E.S.A. Files #3

Christian Warren Freed

Copyright © 2024 by Christian Warren Freed

Cover design by BroseDesignz
Author Photograph by Anicie Freed

Warfighter Books
Holly Springs,
North Carolina 27540
https://www.christianwfreed.com

First Edition: January 2023

Library of Congress Cataloging-in-Publication Data
Name: Freed, Christian Warren, 1973- author.
Title: From Whence It Came/ Christian Warren Freed
Description: First Edition | Holly Springs, NC: Warfighter Books, 2021. Identifiers: LCCN 2024900236 | ISBN 9781957326412 (hardcover) | ISBN 9781957326405(trade paperback)
Subjects: Urban fantasy | Fantasy | Dragons and Mythical Creatures

Printed in the United States of America

10 9 8 7 6 5 4 3 2 1

ACCLAIM FOR CHRISTIAN WARREN FREED

THE LAZARUS MEN AGENDA

'This sci-fi noir adventure thriller has mystery, suspense, and plenty of action. A page turning, fun ride from the first page to the last'- Entrada Publishing

'Reminiscent of Tom Clancy or Stephen King, where you can envision everything happening in an era that don't yet exist but feels as familiar as the room you're reading in at the time.'

'The author draws us into a world full of conspiracy in which those who have everything want even more because human greed for power is too great.'

HAMMERS IN THE WIND:
BOOK I OF THE NORTHERN CRUSADE

'Freed is without a doubt an amazing storyteller. His execution of writing descriptive and full on battle scenes is second to none, the writers ability in that area is unquestionable. He also drags you into the world he has created with ease and panache. I couldn't put it down.'

'Gripping! Hammers in the Wind is an excellent start to a new fantasy series. Christian Warren Freed has created an exciting storyline with credible characters, and an effectively created fantasy world that just draws you in.'

DREAMS OF WINTER
A FORGOTTEN GODS TALE #1

'Dreams of Winter is a strong introduction to a new fantasy series that follows slightly in the footsteps of George R.R. Martin in scope.' Entrada Publishing

"Steven Erickson meets George R.R. Martin!"

"THIS IS IT. If you like fantasy and sci-fi, you must read this series."

Law of the Heretic
Immortality Shattered Book I

'If you're looking for a fun and exciting fantasy adventure, spend a few hours in the Free Lands with the Law of the Heretic.'

Where Have All the Elves Gone?

'Sometimes funny and other times a little dark, Where Have The Elves Gone? brings something fresh and new to fantasy mysteries. Whether you want to curl up with a mystery or read more about elves this book has something for everyone. Spend a few hours solving a mystery with a human and a couple of dwarves - you'll be glad you did.'

Other Books by Christian Warren Freed

<u>The Northern Crusade</u>
Hammers in the Wind
Tides of Blood and Steel
A Whisper After Midnight
Empire of Bones
The Madness of Gods and Kings
Even Gods Must Fall

<u>The Histories of Malweir</u>
Armies of the Silver Mage
The Dragon Hunters
Beyond the Edge of Dawn

<u>Forgotten Gods</u>
Dreams of Winter
The Madman on the Rocks
Anguish Once Possessed
Through Darkness Besieged
Under Tattered Banners
A Time for Tyrants
A Good Day For Crows*

Where Have All the Elves Gone?
One of Our Elves is Missing
From Whence It Came
Of Elves and Men*
Tomorrow's Demise: The Extinction Campaign
Tomorrow's Demise: Salvation
Coward's Truth
The Lazarus Men
Repercussions: A Lazarus Men Agenda
Daedalus Unbound: A Lazarus Men Agenda*

A Long Way From Home+

<u>Immortality Shattered</u>
Law of the Heretic
The Bitter War of Always
Land of Wicked Shadows
Storm Upon the Dawn

The Children of Never

SO, You Want to Write a Book? +
SO, You Wrote a Book. Now What? +

*Forthcoming   + Nonfiction

One

Tavis Halfhand drew his sword, the iron blade singing as it tore free. Drawing a steady breath, the hero watched as a pack of goblins, their green skin dripping ooze and filth, slavered and growled for his blood. They inched closer, hatred for their ancient enemy apparent upon their faces. The ground bubbled where their saliva struck, teeth gleaming each time they called out to one another. Their sounds sent shivers up Tavis's spine. His hands began to sweat. His muscles quiver. The size of their claws alone...

A cold wind blew from below bringing with it the smell of fresh earth. The stone bridge, barely a meter wide, spanned a chasm of a hundred feet before it plunged down. Impenetrable darkness leered, beckoning all to join it. Tavis took a step back, struggling with his fear of heights.

The goblins roared as one and charged.

Gripping his sword, Tavis summoned his courage and bellowed in kind. He would meet the charge the only way he knew how—with blood and steel.

Sarah Thomas closed the laptop and shook her head. "How can anyone read this?"

She long thought her soldier-turned-author-husband could have spent his time more productively, but indulged in his dreams, if for no other reason than it gave him a creative outlet after he left the army. Being an army spouse wasn't easy, but she soon learned that once the army was done with you, they closed the door and locked it. She and Daniel had been stranded for years. It pained her seeing him wander through life now listless, without purpose. For so long he'd devoted his life to a cause, an entity, only to have the rug pulled from under him after he exited the service. He continued asking her opinion, even knowing what the answer would be.

He struggled for years, leaning on her to carry the weight as he failed to find work while only making a meager pension in disability benefits to provide for them. Yet every time the walls closed in, Daniel found a way to step up and beat back the storm. He took care of the kids while she traveled: did the drop off and pick up to and from their private school and spent countless hours driving them to different sporting lessons or events. All without complaint. He told her once that he needed the rigidity, thinking it that slender thread holding him together.

It wasn't until a buddy suggested hitting the local American Legion post for their monthly fish fry, which he reluctantly agreed to, that he realized what he'd been missing. Sara watched the old Daniel return then, brimming with confidence and the swagger she had fallen in love with all those years ago. He blossomed, opening in ways she hadn't seen in years. Their relationship benefited as did his writing. Daniel's perseverance at his craft resulted in a fledgling writing career, until the sparkly vampire trend whipped the rug out from under him.

Instead of retreating, Daniel plunged headfirst into the challenge. His popularity in the genre reignited with his last novel. How couldn't it, considering many of the situations and experiences he wrote about had happened during that strange night spent among creatures who, by every stretch of the imagination, shouldn't exist? She stood at his side through book signings and speaking engagements, all while failing to comprehend the allure of what he did. Daniel often told fans she was his biggest supporter but worst fan—he wasn't wrong.

Sara never developed the taste for what she deemed "silly fantasy." Elves and gnomes? Bah. They were best left to cartoons and children's tales, not grown men with families and lives of their own. At least so she thought until she was kidnapped by agents of the queen of the dark elves. While her darling husband viewed that fateful night as validation for his writing and beliefs, she found his silly fantasies harrowing on a primal level.

Yawning, she leaned back in her favorite chair and stretched her arms over her head. The audible snapping of bones readjusting made the dog's head lift from its comfortable spot at her feet. She smiled. She'd never been a dog person before Daniel and hadn't heard of a Bernese Mountain Dog, but now, after owning four over the course of their relationship, Sara couldn't imagine a day without one. Even if they were more work than both of her children combined. Otto gave a contented grunt as Sara scratched the back of its ears.

"We really need to get him to write about something else, don't we?" Sara said.

Otto cocked its head, as if contemplating how best to answer.

Alone, and in an empty house, Sara only just realized she'd taken to talking to the dogs. She pretended they understood her, offering their unique counsel to her running commentary on daily events. As if doing laundry after a hard day's work offered a mental challenge.

A quick glance out the window showed the first shades of darkness settling. Her stomach growled in emphasis of the time. Giving the dog a last pet, Sara headed for the kitchen.

She didn't like being alone. Not after nearly being killed in her own bathroom as the fallout from their romp across half of North Carolina played out. If not for the taciturn gargoyle, Norman Guilt, Sara might never have slept with the lights off again. Daniel's military training offered consolation, but the sturdiness of her adopted guardian calmed her nerves more than anything. Not that she had any reason to fear. Since that night she hadn't seen or heard from any elf or dwarf or whatchamacallit. At least that she knew of. The fact they blended in with the rest of the world, going unnoticed by almost all, left her rattled.

Frowning at how easily she slipped back into the old fear mindset after reading a few paragraphs of Daniel's recent work, she had to face the reality of the situation, she couldn't plunge anymore into his stories. Her own adventure, limited as it was, proved far more than she desired.

Sara stalked into the kitchen. A pair of wagging tails in search of their expected treats flanking her. Daylight's fading kiss streamed in through the kitchen windows, basking her face in the last heat of the day as she cycled through her options for dinner. With the kids off to her sister's for the weekend and Daniel being pressed into service with DESA, Sara realized she could eat whatever she wanted. Placing the package of chicken cutlets back in the refrigerator, she snatched up her phone and dialed their favorite pizza joint.

Both dogs stared up at her expectantly, giving her pause as she waited for someone to answer. "You guys really like pizza, huh?"

Tails wagged harder in response, leaving her to question just how much dogs understood.

After placing her order, Sara opened a bottle of wine and poured a glass. No matter what she did, little managed to keep her mind off Daniel. His hasty departure left her numb. They'd gone years without hearing from Agent Blackmere or any other mysterious figure associated with the elf clans. Long enough to settle back into a normal routine, or so she thought. At least until Blackmere confronted Daniel at a book signing and dragged him off to who knows where on some secret mission. Aside from that, her only other reminder that life existed was Guilt's Challenger passing by from time to time, a subtle reminder he continued watching over her, but that was it.

What should have been a crowning moment in Daniel's literary career, his first mainstream bookstore signing, turned dark with Blackmere's arrival and request for help. True to form, Daniel leapt at the chance, though he professed his hands were tied and he did so only reluctantly—she knew better. They'd met during the end of his time in the Army, but she'd learned enough over the past two decades that he ached to get back in a uniform and be productive again. Civilian life never suited him and, no matter how much he attempted to convince himself, he missed his time in uniform.

That quiet boundary hovered between them, nestling like an impassable divide. For her part, Sara failed to understand the appeal or why he needed to continue to prove himself. She watched him suffer, helpless to do much more than offer a shoulder to lean on. Daniel had been home for years and continued to remain standoffish around people who hadn't served, often retreating into his shell during difficult times. Her heart ached for him, even if he refused to acknowledge it. Proud and determined to wrestle his demons, Daniel deserved more than a hasty summons in the middle of the night or at a business event that mattered to him.

That Daniel couldn't tell her about it left an ill flavor in her mouth. Hadn't she earned her own right to know at this point with what she had been through? Displeased and pondering how much of her tongue she wanted to give him upon his return, Sara stewed over her wine, slipping another treat to the dogs.

"Where are you, Daniel?"

One of her dogs brushed against her thigh, pushing just enough to let her know he was there. Sara found comfort in the dogs, often treating them equal to their children. Acknowledging she spent far too many hours talking with them, she decided the best thing was to head upstairs and take a nice bath. Few things provided better relief from the day's stress. Draining her glass and leaving it in the sink in favor of grabbing the bottle, Sara headed for the stairs.

The sun dipped below the horizon, allowing a flood of quasi-darkness to sweep in as a light storm broke. Sara found the change disturbing, but only because she knew what lurked in the dark. If half of Daniel's stories were true, from the dragon living under downtown Raleigh to a giant wearing tie-dye, she doubted a locked door and a gun was enough to stop whoever Morgen sent after her. Growing frustrated with the direction her thoughts, Sara did an about face to lock the front door.

She just laid a hand on the cold metal when the doorbell made her jump. Red wine sloshed over her hand, spilling on the hardwood floor while soliciting a mild curse. The dogs started barking. Heart fluttering, she licked the wine from her finger and set the bottle down. Imagination running wild, Sara hated the intensity her life developed in the wake of that one night. Every day was spent looking over her shoulder, expecting one of the elves, or worse, to come for her. She needed a vacation, somewhere far from the political games and internal strife of the elf clans her family seemed to keep getting involved in.

Shaking her head, golden locks sweeping across her face, Sara unlocked the door and cracked it open. What she found, standing on her front step soaking wet from the rain, went beyond anything she imagined, or wanted to see. Disinclined to think ill of the matter, she tried for a smile until she spied the wrapped hilt of what could only be a sword poking over the small man's right shoulder.

"Can I help you?" Her voice cracked.

The man bobbed his head with obvious gratitude. "Ms. Thomas?"

"Mrs.," she corrected, hoping that was enough to make him leave. "My husband will be home shortly if you would care to come back later."

"My apologies, but I'm not here for him." When she stiffened, he rushed to continue. "I've come a long way to see you, Mrs. Thomas. This is a matter of grave importance that concerns us all. My name is Abner Grumman and I need your help."

Sara struggled against the urge to slam the door in his face and lock it. Not again. She didn't want any "silly fantasy" experiences again. With both dogs barking in the background, she felt herself being mired in chaos. Lightning sparked in the distance, followed closely by the dissatisfied rumble of thunder. Every instinct screamed for her to close the door.

"I'm sorry, Mr. Grumman, you have the wrong house." She moved to slam the door.

Abner whipped the sword from his back, waving it in her direction. His pleading look verged on tears. "I'm sorry. I truly am."

A darker voice from behind him shocked her. "Lady, open the fucking door and let us in. Can't you see it's raining?"

TWO

She sat and stared at the waterlogged little man with a sword on the table sitting across from her. The dogs had fallen silent but sat between them with baleful stares. His face whispered defeat, as if the entirety of his hopes and dreams had been ripped away and crushed before his eyes. Sara failed to think of a time in her life when utter pointlessness permeated so thoroughly as to invoke the kind of despair so deep that she saw. Part of her felt for the man. No one deserved the haunting creep of oblivion crawling up their spine.

Conflicted feeling aside, Sara was frowning at the intrusion. Alarms went off, reverberating through the back of her mind. She wanted to call the police and be done with it.

Yet she stayed her hand. Why? Suspicions wormed into her thoughts, threatening to melt her already weakened grip on reality. The man came armed and, despite his pleas for help, failed to provide any reasoning for her to trust him so far. Not to mention the second voice she heard. She thanked living with Daniel for so long. Many of his iron traits wore off on her over the years, including his propensity for profanity, which she quickly learned was an artform when done right. With these words itching the tip of her tongue, Sara contemplated the meaning of this intrusion. And what might occur soon should her decisions prove wrong.

Central to this train of thought was the sword lying between them. Still unsure what happened on the front step, she eyed the sword with suspicion. Had the sword really talked? Her mind refused to accept it. Inanimate objects lacked voice, even in Daniel's books.

Chalking it up to confusion and the unexpected intensity of the moment, Sara settled back into the kitchen chair and drummed a fingertip on her wine bottle. "So, tell me again who you are and why you need my husband?"

Abner licked his lips, gaze flitting between her and the sword. "That is a complicated story. But please, I need your husband's help! I can't keep doing this. I can't. I can't. I can't."

Whoa. Ok, Mr. Crazy. Let's calm down a little and think this through. Damn it, Daniel, why aren't you here? "Settle down. Take a deep breath and start from the beginning." At his nod, she asked, "Who are you?"

"My name is Abner Grumman," he replied, "from Scranton."

"Okay, Abner Grumman. Can you tell me exactly what you think my husband can do for you?"

Abner blinked, cocking his head. "He … he's Daniel Thomas. The author."

"Yes, he is," Sara agreed then offered her best disarming smile often used to end conversations. "Do you have a story idea for him?"

"More like a fucking nightmare."

Her gaze lowered to the sword then away. *Nope. It didn't speak. It didn't.* The hairs on her arms rose as a chill crawled down her back. Face darkening, she fixed Abner with an accusatory glare. "What game is this? Are you a ventriloquist or something?"

Abner hung his head. "I wish I was. But no, this is serious. The sword—"

"Swords can't talk, Abner," she interrupted.

"I have a name!"

"This needs to stop," Sara fumed. *I can't do this.* "How dare you come into my house and insist on playing your little games? All it takes is a phone call to make you regret it."

Laughter, wispy and threatening echoed through the kitchen and Sara started to stand. The dogs growled, hair on end.

"It's not me! I swear!" Abner's face paled. "It's the sword! Ever since I found it the damned thing has been trying to kill me."

"Give me the opportunity, little man."

"I can explain," Abner said, snatching the nearby hand towel and throwing it over the sword.

"You better," Sara said, sitting back down.

"Hey, I can't see!"

Licking his lips, Abner raised an index finger, before pausing. "You, do you know about us?"

"Us?" Sara asked.

"The elf clans. Has Daniel told you about us?"

Here we go. "He has." She decided against giving Abner her history of being abducted by the dark queen, or whatever she called herself.

His shoulders sagged. "That's good. I'm a gnome, though, and used to work at the mall before deciding to look for this."

She followed his pointing fingers back to the sword. "And that is—"

"It all started a few months ago," Abner interrupted. "The clans were in turmoil after the high king's murder. Things were changing. What used to be the status quo devolved into chaos. Some became despondent. Others, like me, found opportunity. Working retail is a steady paycheck but it's not fulfilling. I wanted more. Needed it."

"You got greedy," she clarified.

He shrugged. "Call me an opportunist. Nothing changed for me until one night when I was closing the store. I was just about done when someone started banging on the door. To say the least, I wasn't inclined to open it, leastwise not until I recognized him. Turns out it was an old friend I used to run cons with a few centuries ago. I let him in and, well, I regret it now."

"Friends tend to do that," she muttered, ignoring the few centuries comment. "What did he want?"

"The usual. He had a lead on a score. An easy grab that would leave us both set for life. All we had to do is find it and sell it to a secret bidder." Abner groaned. "Why do I fall for these things? I like to think I'm a good guy. I don't bother nobody, even when they bother me. Mind your own business, that's what my ma used to say. Kept me from getting the plague, didn't it?"

The plague? How old are you? Sara cleared her throat. "Abner, you're spiraling."

"Huh? Ah, of course. Where was I?" He blinked several times, biting the corner of his upper lip.

Sara watched as tiny hairs from his impossibly thin moustache slid across his teeth. *Is he chewing on the hair? Gross.* "Your friend's lead."

Abner refocused. "After I convinced him to keep quiet, I locked the store, and we hurried back to my place—a little one-bedroom place off Creedmoor. It's nice and I don't need much else. That and I can walk to work."

"Abner."

Sensing her patience wearing thin, he adjusted his position, placing both hands flat on the table. "When we got back to my place, he showed me a journal detailing the hidden location of … this."

"I can hear you, stupid."

Abner winced. "The sword has been lost to the clans for centuries, so long many among the new generations don't believe it ever existed … Do you have any idea how much this thing is worth? Fools. All I had to do was figure out the clues and follow the trail. Not hard really. I always liked puzzles. My buddy and I hoped in the car, certain we were about to strike it rich. Neither of us bothered thinking much about the future—what's the point when you live so long? So, we made it up in the mountains, just west of Boone.

"The car gave out somewhere along the Blue Ridge Parkway, forcing us to leave it and strike off into the mountains on foot. In retrospect that might not have been the best decision." He rubbed his jaw with a rueful grin. "The clues took us deep into the mountains. Do you know how many waterfalls we have in this state? A little reminder of what used to be ... Anyway, we made our way to a string of caves that haven't seen the touch of man, or my kind for that matter."

He fell silent, water filling his eyes. "Chester, that was my buddy's name, never paid attention to curses or warnings. He was confident we had found the right cave and just stepped right in. I can still hear his screams..."

"I'm sorry," she said. Sara took a much-needed drink of wine.

"No matter. I was frozen. Couldn't move forward and too afraid to go back. I don't know how long I wound up standing there. Hours at least. Courage finally returned, a slender thread to be sure, but enough to keep me going. The deeper I went into the cave the more my heart threatened to burst from my chest. I've never been so afraid in my life. And I've seen some shit. With no natural light and no one to bounce my doubts off, I stumbled into a chamber and found it—the Sword of Grimspire." He rubbed his hands. "This was it. I was going to be rich ... Turns out I had no idea what I was getting into. This damned thing has wanted to kill me from the moment I touched it."

"Keep tempting me."

"Are you certain that isn't just fear playing on your nerves? We tend to find boogeymen in the shadows, especially when we look for them," Sara suggested. She glanced to the kitchen window, half expecting to see a gargoyle in her trees.

His eyes widened. "You've heard it, all profanity and threats. What else would you call it? This thing has vowed to kill me from the moment I set my hands on it. How am I supposed to process that?"

"He's not lying. I'm going to slice his throat open the first chance I get."

Sara jerked back. Nothing in her life prepared her for this moment. Daniel long ago stopped telling her about his story ideas or plot twists. She lacked the imagination, the spark of curiosity driving his fingers across the keyboard in a whirlwind of fury. Grounded in reality, Sara thought of herself as a simple woman with a grasp on life. Abner and his mad sword were quickly proving her wrong.

"Why?" was all she managed, determined not to address the sword directly.

"Why what?" Abner asked.

"Why does the sword want to kill you? I mean, without a wielder, it's just a hunk of metal. It's not like it has legs or anything. Set the sword down and be done with it."

"I can't," Abner moaned.

"It's the curse! Whoever thinks themselves bold enough to steal my power must suffer a fate of the most hideous designs. That's the rule."

Sara raised an eyebrow. *You arrogant little shit. Let me get my hands on you and it's the bottom of Jordan Lake for you.*

"You see my problem," Abner said when she didn't reply.

"I don't know what I see. This is all too surreal for me, Abner. What did you expect my husband to do for you? The last time I checked he's not an expert on talking swords."

"But he writes the books," Abner blurted. "He should know!"

"I'm pretty sure he doesn't." Sara shook her head. *He better not.* "Besides, even if he could help, he's not here."

Abner thumped his head on the table.

"Stupid. I tried telling you! There is but one way to release the curse and keep your life. I must be returned to the one who created me."

Finally, a break. Sara hummed. "Who might that be?"

"The great and powerful high elf wizard, Sheldon."

The mention of the name elicited another groan from Abner.

"Ok, we have a starting point," Sara soothed. She still wasn't sure if she bought the story or not and wanted nothing to do with either one of them, but letting Abner speak his peace felt the easiest way to get rid of him. "Where is this Sheldon?"

"I don't know."

THREE

"I need a drink." Abner blinked and pointed at the bottle still clutched in her hand. "You have one."

She looked down and frowned. "This isn't strong enough for me either. Do you have any idea what you unloaded on me? How am I supposed to process this? Talking swords! A wizard named Sheldon. I'm a simple woman. I work. I take care of my kids. Nothing in my life says how to deal with whatever you got going on."

"Waaa."

Face twisting in a scowl, Sara jabbed at the sword. "You, you shut up. When I want to hear your opinion, I'll ask you for it."

"Oh, I like her, Abner. Why couldn't you have brought her to find me? She'll be fun to kill."

"I said zip it," Sara snapped, losing patience. "Abner, you want my husband. Not me. I can't help you."

Helpless. Confused. Frightened. A range of conflicting emotions surged through her, threatening to tremble the foundations of all she once thought true. Her experiences with the elf clans proved insufficient for dealing with the reality of the moment. She struggled to understand the situation, knowing a lifetime of thoughts and beliefs lay shattered on the kitchen floor like so many plates casually tossed aside. More than ever, she missed Daniel.

She knew he battled his own demons, but he plunged headfirst into the deep end of the pool, accepting the secret world of the elves and the shady government agency regulating their affairs for what it was without thinking once of what it could do to her. *Where are you, Daniel? Why are you never here when I need you most*?

A muffled cough, the subtle clearing of a throat, brought her back to the present. "What?"

"Sara, like you said, Daniel isn't here," Abner started.

She tensed. *Don't say it.*

"There is something I didn't mention," he added.

She rolled her eyes. "Imagine that."

"I told you he's a dick."

Abner fidgeted, shifting his balance in the chair while looking over his shoulder to the front door. "I'm being chased."

"Of course you are," she hissed, trying not to let him see her looking for her phone. "You didn't think this was an important point to lead with?"

"Would you have let me in if I did?"

She paused. "No."

"I wouldn't either," he admitted.

Sara left the kitchen, heading to the bookcase turned into a liquor cabinet in the front room. Wine wasn't doing it anymore. The clink of ice on glass and the quiet gurgle of liquid pouring followed by a deep groan lost somewhere between frustration and satisfaction echoed throughout the house. *Better. Everything is fine.* In the background, the rain came down harder. Oddly, she found it the perfect night for Abner Grumman's mysterious visit. Just the sort of thing Daniel would delight in writing. When she returned, she found the gnome running his thumbs together, pausing to scratch the nails every third time.

Reclaiming her seat, Sara exhaled a deep breath and stared him in the eyes. "Who's chasing you, Abner?"

"That might take another drink," he warned. "What do you know about lycans?"

"Is that some kind of fruit?" she asked, unwilling to accept what she was being told. Sara handed him a glass of bourbon.

His grunt was answer enough. "Closer to murdering werewolves without a sense of humor."

"Why on earth would werewolves be after you?" Sara decided to play along.

Abner twisted his lower jaw and took a long drink. "You're accepting this remarkably well, all things considered."

"What else can I do? You show up with a psychopath, talking sword and say you're being chased by werewolves." She tossed her hands up. "At this point I might as well let it ride."

"Fair enough. There is a rumor the lycans have united behind a new leader and are seeking the sword to gain enough power to usurp the queen," Abner explained. "These are nasty people. I'm more afraid of them than this sword."

"Let me have at them. You'll learn the true meaning of fear."

Accepting the story, any of it, meant Sara acknowledged belief in their secret world. One night of captivity and the whirlwind adventure taking them halfway across the state wasn't enough for her to jump in. Not like Daniel. She was okay with being in denial. Until now that is. Certain people were born for situations demanding the thorough belief in what shouldn't be. Sara wasn't one of them and wanted nothing more than to kick Abner back into the wet night, with his damned sword, and lock the door.

Sympathy stayed her hand; motherly instinct kicked in. She looked down upon the smaller man, bedraggled and red-eyed, and felt the tug of her motherly instincts. No one, regardless of whether they brought it upon themselves, deserved to feel hunted. Or worse. "These lycans, when did you last see them?"

Another glance over his shoulder and another tremble of the shoulders. "West of Greensboro. I jumped off I-40 when I could. You wouldn't believe how confusing the bypass around that city can be when you're being hunted.

After a quick ride down to Siler City I got on 64 West and … here I am."

She wanted to relax, but his fidgeting behavior kept her on edge. Sara glanced at the door as well. "There's a chance you lost them. Good. We have time."

"Time for what? You're going to help?" His voice rose; eyes brightened.

Jerking back, Sara held up a staying hand. She still found trouble accepting his story. "Not even a little. I'm going to make a call and get you to the right people. This is beyond me." Her face. "Wait, Abner, what if the queen doesn't want the sword? I mean, it was hidden on purpose, right?"

"I never thought about that," Abner admitted. "I really might have made a mistake this time."

"Idiot. I warned you."

Resisting the urge to thump her forehead on the table, Sara finished the last of her wine and rubbed her temples. She needed a way out, yet each new turn threw her deeper into the spiral of madness. Unable to form coherent thoughts, she decided on fixing another drink. After all, the kitchen hand towel did say *shut up liver, you're fine*. The chair scrapped over tile as she pushed back.

The phone rang.

The shrill ring tone startled her, and she dropped back into the chair before jumping up. Heart pounding, Sara excused herself and hurried to reach the phone before it stopped ringing. She prayed it was Daniel. Without giving Abner another look, she went into the other room, hearing Abner repeating,

"Not good. Not good. Not good."

All color had drained from Sara's face at the dial tone. Her hand trembled, threatening to drop the phone as she walked back into the kitchen.

"Sara, what I—"

"We need to go. Now," she whispered.

Abner shot to his feet. "They've found me!"

Sara ran through the house, collecting her keys, purse, and a jacket. Panic drove her, inspired by having seen far too many horror movies after the sun went down. Fiends and ghouls danced in the shadows, beckoning to drag her away to some private hell. The stench of wet dog assaulted her senses as her imagination ran wild.

She looked around, her two dogs watched her in silent judgement from across the room. Their calmness proved little more than a ruse, for she knew they were waiting for her to reach for the leashes hanging on the back of the laundry room door. A new wave of worry consumed her. Knowing they would be safer at home, Sara made the decision to leave them behind.

"Come on," she urged Abner. "Grab that damned sword and hurry up."

"Where are we going?" Abner winced as his fingers curled around the hilt.

"Don't worry about that. Out the back door. Go." Sara turned to lock the front door. She tried, and failed, to avoid the dogs' woeful stares as she ran past them. "Sorry guys. I'll be back soon. I promise."

I hope.

Abner stood in the center of the kitchen. Sara snatched him by the collar, dragging him along. She shoved him outside first, figuring if the lycans were laying in wait he at least had a weapon. The best she had was a small can of pepper spray somewhere in the quagmire at the bottom of her purse.

Night had settled in with earnest, swathing the once quiet street in an eerie haze blurring houses under the glow of orange lights: doors were locked, blinds drawn. Sara struggled to step forward, away from the perceived security of her home. The storm wound down, leaving her street a soaked mess.

She jumped when Abner bumped into her. "Watch it," she hissed.

"What are we doing?"

"Waiting for our ride."

The roar of an engine thundered down the street before he could ask what ride. Abner balked under the angry glare of headlights blazing through the gloom, barreling straight for them. Feeling betrayed, she saw him holding the sword just a little tighter.

The car growled to a stop and a door opened.

"Come on, we're going," Sara said, moving forward.

Still wary, Abner took one step when the bushes next to the house erupted. Leaves and rain blew in every direction, accompanied by the angry snarls of a hairy beast diving for him with open claws. They collide, slamming into the wet siding of the house. Abner cried out.

Frozen, Sara could do little more than watch, mouth agape, as the gnome disappeared beneath an impossibly large animal in a tangle of fists, claws, and teeth. She tried to scream but no sound came out. The sudden rush of a massive body darting past her, whipped her hair around her face.

"Get in the car!"

The deep bellow snapped her out of her daze. Sara turned to run before spying Abner's battered form lying near her feet, the sword sticking over his shoulder. Where her courage arose from, she might never know. Sara reached down, grabbed him by the collar, and began dragging him to the forest green Challenger idling in the driveway. An animalistic scream followed by the crunch of bones and wet smack of tearing flesh sickened her. She focused on Abner, fearing he was already dead. She popped the seat lever and pushed the front seat up to allow her to get the gnome inside. By the time she moved the seat back and took her seat in the front passenger side, scantly finishing buckling her seatbelt, Norman returned.

His massive form slid into the driver's seat with well-rehearsed effort before he reached to close the door. The last thing Sara heard before it slammed closed was the howl of wolves.

Peering into the side mirror, she felt true terror as a dozen figures crowded the middle of the street. The corpse at their center began the slow transformation from wolf to man. As one, the wolves cast their heads back and howled. In their calls, she heard the promise of revenge.

The car sped on, shifting gears. Only when they turned the corner and were several blocks away did Sara sink into the leather seat. "Thank you, Norman."

The gargoyle, Norman Guilt, grunted and hit the gas.

FOUR

Sara usually didn't appreciate the power of a classic muscle car. They were too loud. Too arrogant. She found most of the drivers, especially young soldiers blowing their paychecks on a range of Mustangs and Camaros, compensating for something. Tonight however, she gripped the handle on the door for dear life while silently urging Norman to go faster. They wound through the quasi-city streets, barreling through the outskirts of Raleigh. To where remained unknown and, given the way the night continued devolving, Sara didn't want to know. Any place without those werewolves felt right to her.

Stomach in turmoil, she managed to look into the back seat at the prone, unmoving figure of Abner Grumman. She tried to see the rise and fall of his chest, but the darkness of the cab proved impenetrable. "Is he alive?"

"He lives."

The careless disregard in his tone soured her. "How can you know? You haven't even looked at him."

"Sara Thomas, our kind disintegrate upon death. There are no bodies to bury. No funerals to attend. When we stop breathing, we stop existing," he replied. "You know this."

She felt the snap deep inside as pent-up rage broke through the veneer of propriety. "Excuse me for not remembering proper elf etiquette! You may not have noticed but I was being attacked by a fucking werewolf! And don't get me started on that sword!"

"Oh please, start on me. I can't wait to see what nightmares we can create together."

The Challenger rolled to a stop at a red light and Norman finally gave the gnome a proper look. The sword jutting over his shoulder gave the gargoyle pause. "So it's true. The sword has been found at last. We are in danger."

"And?" Sara snapped. "That's it? That's all you have to say?"

"This is beyond my abilities, Sara Thomas. I was assigned to ward over you, not deal with the venom in the sword of Grimspire."

"What are we going to do? Daniel isn't here. Do we call DESA?"

Norman shook his head. The scrape of hair and flesh across the supple leather seat made her hair stand on end. "Your government will attempt to take the sword and hide it, ignorant of the danger it possesses. No. This is a matter for the elves. One I am not equipped to handle. We need help."

The light changed, vibrant green bathing the front seat. Sara stared out the windshield as the city blocks sped by. Without knowing where they were going, all she had were familiar establishments and street names to go by. They passed the most famous hot dog stand in Raleigh on the left before Sara realized they were heading for downtown and, she suspected, the one place she never wanted to see again.

"Where are you taking us?" she asked finally as the handful of skyscrapers marking what, from a distance, proved a scenic view of downtown Raleigh hove into view.

Norman, for his part, remained silent.

"There has to be another way." Sara shook her head as realization set in. The car slowed to the speed limit and proceeded into the parking deck across the street from the Wells Fargo building.

"I'm listening," Norman challenged. When she failed to respond, he cut the engine and got out. "We must hurry. Our enemy is relentless but even they will not dare enter the Queen's sanctum."

Sara hurried to join him. "What about Abner?"

"I will carry him. Go ahead of me and be swift. I sense more afoot this foul night."

She obeyed, waiting long enough for Norman to hoist the stricken gnome, and sword, over his shoulder and head for the street.

The rain had let up to a mere drizzle. Soft winds blew debris down South Salisbury Street under the watchful gaze of darkened windows and the soft glow of changing lights. Sara preferred this part of the city during the street festivals when it was filled with crowds, music, and laughter. Leading the way, she crossed over to their destination and headed for the front doors.

"Not that way," Norman called. "We go in through the side."

Sara frowned but said nothing. There would be a time to unleash the fury of her thoughts later—if they survived.

Side by side, they worked around the slender side street to a portion of the wall made to look like a door. Norman took the lead and pressed into the brick, rewarded with the hiss of a panel opening. Keying in his code, the gargoyle waited for a secondary door to slide open, revealing a short hall with an elevator beckoning.

"Are you sure this is safe?" Sara asked more for personal edification than concern. Standing beside him made her dangerously comfortable.

He ignored her and tromped into the elevator.

Abner groaned as his head struck the cold metal paneling, but the gnome didn't wake up. The sword remained conspicuously silent.

"Follow them. We must be sure what they are after," Morgen said. "Viviana, ensure my daughter remains safe. We cannot have that criminal linking up with her. The stakes are too high."

Hanging up, the queen of the dark elves and de facto ruler of all the clans in the wake of her estranged husband's assassination, resumed her lonely vigil over the city. Out of every place in the world developed since the rise of man, she found this the closest to home. Reminiscent of the ancient capital of the elves, before the schism tore their civilization apart, it presented a city on the cusp of change. Her view dominated central North Carolina for miles, soothing her fragile nerves in times of crisis such as this.

News of Xander's escape wouldn't take long to spread, fueling the flames of dissent and sparking a new front in the never-ending civil war. The former champion of light proved the vitriol those seeking power rallied behind.

How many more needed to die for the empty glory of one man? Can the clans withstand another onslaught or am I doomed to be the ruler of a dead kingdom bereft of hope? A lifeless entity burdened by the ghosts of the past even as the future burns and dies. Would that Alvin were still alive and we reconciled our differences…

A knock disturbed her, punctuated by the distant cut of lightning. Morgen sighed. "Yes, Aislinn. What dire news do you bring me this time?"

Coughing, the younger elf lowered her eyes and blushed. "Norman Guilt has arrived, your majesty. He bears news demanding your attention."

"They all do," Morgen remarked and waved off her assistant's concern. "What can be worse than my potential son in law's escape from prison?"

"Ma'am, its best if he tells you himself. There is another small matter, however," Aislinn hedged. "He brings the wife of Daniel Thomas with him."

Wonder of wonders. Can this night get any worse?

They sat and they stared. No one spoke. No one wanted to, nor did they know what to say.

When last they met it had been fraught with thinly veiled threats and the promise of a violent demise. Perhaps not Morgen's best hour but a necessary one. Enemies, if by the spur of chance, Morgen knew there'd be no room in her heart for forgiveness had their roles been reversed. That they found themselves approaching a tepid, favorable arrangement might have piqued her curiosity if not for other matters consuming the elf clans.

Her gaze flit between the staunch gargoyle her late husband detailed to protect the human and Sara. Huddled in the far corner, now asleep on a pale-yellow couch was the gnome Abner, and the sword. Morgen's mind struggled to comprehend how both were now in her presence. Their worlds never should have mixed.

Trapped between conflicting thoughts, Morgen laid her palms flat on the table and made a show of running them across the faux wood table. "Sara Thomas, to what do I owe the pleasure?" she began, deciding on empty pleasantries in an attempt at placating the fire smoldering in the woman's eyes.

"Pleasure is the last thing I'd call it. If you remember, *your highness*, the last time I was in your presence you threatened to kill me," Sara sniped.

"Yes, well, circumstances change as needs must. That you are here speaks volumes to the level of danger in which you find yourself." Shifting her focus to Norman, Morgen asked, "What hunts him?"

"Lycans."

Morgen stiffened, the slightest movement before regaining her composure. "Are you certain?"

"I killed one before we escaped, though whether it is a rogue element or at the behest of their chieftain remains unclear," the gargoyle replied. "They seek the sword."

Morgen stared at the plain hilt, wondering what the fuss was over. Elfkind had more magical imbued weapons than easily counted. She had hoped this one was gone and forgotten. What made the mad genius behind this sword special? Bane more than blessing, she feared for the continuation of her people should the sword fall into the wrong hands. Werewolf hands. "Ah yes, the wizard's mythical creation. Fool. He never should have wasted his time with it. All that weapon's done is wreak havoc among us when we need it least." She snorted. "We should smelt it down and strew the remnants in the Cape Fear River."

"I can hear you, you know. Touch me and I'll murder every last one of you."

"Cute," Morgen replied.

Sara shrugged. "It has an attitude."

"It always has," Morgen clarified.

"I have a name."

This is a first. Are we supposed to be friends now? She tried to kill me once. Why me? What did I do to deserve this? Sara decided to lay it all on the table. Only one of them had the right information necessary to get out of this jam and she didn't see the need to be a part of it any longer. "Can I go home? There's not much I can do here. The sword is with you. What more do you need from me?"

"The lycans won't leave you alone until they obtain the sword," Norman answered. Regret weighed his words down. "We must get this sword to safety before you will be free from their mangy curse."

"No. I'm done." She shook her head, resolute in her decision.

"Norman speaks true. Lycans are ruthless in their pursuit. Once they latch onto prey, they are unstoppable," Morgen added. "It appears you are in this whether you wish it or not."

Cold realization struck. Sara wanted to run. To flee as far as possible until Daniel returned. Pleasing as it sounded, it proved little more than an empty wish. She opened her mouth to speak when a thought struck. "I need someone to take care of my dogs."

"Excuse me?"

"My dogs. They are home alone with no one to take care of them."

Morgen squinted. "I fail to see how this is an issue. There are more important matters at stake."

"I'm not doing anything else until I know my dogs are taken care of," Sara insisted.

Failing to understand the complexities of humanity, the elf queen sat back. "Very well. I shall detail one of my assistants to see to your … animals. Tell me though, what do you think you are about to do?"

"Nothing I want to. It seems fate is ignoring me tonight."

"Perhaps that is true of us all."

FIVE

The smell of wet dogs choked the area. Huddled beneath the overpass on Lake Wheeler Road, part of the historic Yates Mill Park, were eleven men and women. Breathing hard and filled with hatred, they snarled and snapped at each other. The rain had finally broken, leaving the sky a scattered mess of darkness and clouds as the half-moon struggled to reclaim its domain. A chill settled in, burrowing down to the bone.

Laid out on one of the large stones close to the old water wheel, was the corpse of their fallen. Mangled and broken from his failed assault with the gargoyle, he paid the ultimate price for his arrogance and shamed his clan. What remained of his body became a warning for the others should they seek individual glory over that of clan honor. Drying rivulets of blood ran down the rocks to be lost in the small pool under the dam. An arm had slipped from his chest to drape across the moss strewn boulder.

"He deserved a better death than this," snarled a scar-faced man with a black mohawk. His taloned claw jabbed at the corpse.

A female with wild red hair running down her back snapped, "We know this, Spike! That ain't the point. No one said a fucking gargoyle was going to be there."

Snarls and grunts swept through them in a chorus of agreement countered by an undercurrent of rage. The pack may be family, but there were differences of opinion surfacing that threatened to tear them apart.

Spike paced up and down the boards spanning the stream leading into the cow pastures across the street. "I say we hunt that stone monster down and get revenge now," he growled, "Sword be damned."

"You know what we need the sword for," a thin man with sandy blonde hair and covered in tattoos said. "Gruff said—"

"Gruff ain't here, is he, Good Boy?" Spike interrupted.

Good Boy stood his ground. "Don't matter. We got orders."

"Stand down, Spike. You know what happens when we don't play nice," the redhead female warned.

Spike whirled on her. Hatred in his yellow eyes. "Easy, Princess. We all know you're Gruff's pet. Maybe you need to roll over and beg for a treat, but I'm not taking it. Not this time. Spot's death is a step too far. He d—"

The wail of a lone wolf up the hill cut him off. Heads snapped, snouts lifting to the light breeze pushing south. Several members of the pack began bouncing, their sneakers slapping wetly on the rocks.

Princess titled her head back and offered a reply.

The chorus of frogs along the banks of the nearby lake went silent as the pack gathered and, as one, turned to face the trail leading down to them.

A shadow fell, cutting the pristine pale moonlight. Instead of going down the trail, Gruff snuck behind the old mill wheel and marched to the center of the small dam. A massive man, he stared down at the broken body. His snarl curled his lip, showing off a large canine fang of purest white. His heavy muscles bulged beneath the Carolina blue track suit.

"Why is he lying there like a piece of meat?" Gruff demanded.

Princess cast a sidelong glance at Spike, smirking when the upstart bowed his head and took a step back. *Coward*.

"Gruff, we were being hunted."

Crouching, the pack leader leapt down and landed beside Spot's body. Gruff knelt to lift his friend's head, touching forehead to forehead. He closed his eyes, remembering the good times while privately vowing to get revenge on those responsible. Satisfied he'd paid his respects; Gruff rose to his full menacing height and confronted the pack.

"Who did this?"

"A gargoyle," Princess replied. "He was protecting the gnome."

Gruff cocked his head. "That doesn't sound right. Why would a gargoyle sit by and watch without getting involved before now?"

"Because you weren't here," Spike glowered.

Gruff snapped his jaw. "Say again, whelp?"

Finding his courage, Spike pushed past Princess. "Where were you? We needed you and now Spot's dead. You're the pack alpha. You shoulda been there."

The pack fanned out in a half circle, careful to give them plenty of room. Only Princess remained within striking distance.

"That sounds like a challenge, Spike. Are you challenging me?"

Spike brought his hands together, cracking his knuckles. "I guess I am."

A hushed silence fell over the group. Tiny hairs stood on edge. Fists clenched. The pack tensed. Anticipating the next fight. To their shock, Gruff cracked an uncanny smile. His teeth glowed in the night, framed by his thick salt and pepper mane and the gold chain peeking out from the white tank top under his jacket.

Spike cocked his head in confusion.

"Good." Gruff launched at Spike, transforming into wolf form in a blur.

They collided, claws and fists slashing and pummeling. Fur ripped free. Flesh tore. The stench of fresh blood antagonized the pack, whipping them into a frenzy of howls and chants. Both now in wolf form, the two battled for control of the pack and the right to exact revenge on the gargoyle, and the gnome. The snap of a bone increased the unleashed rage.

Spike's jet-black fur, now marred red, clashed with the grey and black of Gruff. Weaker and smaller, Spike scrambled away, making for the old railroad ties used as steps leading up the slope and to the mile long trail circling the lake. He gained the second step when Gruff pounced upon his back. Twisting to bite, Spike's efforts were rewarded with a massive paw swiping across his face, slamming his skull down to the wet earth. His body went limp, unconscious.

Gruff stood atop the body and howled.

The pack answered.

Shimmering, his figure blurring, Gruff transformed into his human guise. Breathing hard and sweating, he paused to tuck his chain in. The pack leader glared down at Spike, kicking him to see if he still lived. The shallow rise and fall of his chest confirmed it. "Next time try harder, Spike," Gruff snarled. He turned to the others. "Anyone else want to challenge me?"

Heads lowered, refusing to meet his gaze.

"I didn't think so. Princess, tell me more about this gargoyle. Do you know who it was?"

She took a moment to tie her hair before joining him. "No. He came out of nowhere. We tracked the gnome to a house in the suburbs and were preparing to strike when a dark green Challenger showed up. Next thing we knew he and Spot were fighting and, well, you know the rest." Princess gestured to Spot's now cold body.

"Green Challenger, eh?" Gruff rubbed his chin, frowning as his hand came away coated in sweat. "There's only one of the guardians who drives a car like that, but what was he doing following the gnome? It doesn't make sense. Where did he take the gnome?"

"We lost the trail somewhere in the Boylan Heights area," she answered. "They weren't alone. They had a woman with them."

"A woman? What woman?"

"We don't know."

Gruff failed to find any significance with the human involvement, though he found it odd Abner would go to a human over one of his own kind. "Did he have the sword?"

She nodded. "Wrapped up and slung over his shoulder as if he might use it. Gnomes have always been useless."

"Doesn't change the fact the little bastard got to the sword before us. Or that he's likely on his way to Morgen. If she gets the sword..." He let the thought fade, the consequences too dire to accept.

The lycan clans had suffered during the reign of the elves. Beaten down and pushed to the brink of extinction, they needed the sword to fulfill the prophecy and reclaim their right to the throne. Gruff felt his future crumble under the weight of impossible scenarios he, and the others, were powerless to arrest. An inglorious end to a strangled existence.

"Princess, take two others and head to the Wells Fargo building. If Guilt took the gnome there, I want to know. And if he is there, don't lose the scent again. We're not going to get another chance at claiming the sword. Am I clear?"

"Yes," she answered before pointing at the set of twins ever standing in her shadow, though for what reason she hadn't deduced. Might be lust, might be the hunger for power. Regardless, she didn't care. They were the pack's top hunters and her most trusted disciples.

The trio bounded up the trail, disappearing behind the curve. The groan of an engine turning over echoed across the lake. Soon the red glow of taillights bathed the area.

Satisfied his orders were being met, Gruff told the others, "See to Spike's wounds. I don't want him dead, yet. And dispose of Spot. I'm tired of looking at him."

Field Agent Cecile Barnabas hated her life. Since the debacle resulting in the assassination of the high king, she'd been assigned to the small, newly established, office just west of Raleigh. Day after day she stared out her window, the only one afforded to her, gazing at the disturbingly arrogant Canadian geese strutting into the road, daring a car to hit them. Thus far, not a car took up the challenge. She wished she had the audacity to.

Nothing happened in Raleigh. Nothing worthy of the years spent training, learning, and attempting to prove herself as a valuable asset to D.E.S.A. The Department of Extra Species Affairs thought they kept a close watch over the elf clans, but no one foresaw Xander and Gwen's betrayal and attempt at usurping the thrones of both the light and dark clans. Cecile had been in Washington when it went down, mired beneath a mountain of paperwork and longing for a change. She leapt when Agent Blackmere offered her the assignment in North Carolina. Little did she know it would prove interminably dull and as far from her vision as possible.

Crumpling her tenth sheet of typing paper of the evening, she closed one eye and clamped the end of her tongue between her lips. "One. Two. Three."

Cecile arced the paper into the trash can beside the office door and jerked a fist down in triumph. "Ten for ten. I ought to be, considering I'm stuck here between Carolina and Duke."

Another day of no calls. No urgent emails. Two days ago, Blackmere arrived and took Daniel Thomas away on a secret mission up north. Why he didn't ask her to go irritated her. She was a field agent after all, not an office one. Instead of earning her paycheck, Cecile remained confined in little more than a cell, wasting government resources with casual disregard.

The phone ringing jolted her, it being the last thing she expected, especially so close to clocking out for the day. Cecile glanced out the window for the thousandth time, surprised to find the sun had set.

"This is Agent Barnabas," she said after calming down enough to answer the antiquated landline phone D.E.S.A insisted on using.

She listened, eyes widening, as the caller spoke. She felt her flesh dampen even as her heart thundered in her chest. Her foot started tapping uncontrollably, slight at first before breaking into a fever pitch symphony.

"Yes, I understand. I'll handle it immediately," she replied and hung up. *At last!*

SIX

Sara paced when she became nervous. She was nervous now. With the promise of blisters forming because she'd worn the wrong shoes, she had never felt more alone or afraid. Setting aside the fact nothing made sense, Sara longed for Daniel. With him, she was unstoppable. Without him, she was stoppable. Or was she? Pausing midstride, the slightest spark of wonder crept into her thoughts. The eternal question of *what if* took root. What if she was strong enough to deal with fantasy creatures who, by all rights, shouldn't exist? What if she had the power to not only help Abner but ensure the wretched sword was returned to its creator? What if.

Maybe, just maybe, she had her own story to tell. One not needing the iron strength of having her veteran husband to lean back on for support. Her mind drifted back to the last part of Daniel's new book she snuck a peek at. His hero had the nerve to stand upon the bridge alone against a horde of bloodthirsty foes. While she didn't know what the rest of the night, or this adventure, held in store for her, Sara envisioned standing in his place. Her heart beat louder. *What's the worst that can happen? I mean, I could die and that doesn't fit into my plans, but do I really want to live with the regret of knowing I had this one perfect chance to search for who I am? A flash of guilt gnawed at her when she thought of her children. Better they weren't involved.*

"You look pensive."

Jarred back to the moment, Sara jumped at the baritone of Norman's voice. "Do you blame me?"

"No. Were our roles reversed I too would find it difficult to accept," he admitted. "Daniel knew this, I think."

"It's easier for him. He has the uncanny ability to fall back into what he calls 'deployment mode.'"

"I understand." Norman took a seat on the sickly yellow upholstered couch and clasped his hands together. "I have fought in many wars. My kind has been hunted to near extinction. Dealing with loss or the prospect of death is easier when you are meant to be in a warzone. There is no time to think of home, of family. Doing so will only see you killed faster. Emotions do not serve us well in intense situations, Sara Thomas."

She viewed him differently for the first time. In place of a menacing figure with a violent agenda she saw a creature with an impossible heart. A continued push and she might find the gargoyle bordering on tears. The idea proved as amusing as it was sad. "I hear what you're saying, Norman, and I appreciate your insights. I do, but I need to work through this on my own. I'm not a soldier. The hardest thing I ever had to do was watch my husband go off to war. I just can't—"

Norman Guilt stood and wrapped his arms around her in a tender embrace that shocked her, more so when she accepted the hug and returned it. Her knees buckled as tears burst free. Leaning into the gargoyle's chest, Sara wept.

"How very touching. Two separate species finding the strength to overcome their differences and become friends." Morgen's voice shattered the fragile illusion of the scene.

Wiping her eyes with the heels of her hands, Sara faced the queen. "Jealous? I don't seem to recall you having accomplished the same."

Morgen clicked her tongue on the roof of her mouth. "The gnome is awake. I need both of you to come with me."

Stings, doesn't it, bitch? Sara adjusted the scrunchie pulling her hair back and met the queen's withering glare. "We should go. I'm ready to go home."

Morgen glanced up at Norman as he passed, a twinkle in her eyes. "You big softie."

Grunting as he passed, the gargoyle refused to meet her gaze.

They joined Sara in the main lounge where Abner stood looking out the window. Off to the side, ignored and swaddled in rags, sat the sword.

"Abner Grumman, do you know who I am?" Morgen asked, her tone stiff, authoritative.

The gnome spun, eyes widening. "I... I..."

She offered a thin smile reserved for visiting diplomats and those assuming to be her betters. "Allow me. I am Morgen."

Lower lip quivering, Abner smoothed down the wrinkles in his shirt. "Uh, hello."

Leaning close, Norman growled, "She's your queen, idiot."

Abner flushed and made an awkward attempt at bowing. "Uh ... yes, yer majesty."

Forcing herself to keep from rolling her eyes, even as a light giggle escaped Sara, Morgen waved him off. "Oh stop. Norman, if I had wanted to introduce myself as such I would have. Now the poor man is stricken by fear. Abner, take a seat. There is much we must discuss and you, troublesome gnome, are much of it."

An annoyed look flashed across his face before he regained control and sat opposite her. She watched as glanced at the sword then away.

"Yes, the Sword of Grimspire. It is the source of our problems this night, thanks to you," Morgen began. "Why is it here? In my presence?"

"I ... ah ... well..."

"Save it. I'll tell you why. Because you got greedy. You thought by finding the sword, which was purposefully hidden from the clans, you'd find the right buyer and make a fortune. Stop me when I'm wrong." At his silence, she continued. "Only, when you got your grubby little hands on it you found more trouble than you expected. That sword, Abner Grumman, was never meant for average hands. Forged during our darkest times, when the clans were still whole, it was a symbol of power and justice.

"My husband and I had a mighty empire, long before the rise of humanity. Together, with the sword, we beat back the hordes of supernatural monstrosities threatening to drive us to extinction. Like all good things, we soon discovered the sword was more than it appeared. Each life taken became part of it, until madness imbued its soul. Anger, hatred, and jealousy made the sword dangerous. The decision was made to secret the sword away, so that none would succumb to the darkness within. Thousands of years passed and you, of all people, have returned the sword to light and, in doing so, made yourself a target."

Morgen paused to take a sip of wine from the glass she had almost forgotten she had. She thought of offering to the others before continuing. "You have placed us all in danger through your ignorance and greed. What exactly did you hope to accomplish? That your buyer didn't know what the sword means or what it can do?"

Fumbling with his fingers, Abner failed to reply.

"Precisely! Humanity would tear itself apart should they gain the power in that weapon. Worse, the lycans now know you possess the sword and will stop at nothing to claim and at last make their bid to regain control of this world." She tsked. "Your ignorance has damned us all."

"There has to be something we can do," Sara said. Her side glare at Abner for involving her spoke volumes and amused the queen.

"Perhaps," Morgen replied through pursed lips. "If the sword can be returned to the man who created it, and he can be convinced to see you, the sword might be sent away once and for all."

"Away?" Sara asked.

The queen paused. Elfkind had secrets, dark and terrible ones no human, especially not the wife of an author who seemed intent on bringing those secrets to life through works of fiction, should know. Still, for all the doubt stemming from associating with mortals, Morgen found a quiet strength lurking within Sara, waiting to be unleashed.

Her mind flashed to the events happening in upstate New York and the potential fallout should the operation go wrong. Having to deal with another crisis, one with the inherent ability to bring her world to its knees, stole her focus from Xander's escape and the veiled threats of the prime minister. She needed solutions. Answers. And she needed them fast. "I'll leave that to our friend, once you find him."

The lack of explanation frustrating her, Sara leaned forward on her elbows. "I don't have time for games. My life, my family's life is in danger, and you insist on playing a verbal shell game. Abner already told me about the wizard. Where do we find him?"

"That is another matter altogether. Sheldon has ever been a recluse, even before the schism. No one has seen or heard from him in centuries, though there is one who may know. How far are you willing to go to be free from this nightmare?"

Sara tensed. Until now she hadn't given much thought beyond escaping Abner and the sword and returning to the mundanity of her life, as if that was possible. The promise of finding adventure of her own, combined with the lure of stepping out from Daniel's shadow in the world of the elves proved too much to ignore. Sara came to realize she needed this. Why remained hidden, however. A surprising sense of peace settled over her tepid thoughts, calming her as the decision made itself for her.

"Enough to ensure my family is safe," Sara replied.

Looking pleased, Morgen smiled. "Good. There is a man to the east of us who may help. A recordkeeper from the old days, he alone knows the wizard's location. Find him and you can end your troubles, at least for this night."

"Great. Where do I need to go?"

Morgen finished her wine. "Patience, Mrs. Thomas. You'll need more than a healthy attitude with a pack of lycans on your scent."

"I will escort her," Norman announced. "And the gnome."

An audible sigh escaped Sara.

"You know where to go?"

He nodded.

Morgen settled back into her chair. "Good. Speed is your ally. Stay ahead of the wolves. The sword must stay out of their hands at all costs, Norman. No sacrifice is too great. None."

"I understand," the gargoyle replied. To Sara he said, "We should go now."

Morgen watched them leave. Her part in their story ended, at least for the moment. A woman who left nothing to chance, she wished she hadn't sent her most valuable asset north to handle Xander and her wayward daughter. Collecting her wine, she sauntered to her favorite spot to absorb the sights of the night while thinking of the myriad ways it all might yet go wrong.

She hated leaving anything to chance.

"Where are we going, Norman?" Sara asked in the elevator down.

"To the coast, but we need help first. I cannot ward against a full lycan pack alone," he told her. "We need reinforcements."

"You're expecting a fight."

Another nod.

Fretting at their side, Abner bobbed his head. "I'm really, really sorry about this. I am."

"Save it for after we get rid of this sword and get home," Sara snapped.

Rebuked, the gnome fell silent.

"Norman, where are we heading to first? If those wolves are out there hunting us…"

"They are. Of that I have no doubt. We are going to the science museum. I have an old friend perfect for the work ahead," he answered. "If he's willing."

Museum? Resisting the urge to ask whether his friend was a dinosaur's skeleton, Sara felt it prudent to remain silent. At least for the time being. A thought struck and she reached out to touch Norman's forearm. "Norman, who did you think Morgen will get to watch my dogs?"

SEVEN

The North Carolina Museum of Natural Sciences was part of a sprawling complex of various museums often referred to as the *Smithsonian of the South*. Sara never understood the reference considering Washington D.C. was below the Mason-Dixon Line. South was south for a New York girl. That being said, she thoroughly enjoyed seeing the wonder fill her children's eyes as the roamed amongst skeletons of creatures long extinct, a meticulous butterfly garden, or learning about the impact of hurricanes on the state. Personally, she felt no need to return to the history museum across the street or the museum of art a few miles down the road, but the science museum held a special place in her heart.

Why Norman took them the few blocks up the street to the closed museum remained a secret. She learned long ago the gargoyle, taciturn on his most talkative days, preferred the objectivity of silence when dealing with others.

Leaving his Challenger in the parking garage for fear of its obnoxious engine alerting the werewolves to their location, they hurried on foot under the watchful boughs of ancient oaks. They skirted around the state capital building, ignoring the gaze of the various statues lining the manicured lawn. This late at night there was little traffic. A cascade of red and green washed the building facades and puddles up and down the two main arteries of the city.

Sara had lived in the area for years and could count the number of times she'd walked through downtown on one hand. Accustomed to suburban living, she never found the taste for crowded streets filled with the noise and trapped exhaust of thousands of cars. None of that mattered now. Her thoughts focused on escaping the threat at hand.

They crossed East Edenton Street, slipping between the twin museums. Sara headed for the front door before Norman stopped her. She followed his gesture and hurried to the front street, guessing he intended on bringing them in through the maintenance entrance. Her suspicions proved true as they scurried under the famous globe structure built into the museum's face. Norman led the way with powerful strides. Sara matched him, though had started breathing heavily. A handful of steps behind, Abner and the sword struggled to keep pace.

They had just rounded the corner when the distant howl of a lone wolf echoed. Norman pressed them against the building, his stone eyes scanning the streets for sign of their pursuit.

A second howl echoed back, much further away.

Time was up.

"They are closing," Norman explained. "We must hurry."

Dramatic undertone aside, Sara agreed. "Where is the door? We're too exposed out here like this."

She swore she caught the stench of wet dog. It was becoming a recurring torment. Not for the first time this night she longed for a weapon. A stick. Anything to give herself a better shot at survival.

Norman waved them forward and the tiny band inched toward the bay door just ahead. He turned, putting finger to his lips before slinking up to the door. A stiff breeze funneled down the street, blowing under his battered leather jacket. Bringing her hand to cover her face from the sheet of leaves and debris barreling toward her, Sara failed to see Norman disappear.

Cursing, Sara decided she and Abner were too exposed. Snatching his collar, she dragged the gnome after Norman. They hurried down a gentle slope to the loading bay door. Fretting at the prospect of being trapped, Sara eased into the shadows and watched the road. A trio of cars raced by, screaming south toward I-40. The rattle of chains behind them startled her. Sara reached for the gun she didn't have. *Shit. This is going to have to change, for my sanity if nothing else.*

Norman poked his head out and waved them forward. "Hurry," he urged.

Once inside, Norman pulled the door down and hit the locking lever with his foot.

"Where is your friend?" Sara asked.

"Upstairs. Third floor."

Finding it odd, she followed him as he began to walk. "Does he know you're coming?"

"He does," Norman said as he led them through the back hallway before emerging in the first-floor room containing the hanging skeletons of whales and other sea life.

They took a pair of escalators up to the darkened third floor. Norman unerringly led them past the insects and butterfly garden, meeting the gaze of the museum's sloth hanging from one of the trees. The gargoyle took them past the giant skull of a tyrannosaurus rex and into the dinosaur exhibit. Up a small flight of stairs and they came into a large room overlooking the northside of Raleigh and a series of dinosaurs brought to life by artisans years before Sara considered making North Carolina home. There, seated on one of the benches was a hulking figure she never expected to see again.

"Bert, we made it," Norman announced.

The troll rose and, towering over them, tilted his head to the side, cracking his neck as he stopped a pace away. Deep set eyes took in each. The rise and fall of his chest thrummed with the thump of his heart; Sara shrank away and Abner whimpered from behind. Then, unexpectedly, Bert broke into a smile.

"How have you been?" Sara asked, taking a seat beside the troll. While lacking any feeling of friendship or companionship with a man who once tried to kill her husband and kidnap her in the name of the queen, Sara found a measure of comfort in being so close to him again. So much changed that night, including her opinion of Bert. After all, he went from an unwilling villain to losing his brother and helping Daniel and DESA save the day. Somewhere along the way they formed a loose friendship. How many others could pull themselves from the depths of despair and find a new life?

"Trying to stay busy. Norman got me a job here as the night janitor," Bert said. "Don't pay none too well but I like talking to the dinosaurs." He sighed. "Sara, I miss seeing them roam the earth."

Seeing them? How old are you? How far back does elfkind stretch? Were they at the dawn of time? "I always liked this part of the museum. It reminds me of just how small we all are."

"Yup. Lou was always the thinker. I liked to smash stuff," he replied.

She remembered what Daniel's car looked like after Bert *smashed* it. "I'm sorry about your brother."

He hung his head. "Lou was a good guy, ya know? Always thinkin. We was good together. Him and me. I miss him."

"I didn't get the chance to know him," Sara said softly.

A brightness shined out his eyes. "You woulda liked him. Ma always said he was the smart one."

She smiled. "I'm sure you're plenty smart on your own, Bert."

"Norman says you're in trouble."

She nodded. *There's the understatement of the year.* "A little."

"Daniel not here?"

"No, Bert, he's not."

The troll scratched his jaw, tracing along an old scar. "Norman says you need my help."

"If you're willing to give it," she replied. "We can use it. There are some bad things chasing us."

"Werewolves."

Surprised Norman managed to provide Bert with so much information over a brief phone call back in the car, Sara said, "Yes. Nasty brutes." She debated on admitting it aloud before adding, "Bert, I'm scared."

Making a show of cracking his knuckles, flakes of dry skin showering off, Bert said, "I don't like the doggies. I'll protect you. For Daniel."

"No, Bert. For Lou." She wasn't certain but thought she caught the shadow of a tear crowding the corner of his eye after she spoke.

"The building is secure, for how long remains to be seen," Norman announced as he returned from his sweep. "Where's Abner?"

"He went across the bridge," Bert replied.

Together, they went across the small walkway connecting the main building with the more scientific center of the museum. Passing under the judgmental gaze of a mastodon skull, complete with curled tusks, they found Abner sitting in a sunken amphitheater area used for short movies and presentations. The sword leaned against the back of the seat in front of him.

"Abner, we need to talk," Sara said just loud enough to not startle him.

"I know," he replied, never taking his eyes off the sword. "Do you think it can?"

"Can what?"

"Kill me."

Sara groaned. They didn't have time for this. "Abner, we have a pack of bloodthirsty werewolves after us, after you. I don't think a shit talking sword is top of your list of concerns."

"I heard that."

The sword's voice was muffled from under the wrappings Morgen had placed on it. As much as Sara wanted nothing more than to toss the sword in the depths of Jordan Lake and be done with it, doing so only prolonged the inevitable conflict between elf and lycan, not prevent it. Reluctantly, she admitted doing so wouldn't guarantee her family's safety. Only one option remained. They needed to get on the open road, away from the confined spaces of Raleigh and return the sword to its creator. That simple.

Only she doubted it would be.

"We have a plan and now we have help. I need you to keep it together long enough to see this through," she told him. "Bert here is going to ensure nothing bad happens."

"I gave my word, I did," Bert growled.

Norman stepped between them. "We need a new vehicle. I can't fit everyone in my car."

Amused at the thought of Bert's immense form squeezing into the small cabin of the Challenger, Sara knew they were about to sacrifice speed and power, the two things they needed to get them on their way.

"I got a truck! A big one too." Bert beamed. "When do you want to leave?"

"Now," Norman said.

Agent Cecile Barnabas crouched in the middle of the empty suburban street. Rain washed most of the evidence away, but she found a small spattering of blood left behind from whatever happened outside the Thomas house. Giddy with excitement at being associated with Daniel and his wife, she saw the golden opportunity of escaping her desk job and getting into the field because of them. When dispatch called, they failed to tell her whose house she was going to, only that an incident threatened to undo the extraneous containment protocols D.E.S.A. had with the elf clans. Realizing where she was, whose house, changed it all.

The glint of streetlight on an alien object caught her attention. Flashlight in hand, Cecile moved to investigate. She kneeled, using a pen to lift the tangled mass from a small clump of debris trapped on the lip of the storm drain. Bringing it close, she inspected the item and felt her heart sink. "Oh, that's not good."

Together with the bloodstains in the street and signs of struggle, the handful of fur drew her to the only logical conclusion. One she never expected, nor wanted.

Cecile gave the Thomas property a final check before hurrying into her truck. Washington needed to know her findings, fast. The last thing any of them needed was a pack of werewolves running loose. Finger dangling above the call button, a second thought occurred to her. Why were the wolves after the Thomas'? Where did they all go?

Too many unanswered questions plagued her. Cecile considered herself a practical woman who, until passing the extensive series of tests and evaluations required to get her job, didn't believe in fairy tales or monsters. The world turned out to be much darker, more dangerous. She prided herself on doing her part to ensure humanity was kept safe from the creatures of the night and those who belonged in the forgotten annals of myth and legend.

Already knowing what Washington would tell her, Cecile started thinking outside of the box D.E.S.A. liked to keep everything. She needed to find the werewolves and Sara Thomas. After that she could get to the task of figuring out why those two were colliding in the suburbs of Raleigh. The only problem was she didn't know where to start. Frustrated, she started thinking the mission of her dreams might prove her undoing unless she could catch a break.

Digging into a pocket for her cell phone, she hit the button and made the call.

EIGHT

Packing into Bert's van, complete with a vintage airbrushed scene of a wizard riding a unicorn in a thunderstorm with a purple background, because of course he did, Sara felt like she was now part of the Scooby gang off to solve a mystery. The back seats were ripped out, replaced with a long couch on one side. Across from it was a small refrigerator and a cabinet for food. The television mounted to the corner by the back doors was just large enough to make out individual video game characters Abner discovered after taking his seat. Finishing the nostalgia was a plush carpet of emerald green.

The only thing missing is a lava lamp. Sara shook her head, marveling at the pristine condition the aged van was in as well as how clean it smelled. Too clean almost. Taking a spot beside Abner, she stared at the dancing hula girl glued to the dashboard. She wanted to laugh at the absurdity of it all. For a secretive race who shouldn't exist, they took every opportunity to enjoy a passing phase of modern culture.

Bert seemed indifferent to her amusement. To him, this was a way of life.

The troll strapped on his seatbelt and looked back. "Everyone set?"

"As we'll ever be, Bert," Sara replied.

Gunning the engine, he slapped his hands on the steering wheel. "Great! Where are we going?"

All eyes turned on Norman.

The gargoyle stared out the windshield, waiting until the van pulled onto the main road and headed south. "Fort Bragg. I need one more gun before we head for the scholar."

"You mean Fort Liberty," she corrected.

His silence was answer enough.

The van roared down the street, a cloud of exhaust fumes trailing after. Bert pulled on to I-40 and headed east without further instructions. Sara was impressed. He knew how to get around.

Norman constantly checked the mirrors, his hand curled around the handle of a snub-nosed revolver. Combined with the blips and beeps of the game Abner immersed himself in, Sara found the scenario beyond surreal. "Norman, I need a weapon if I'm going to defend myself."

"I got your weapon right here, lady. All you have to do is take me from the gnome and I'm yours. Oh, what fun we'll have!"

Ignoring the sword, she pressed, "I mean it. You can't watch me all the time. What happens if the werewolves attack me when you're occupied?"

"Can you handle a gun?" Norman asked without looking.

"Well enough. Daniel taught me."

He nodded. "When we get to Fort Bragg, I will take care of it."

"What about me, Norman? Do I get one too?" Bert asked, almost too gleefully.

"No."

"Not fair!"

The gargoyle's head turned, fixing the troll with a glare. "You don't need one, Bert. You have enough strength already."

Confusion twisting his features, Bert eventually said, "But Lou was killed by a gun. He didn't deserve that."

"No, he didn't, but you having a gun won't change anything," Norman reiterated. "Besides, I doubt the lycans have human weapons."

Struggling to recall what little lore she'd learned over a lifetime of watching bad movies and listening to Daniel rant about it, Sara frowned. "Norman, how do we kill a werewolf? Do you have silver bullets, or do we just yell '*bad doggie*' and smack them with a newspaper?"

"Do you have any idea how rare silver bullets are? The process is easy enough, but finding the right quality and grade of silver is not," Norman answered. "These are foolish questions, Sara Thomas. I would have thought Daniel did a better job teaching you our stories."

"He didn't write about werewolves," she snapped. Still, rebuked, she sat back and left the odd pair to the driving.

However, watching Abner plow, unsuccessfully, through whatever level of Mario proved equally unappealing and her mind and eyes soon wandered to the sword. Propped against the back doors, the sword remained hidden within the wrappings, added by an old burlap sack Bert had in one of the unmarked museum storage bins. She didn't ask. Some questions required no answers.

While the sword demonstrated a natural vehemence, Sara wondered how any creation could hold such abject hatred. The brief glimpse she had of it showed an intricate weapon better used as a collector's item, ornate and gilded; one deserving to be in a great museum. Nothing suggested the spiteful entity lurking deep within the folded steel. The more she thought on it the more questions arose. How could a sword speak? It didn't have a mouth or eyes. Was there some transcending presence, perhaps a damned soul, trapped within that imbued the magic from days long past?

Oh bother. I'm sounding like one of Daniel's silly books now. There must be a trick to it. A figment of our imagination compelling us to think it's alive. She wanted to ask. To learn the secrets of the blade. But who could she trust to provide an accurate answer? Bert didn't know much about anything, leastwise he pretended so. Norman refused to say more than he deemed necessary. And Abner was more afraid of the sword than her. That left one option.

Biting the tip of her tongue, Sara considered reaching out to touch the sword. Not hold or claim, just touch. Learn those twisted secrets making the sword so angry and, if time was on her side, find a way to free whatever being was inside. Her hand crept out, seeking the ancient hilt. A satisfactory hum urged her on. She wanted to feel powerful. To not be afraid of the wolves in the night threatening her and her family. She wanted to know what it was like to stride around the world and have others quake in her passing. The world needed cleansing and she meant to be the tool to do so…

"Don't," Norman's gravelly voice stopped her, inches from the sword.

Sara jerked. Eyes widening, she pulled her hand back.

"The sword will twist your thoughts, playing on your darkest desires until it takes over your mind and turns you into a creature none will recognize. It is a twisted game."

"I wasn't even thinking about that," she replied. She felt the sword's subtle pull. A quiet hum in the back of her mind, warm and soothing as a summer evening.

"Your intent does not matter," Norman countered. "The sword has been imbued with what your kind might call a demonic entity. That malevolent spirit pushes the boundaries of depravity. You would not notice the decline at first. Its will would manifest until you no longer recognized the difference between right and wrong. Instead of a benefactor you will become a tyrant, like all the others."

The mechanical sounds ceased as Abner paused his video game and swallowed hard. "You mean…"

"Yes, Abner Grumman, you would become an agent of evil and the Old Guard would be summoned to deal with you."

"What are the Old Guard?" Sara asked.

Abner couldn't help but shift his gaze to the burlap wrapped sword clanging against the metal paneling before he resumed his game.

"They are the best of us. Defenders of the crown and throne. Men and women from all races sworn to protect the monarchy. They are ruthless when pursuing a task, not stopping until all threats are eliminated," Norman explained. "Having them involved is a death sentence for all."

"Including you?"

"Yes," he said after another mile flashed by.

Sara stared at the empty road; thoughts lost in the dull glow of headlights as the miles sped by. With midnight fast approaching, she found fewer cars on the road. This part of the interstate, several miles removed from Raleigh proper and the congestion of the suburbs, she couldn't remember ever seeing a heavy flow of traffic. Normally the prospect of a faster travel time enthused her, but here in the darkness of the night she found it intimidating. Shadow images of wolves racing alongside them, red eyes gleaming with hunger, haunted her.

A sign announcing the merger with I-95 and, from what she knew thanks to experience, the thirty-mile run south to Fayetteville, brought no relief. The thrum of wheels chewing up the pavement combined with the roar of an engine past its prime conjured fresh images in her head. The last time she felt this little in control was when Daniel left to confront his then literary agent. While events spiraled, she pretended to remain stalwart for their children. Then came her kidnapping and her first run in with Morgen. Curiously, she failed to recall any monstrous bodyguards lining the walls like vicious henchmen.

Balancing between the twin threats of a sword wanting to kill any who touched it and a pack of bloodthirsty monsters roaming the night, Sara longed for a return to normalcy. Yet each bit of progress she made in turning her mind back to what the rest of the world deemed sanity, she failed to shake the allure of endless possibilities in adventure and intrigue should she become fully vested in this clandestine world existing alongside her.

She found herself longing for Daniel's calming presence. "Norman, do you know why Daniel was called back by DESA?" she asked after reaching for her phone.

"I have heard whispers," the gargoyle confirmed.

Hope blossomed within her. "Can you tell me?"

"I'm not supposed to, but he has been called to help track Xander down after the champion escaped his prison cell."

Xander? The fallen champion who helped Gwen kill her own father? Instead of finding comfort in the prospect of her husband swooping in to rescue her from whatever it was she was involved in, Sara found herself worrying more about Daniel and the vengeful madman sworn to get his revenge on all involved in stopping his plans. Werewolves on the run suddenly didn't seem so bad after all.

Unable to stop pacing, Gruff scratched the side of his face. He hated waiting. Hated not knowing. The pack leader spent decades working his way through the packs until he finally collected enough support and power to make his bid for power. The silver hair on his chest poking up from his v neck, Gruff ached to transform back into wolf form and be free of mortal constraints. Free to run wild and tear into his prey. Until he received word from Princess, he was resigned to pacing and swelling with rising hatred and anger.

The phone ringing caught him by surprise. The lycan halted midstride and answered, "Tell me."

Listening, Gruff felt his pulse quicken. His right hand elongated, fingers turning to claws, before he caught himself.

The others, until now keeping well clear of their leader, crowded closer. They felt his heart thundering. The rise in adrenalin surging through him. This was it. The moment they'd waited for since the ill-fated attack on the gnome earlier that night.

"Keep tracking them," Gruff ordered. "I'll bring the rest of the pack and meet you."

Hanging up, he turned to his pack, a triumphant grin stretching his face. "Mount up. Princess is on their trail. We dine on gnome tonight and claim the sword!"

Tilting their heads back, the pack howled and raced for their cars.

The hunt was on.

NINE

With night dragging deeper, Agent Cecile Barnabas turned her headlights off as she pulled off Lake Wheeler Road and onto the small side road leading down to the historic Yates Mill Pond Park. Situated in a quiet park of Wake County more populated by cows and farm life than people, the park dated back to the 1750s. Today, it was a minor attraction for families and historians. Tonight, it was the scene of the one lead her teams back in Washington provided.

She contemplated cutting the engine and gliding down the slope to the parking area to reduce her sound profile. Without knowing if the lycans were still on site, Cecile chose caution over the guns blazing approach. She calmed slightly as her government issue sedan cruised around the final corner and entered the parking lot. No other cars were here, as far as she could tell. Breathing a heavy sigh, she parked then took a moment to ensure her weapon was loaded and on safe. *You can do this, Cecile. Just like training. Follow protocol. Follow the rules*.

Cecile closed the door as soft as possible, wincing at the click sounding louder than a gunshot to her ears. Gun hand trembling, she stalked across the short parking lot, slipping between the buildings nestled against the lapping shores of a small lake. Another time and she might have found the area enticing enough to explore, perhaps take her boyfriend and make a day of it. North Carolina State University ran a creamery just up the road. The sort of experience city folks could go to and proclaim they got to eat their ice cream while watching the cows responsible for such dairy delights.

A car roared down the country road. The red glare of taillights as it slowed just enough to make the soft right turn brightening the area. Cecile's finger slipped into the trigger well. Her thumb danced over the safety. *Get it together, woman. You've been through worse*. Only, she hadn't. This was the edge of the map for her. Uncharted territory beckoning her further. A twinge of excitement collided with the nervousness ready to break free and run rampant through her mind and body.

She followed the path down to the mill and the rocks below. The stench of wet dog choked the air, but she failed to find any werewolves lurking in the shadows. Cecile did a quick sweep through the immediate area and, after finding nothing but tracks, holstered her weapon. Disappointed, she ran through a series of steps to secure the location and search for clues. With her quarry already gone, Cecile felt her opportunity to nab the big collar slipping through her fingers. Knowing her career was defined by her actions, she shrugged off the moment of uncertainty.

Turning to leave, she caught the slight glint of metal under the invasive beam of her flashlight. Squinting, Cecile inched closer to investigate. The ground turned into muddy slop once she got off the trail leading under the bridge. Thankful for wearing a sensible pair of sneakers, she stepped off the wood plank crossing the small stream runoff. The area looked disturbed. Closer inspection showed a large section had been overturned, looking dug up. She kneeled next to the object, slapping a palm across her mouth to stifle the escaping gasp.

It was a ring. A wolfs head. The sigil of the clans. It was also attached to a finger which was still attached to the hand poking out from the fresh dirt mound. *Yes!* She had proof the lycans were on the move. Unlike elves or dwarves, werewolves did not dissolve into ash upon death. She supposed it made sense; all things considered.

She frowned as only some pieces slipped into place. Stepping back, she made the call she didn't want to. "This is Barnabas. I have a body. Lycan. But nothing else. He was buried and left behind. No idea where the pack went or what they are after yet."

"Agent Barnabas, you do know the lycans are all chipped, right?"

She paused. *Microchipped? Like a dog*? Humane or not, that bothered her. "No, I wasn't aware of that. Not that it matters much. I don't know what pack this guy belonged to or where he came from."

"Easy fix. Give me a second."

Frustrated with the secrets being kept, Cecile felt her stomach twist as she stared at the hand. A million thoughts clogged her mind, preventing her from thinking clearly. Out of all of them, the image of a lycan in human guise kicking a leg out as it was shocked by the collar around its neck for attempting to leave the yard stuck. She snorted a giggle.

"Got it. Do you have your issued tablet?"

Stirred back to the moment, Cecile replied, "It's in the car, yes."

"Good. This guy's name is Spot. He runs with the Blue Ridge Pack. They're a long way from home. Out of their territory."

She didn't know who she was talking too, only the man on the other end of the line proved equally infuriating and annoying. *Spot? You've got to be kidding me. Who did he run with, Fido*? "How do I track them?"

"I'm sending you a link now. Won't do much more than show you where they are but at least it's a start."

"Copy, Washington. Barnabas out." She hung up, unwilling to hear anything else.

A recovery team would already have been dispatched, ensuring no civilian would stumble upon the body in the morning or beyond. Raleigh being a generally low crime city compared to the larger ones, the last thing she needed was to waste time mitigating the murder of a creature who shouldn't have existed in the first place.

Cecile hurried back to her car. Call it intuition. Call it a hunch. Whichever, she felt she knew she stood upon the cusp of something momentous.

Setting his glasses on the keyboard and pinching the bridge of his nose, Darryl Wallace took a string of depths breaths. He'd been with D.E.S.A. for a number of years, providing tech support for several operations. Until tonight he had missed every major action, including the North Carolina debacle several years ago. He slipped on his shoes and straightened his tie. The information he'd just learned needed to be acted on immediately. A storm was brewing. He felt it and, by some strange twist of fate, he was at the precipice of finally getting his legs under him with the agency. He would break his bad streak. Awards, promotion, and glory awaited.

Darryl headed to his supervisor's office. *Tonight, Darryl Wallace you are about to be somebody!*

"What do you want, Wallace?"

The giddiness fled. Darryl suddenly remembered no one, including himself, enjoyed going to this particular supervisor. She was a bitter woman shoved into a menial job after a string of failures as a field agent. Instead of being let go for her incompetencies, the powers that be decided she could best serve the agency in a middle management position without direct contact with any critical aspects associated with the secrecy of the elf clans.

Fortunately for Darryl, or maybe unfortunately, she listened as he detailed his conversation with field agent Barnabas, quietly absorbing developing events. A wicked glint danced in the corner of her eye.

"Good work, Wallace. Monitor the situation and report every update. We can't afford another nightmare like the last time that infernal state got out of control," the supervisor instructed. "I'll relay to higher."

Darryl stood in the doorway, blinking as he processed his orders. A surge of disappointment rose.

"What?" she asked.

Blinking again, he replied, "Er, nothing."

"Then get back to work. We don't have all night."

Violent Meyers glared at Darryl's back as he loped back to his cubicle. With a little luck, she would never have to deal with incompetent menials like Wallace again after tonight. Concealing her laughter, she finally saw the golden ticket she deserved and was willing to do anything in her limited ability to claw her way free from this obscure hell and back into leadership's good graces.

The Department of Extra Species Affairs was established in the aftermath of World War I when the world became smaller thanks to new modes of transportation and communication. Up to that point the elf clans walked among humans with immunity. Their purposes seldom crossed, leaving humanity without a clue they were not alone in the world. Through the years it became a haven for those obsessed with fantasy and the supernatural. For those who didn't quite fit in with acceptable society. The kind who stared at the stars and asked if we were alone.

After the near societal collapse of the early 1970s D.E.S.A. shifted to a more bureaucratic role, replacing the mystics and dreamers with those based on logic and their ability to reason. A military arm of field agents, trained in every modern tactic United States special forces received, fanned out across the country, posing as the harmless vacuum salesman, the plumber, or the friendly neighborhood butcher. Each cover story was immaculately created to allow agents to blend in and observe.

The agency shifted again in the aftermath of the 9/11 terror attacks. Fearing the enemy might attempt to seduce the fringe of the elf clans to joining the cause,

D.E.S.A. clamped down on the clans and maintained a more permanent presence. To date, only a handful of the highest-ranking officials knew of its existence, with presidents failing to be included. This did little to stop those like Darryl Wallace from finding a home and living his dream.

Making his way back to the false security of the blue walls of his cubicle, Darryl struggled with knowing he had done the right thing by reporting the event to Violet and the predatory look in her eyes inspiring a fresh wash of perspiration. Days like this when the deodorant wore off a long time ago, he knew he couldn't yet go home. Not until he saw how matters played out and whether he could trust his supervisor. He logged back into his computer, hands hovering over the keyboard.

"Hello! Darryl!"

He pushed away from his desk, eyes wide as he looked upon the man leaning against one of the chest high walls. "Huh? What's up, John?"

"I asked if you wanted to get a bite to eat with us," John replied with that winning smile capable of swooning women and making babies laugh. Darryl was immune though. "It's break time."

You couldn't have just texted me? Damned near gave me a heart attack sneaking up on me like that. "Sorry. I gotta stay and monitor a potential situation developing in North Carolina."

John hummed. "It's always that damned state, isn't it? Maybe we should just evict those elves and send them back to Europe." When Darryl didn't comment, he continued. "Ok, have it your way. We're doing Thai this time. Maybe I can bring you back something?"

"Sure, that would be nice," Darryl said, watching John depart.

With a quick wave, he resumed the dark corridor his thoughts found themselves winding down. What if he couldn't trust Violet? Who could he turn to when it all fell apart and the higher ups dropped the hammer on him? Darryl pulled up the private document he'd been building for years, praying it might do him some good should it fall out that way.

TEN

The van rumbled on through the impenetrable darkness. Abner, having grown bored and seeming to run out of adrenalin, had fallen asleep a few miles back. He snored softly on the couch, oblivious to the world. Sara felt her eyes grow heavy, the weariness of the day settling in. As much as she wanted to give in and tilt her head back for a little sleep, she found the act harder than usual.

"…going down the onl—"

Rolling her eyes as the troll strangled out the old 80s song, Sara yelled, "Bert! I have a headache. Could you turn it down please?"

Bobbing his head, locks of greasy hair sweeping over his collar, the troll complied. "Sorry, Ms. Sara. This was jus Lou's favorite song."

A pang of regret awoke. She didn't know what he went through that night his brother died, and not knowing opened a line of sorrow she couldn't escape. Sara reached out to touch his shoulder. "I'm sorry, Bert. I am, it's just been too much for me. This isn't my world."

"Aw, I know. Me and Lou was gonna mess your husband up like Morgen wanted but we found him nice enough, ya know? I like Daniel so that means I like you too."

"Thank you, Bert," she said, unexpected sentiment seeping through her words.

"I got some water and aspirin in the fridge if you need it."

She thanked him again and rummaged through the small fridge. That's when she first heard it. The low whine of engines closing in at high speed. Still miles from their exit, that meant one thing. Sara downed the aspirin and looked out the back window, only to find the window covered by the television and a poster of a band she didn't know.

The whine turned into a roar. Multiple roars.

Norman's voice cut the tension, "They have found us."

How? Failing to understand the odds of being tracked so quickly, Sara slid up behind the front seats. "What are we going to do?"

"Hold on!" Bert hollered.

The van lurched as he depressed the gas. Whatever the troll thought was going to happen in his heroic attempt at losing their hunters, failed to materialize. The van was too old, too tired, and lacked the power to out race the dozen or so motorcycles closing on them. She caught the glint of wild glory in his eyes and knew telling him otherwise was pointless. Best let him enjoy his moment while it lasted.

"What are we going to do?" she asked.

Norman unbuckled his seat belt. A trio of bikes raced by, crossing in front of them several times. Others pulled up on either side of the van, boxing them in. Shouts and growls roared over the scream of engines and squealing tires.

"Bert, slow down so I can open the door," Norman ordered.

The troll balked. "Are you crazy? Slow down! They'll kill us, Norman."

"Not if I kill them first."

The van slowed and Sara watched as the trio of bikes sped ahead.

Norman gave her a final look, pausing to offer a grim smile, and shoved his door open. She'd never seen a gargoyle before, leastwise not one in his original form. The blur of energy as Norman Guilt transformed into a winged creature, solid grey and menacing with fangs and horns, twisted her stomach. The door slammed shut. Sara stared after him, mouth agape. *This isn't how Daniel wrote him...*

She swore she heard Norman growl to speed up. So did Bert. The van's engine gave a valiant bellow, vomiting a cloud of black smoke as it picked up speed.

Bert chuckled. "Hold on, this is going ta be fun."

Sara barely grabbed the back of his seat before the van shifted left. The crunch of metal on metal and shower of sparks blazed in the night as they collided with one of the bikes. Sara watched machine and rider tumble away—one down.

The bikes in front realized something was wrong and wheeled around.

"Bert, are your windows bullet proof?" Sara asked after spying the small, dark objects in the riders' hands.

"Nope, why?"

Shit.

"We're going to die!" Abner squawked. The sword snickered at the promise of battle.

Gargoyles, contrary to popular myth, despised sitting still. They were creatures of action. Children of the hunt. They ranged across the wild places of the world where men dared not go, stalking their prey and instilling dread before swooping in for the kill.

Norman lamented their demise and relegation to ignominy in pop culture. Instead of being the stalwart hunter killers of the elf world, they found their fangs pulled. But not now. Now Norman could be his true self without regret or fear of reprisal.

With a fifteen-foot wingspan, Norman rocketed through the night sky. Curved fangs jutted below his lower lip, framed by a thick forehead and shallow cheeks. His skin was stone grey after a summer shower. Tufts of black hair peppered his arms and legs, obscene among the corded muscles. In his natural guise, he was the heart of vengeance. Claws outstretched; he drove into the nearest rider.

Claws pierced flesh above the leather collar, lifting the lycan up with a scream. Norman surged higher. The flap of his leathery wings causing the beat of nightmares. Once he deemed they were high enough, the gargoyle cast down his enemy and plunged toward the next. The werewolf crashed into the pavement with a sickening crunch. A pair of lycans had leapt upon the van and were crawling toward the windshield—Norman dove.

The van rocked as he landed, claws piercing metal as he anchored himself in front of the advancing werewolves. He crouched and braced for their charge. The man on his right blurred into wolf form. The woman on the left tilted her head back in wild laughter. Norman found it odd they longed to test their martial prowess on him even as he welcomed the challenge.

Lashing with both front paws, the wolf struck Norman's chest while his human companion lunged for his legs. Neither expected the merciless beating of wings driving them back. In the process of falling, the human blurred into wolf form, long nails raking across the van's metal roof in a shower of sparks. Her lower half slipped over the edge with a thump before she arrested her fall and pulled herself up.

The male wolf lunged again, jaws stretching for Norman's throat. The gargoyle met the charge, snatching both paws in his massive fists and slamming his forehead into the wolf's face. Teeth and blood burst from the wolf's mouth, followed by a ragged scream. Norman head butt the wolf again, and again until he heard the telltale sound of a neck snapping. He discarded the corpse over the side and attacked the recovering female. Seeing her time already past, she snapped her jaws and spat before turning and leaping clear of the speeding van.

Breathing heavy, Norman rose to his full height, chest heaving from the exertion. The first bullet struck a heartbeat later, hitting the near armor of his upper wing. Snarling, he rolled his shoulders and turned to meet the new threat.

"Look out!" Sara shouted.

Bert clenched the steering wheel with both hands and ducked a split second before a hail of gunfire smacked the van and windshield. Sara dropped to the floor and clamped her hands over her ears. Glass chipped under the thunder of impacting rounds. The engine whined as if eager to escape.

From the couch, Abner squawked and jumped up. Sara grabbed one of his ankles and jerked his legs out from under him. His head bounced off the carpet to the laughter of the sword.

The bikes sped closer, sensing the opportunity to kill. All it took was one round to incapacitate Bert, a lucky one to kill him, and they would be dead. Poking her head up just enough, Sara saw the dark mass blast in front to knock two of the three riders off their bikes. One slammed into the van, bouncing off in a twisted piece of scrap metal. The third rider avoided Norman's attack and continued firing into the side of the van as they passed.

Sara found her courage and slipped into the passenger seat. Hands trembling, she checked behind and was surprised to find the werewolves were getting further behind, circling around a shape on the road. "Bert, you can slow down."

He shook his head, continuing at full speed. "Nope. Not happening. They're sneaky, them dogs. We gotta keep moving, until Norman gets back."

They continued another mile south before finding Norman, back in his human guise, waiting on the side of the road. Popping open the side door, the battered and bruised gargoyle stomped inside and all but collapsed on the couch.

He turned to meet Abner's stare. "What?"

The gnome gulped. "You look terrible."

Sara let slip a laugh.

The van stuttered on.

Gruff found a disturbing trend materializing with his pack: They were dying at an unprecedented rate. Should it continue, he wouldn't have the manpower to take the sword. Not with that gargoyle protecting it. Four more lycans died in the van assault, their bodies lined up on the side of the road. They were his friends. His followers sworn to support and defend him through the good times and the bad. None expected to die hunting a monster.

Removing his helmet, the pack leader dropped his kickstand and glared at the survivors. Several were beaten. He noted the heavy bruising on Princess' face and neck, silently comparing it to the ruined face of Henry as he lay dead, locked in mid-transformation. The others kept their heads down, refusing to meet his gaze.

"How did this happen?" Gruff demanded. "I grow tired of seeing my pack slaughtered by that goddamned gargoyle."

"We had them," Princess insisted. "If Guilt had stayed in the van the sword would be yours already."

Gruff snorted. "I keep hearing that. The only thing we're getting is killed."

"We've never fought a gargoyle before, Boss."

"Clearly," he ignored the speaker. "Push the bikes into the ditch and dispose of the bodies. We need to keep moving. Princess, you up for taking tail again?"

She started to nod, stopping abruptly as pain twisted her features. "Enough. Give me one to drive."

Gruff looked at Good Boy and jerked his head. The smaller man went to stand beside the second. "The rest of you, get this cleaned up asap. I don't know where they're going but we can't let them get too far ahead." He sucked in a deep breath. "I want that sword. Whoever brings it to me, and the gargoyle's head, will be named pack second."

He ignored the hateful glare Princess fired at him as the remaining pack burst into action, knowing the sooner they cleared the engagement area the sooner they were back on the hunt. The promise of blood spurred them as much as his promised punishment should they fail. Less than a minute later the single cab truck rolled up; Princess and Good Boy got in, peeling off with a squeal. With more power and in better condition, finding the van wouldn't be an issue. Gruff just hoped they had enough sense to stay back to not arouse Guilt's attention.

He watched them go, wondering how much more his pack had to suffer as they forged their destiny.

The future of the lycans was at stake.

A future in which Gruff planned to be king.

ELEVEN

Clanking down the street with more rattles than before, Bert guided the van off the interstate and into the sprawling monstrosity known by countless soldiers as Fayetteville. A true army base town, whenever those units stationed at the former Fort Bragg deployed, the city became a ghost town. Sara first met Daniel here after one of his deployments and, though they only lived an hour north, vowed to never return here unless she had to.

To her surprise, much had changed in the past decade and a half since they bought their first home together close to the base on Cliffdale West. They drove past a string of faceless gas stations, closed convenience stores, and over the bridge beyond the county courthouse. Sara recalled the old days of Korean drinky bars, drug dealers roaming the streets, and prostitutes lingering outside of infamous strip clubs comprising downtown Fayetteville. Those wild days were gone at last.

Seemed that city leadership finally swooped in and enacted gradual changes for the benefit of all; Daniel had mentioned they were planning to once in a passing conversation. Now small businesses, craft breweries, and a brand-new police station were sitting over the ashes of past debaucheries that transformed Fayetteville into a place to visit. It too appeared that the old bars were torn down and the Airborne and Special Operations Museum was created after all. At last, the brave soldiers who risked their lives by dropping from the sky were given a proper memorial they could be proud of.

Seeing this did little to subdue Sara's dislike, however. Some hurts refused to go away. "Will this contact of yours help us, Norman?"

The gargoyle, already taciturn, hadn't spoken since their encounter with the werewolves, prompting her to wonder if his heart was in this. She'd never taken a life and had no aspirations to do so but recognized the effects. They seldom spoke of it, choosing to hide their pain by burying those memories deep inside and refusing to look within lest they become consumed by it. She knew better than to ask Norman, just as she learned to not ask Daniel. The gargoyle had been alive for countless years, no doubt participating in his share of mayhem. Yet for all that, Sara learned the elves had a certain human quality among them.

Norman turned away from the television, blinking twice before answering. "That depends on his mood. He's a former team guy with little tolerance or patience."

"Where have I heard that before?" Abner muttered.

The gnome hadn't relaxed since the ambush. More than once Norman's growl stopped him from bouncing his foot. Sara had heard him debating in harsh whispers with himself about abandoning the sword and knew he was close to attempting to do so. She felt for him, even if this was his fault.

"Sounds like a pleasant disposition," Sara commented before Norman went after the gnome, again.

"He's the right one to have in a fight," Norman said. "Head over to the Crown. He likes prowling the rooftops."

Prowling the rooftops? Sara turned away so he couldn't see her frown. "The Crown it is."

Years ago, Cumberland County and the city of Fayetteville came to an agreement to construct the county's premier venue for sports, concerts, and more. The Crown Coliseum was the result. Capable of holding ten thousand, it played host to hockey, music, and arena football for years. Situated on the fringes of town, it was the perfect place for their clandestine meeting. The last time Sara had been here was when Daniel had a booth at the local ComiCon. It wasn't her crowd, a fact she reminded him of repeatedly during those two, and only two, days she helped. That was the last time she volunteered to go with him to an event.

The van rumbled on. Sara smirked at the thought of breaking her vow and returning to the scene of one of the most confusing events of her life.

Pushing close to midnight, the van pulled into the parking lot. They were unsurprised to find it empty. Following Norman's guidance, Bert rolled the van up to the docking doors and cut the lights. Both he and Sara peeked out the windows, hoping to catch a glimpse of the one they'd risked their lives to find. While Bert seemed to know who he was looking for, Sara's imagination began to get away from her.

"You won't find him," Norman told them. "Not unless he wants you to."

"Won't keep me from slicing his head off. Someone take this towel off me."

"He does know we're coming, right?"

Norman nodded before opening the side door and stepping out, his back a string of snapping as he stretched. "I should go alone. He does not enjoy surprises. I'll be back."

Irony aside, Sara found his promise hollow. The werewolves were still out there, presumably hunting them. What would happen if they struck when Norman was off stalking his friend? She looked at Bert. The troll was massive and capable of handling his own, but against a pack of rabid wolves how much could he accomplish before they swarmed over them and took the sword?

"Norman, I…."

Too late. Blurring into his gargoyle form, he was airborne before she finished. The van rocked, buffeted by the sweep of his wings. Unable to contain her frustration, Sara punched the dashboard.

"Uh, I wouldn't do that. The dashboard fell off the last time I did that," Bert told her.

She found the comparison ridiculous and instead changed the subject. "Bert, do you have weapons?"

He beamed. "Nah, I was always more of a baseball bat kinda guy. Ma always said I was good with my hands."

Doubtful his enthusiasm for fist to fist was enough to ward off a pack of bloodthirsty werewolves already angered from losing several of their own. Sara, remembering Bert's warning, lowered her forehead to the dashboard with a slight thump. The hula dancer danced beside her.

Perfect.

Norman Guilt sailed over the round roof of the coliseum. His perfect night vision failed to produce any sign of his quarry. Tucking his wings, he circled around for a second pass. He felt the sizzle of the round blasting inches from his head before the shot rang out. Norman lowered his head and dove, claws extended. A second and third round flashed past before he collided with the shooter. Bodies tangled, Norman wrapped his arms around the target and pinned him down. The sniper rifle skittered away through pools of rainwater.

Norman caught a knee in his groin before being kicked off. He flipped over the shooter's head and landed on his back. The shooter was already on his feet and reaching for his rifle by the time Norman regained his feet. Funneling his rage and frustration over the night's events, Norman leapt forward and crushed the shooter into the roof. Grabbing the man by the unkempt hair tied back with a camouflage bandana, Norman slammed his head twice before rendering him unconscious.

Breathing heavily, Norman rose and looked around, ensuring there wasn't another shooter lurking in the night. Satisfied the area was secure, he grabbed the rifle and slung the body over a shoulder before sailing back to the ground and his waiting companions. The clouds were starting to break, revealing the baleful glare of the full moon in all its glory. The implications ran through Norman's mind as he delivered his package.

"What's this?" Sara asked.

Norman, back in human form, rubbed the growing bruise on his jaw. "Our help."

Eyebrow raised; Sara didn't ask the obvious question. Instead, she asked, "Is he still alive?"

The gargoyle grunted. "Damned fool almost killed me."

"With friends like that," she quipped.

"What about them?" he asked.

"Never mind. Are you sure he will help us after your, ah, altercation? He doesn't look like anything special."

"He doesn't have a choice," Norman growled.

"Lovely. Do we tie him up and throw him in the van or wait for him to wake up? Those wolves can't be too far behind."

"The pack will have taken time to see to their dead before continuing pursuit, but you are correct. They will still be on our scent before long, if they ever lost it," he explained. "Tying him up will prove problematic. Best we leave him here and wait."

Not liking it but failing to see an alternative, Sara sank back into the passenger chair. It didn't take long before boredom overrode fear, and her fingers drummed a forgotten tune on the dash. Bert stood beside her, leaning against the van like the poster boy for a 1970s car commercial. After placing the rifle in the back with a rattled Abner, Norman began to pace.

Sara didn't know how much time passed before the man on the ground stirred. Groaning, he reached to his forehead and rolled onto his back. Surveying his surroundings, he pulled himself up to a sitting position and glared at Norman. "You didn't have to fucking hit me so hard."

Norman replied, "You didn't have to shoot at me."

Spitting a mouthful of blood, the man snorted. "If I wanted you dead, you'd be ashes drifting to the ground right now, *old friend*." He eyed Sara then Bert and then the gnome. "You going to introduce me to your friends or what?"

"Uther, meet the team."

"Uther?" Sara asked.

"Yeah, like King Arthur's father," he said. "Only I ain't royalty."

"You're a royal pain in the ass," Norman muttered. "The queen still wants your head for that stunt in Brussels."

"Brussels? That was three hundred years ago," Uther replied. "Damned elves. They never forget, do they?"

"You did nearly get her entire family killed."

"How was I supposed to know Napoleon had patrols that far out?" He shrugged. "Anyway, where did you get this rabble from and what do you need with me?"

Norman explained their current situation, emphasizing the determination of the werewolf pack. Uther listened his gaze never leaving Sara. That predatory lingering made her flush, unsure whether he wanted to kill her or not.

"Let me get this straight," Uther drawled. "This little shit found the sword of Grimspire, brought down the wrath of a rogue pack of mutts, and got this hummie involved."

"My name is Sara."

"Whatever. Just because your husband is famous doesn't mean I respect him," Uther snapped. "What's the bottom line?"

"We need weapons and an extra gun to get us to the wizard," Norman intoned.

"I got the weapons and don't have a problem being a gun," Uther said. "But this isn't going to be as easy as you think."

"Why not?" Sara asked. Sensing him trying to shove her aside, she needed to establish her place in the group. Whether Uther liked it or not.

Glaring, Uther said, "I know where the man is you need to find the wizard and he don't talk to people without a tribute."

"What's the price?" Norman asked.

Uther snorted. "An ogre's egg."

Bert gulped and shook his head when Sara opened her mouth. *Ogre?*

"Where do we find one?" Norman asked.

"There's a nest down under an old railroad bridge close to downtown. First, we need to get my gear. I got a connex on base. Best we hurry before the doggies catch up."

They piled into the van, Sara begrudgingly taking a backseat with a scowl, and with Uther's directions pulled onto All American Boulevard, racing toward the second largest army base in the United States.

Night dragged on, oblivious to the stares and silent judgments being passed around by those within the van. Only Abner ignored the stress by diving back into his video games. The sword of Grimspire rested behind him and it was there Uther's gaze went. Sara watched the light dance in his eyes as his fingers itched. She didn't trust the newest addition. Not one bit.

TWELVE

Sara found it odd when the gate guards failed to question their odd menagerie filling up the van as it rolled onto base. Normally they would be forced to stop, get out, and wait for security to check the vehicle before being issued a temporary pass. Instead, Uther waved his badge, and they were welcomed with a salute. As much as she wanted to question how, she held her tongue. Tensions remained high between them and, regardless of her initial sentiments, Sara knew they needed the man if they had any shot at getting to the wizard first.

Without knowing more than the vague little Norman told them, Sara felt her skin crawl. Uther projected a level of violence simmering beneath his skin, waiting to burst free. She'd heard Daniel's stories, often choosing to slide them into the category of fantasy and embellishment. Until now she refused to believe any living being held that much anger inside. Unsure whether Uther was a villain or not, she decided to hold her tongue. For now.

The van drove past the South Post PX, hooking left on Chicken Road before heading out toward the field training area.

"Where are we going? Main post is back the other way," Sara asked, suspicious.

Uther grunted. "You don't think I'd keep an arsenal in the heart of the base, do you? I have been stationed here for a long time, in one guise or another. I have a connex positioned out at Camp McCall. All the weapons we need to kill the puppies."

Knowledge of the former Fort Bragg limited, Sara vaguely recalled Daniel mentioning how Camp McCall, attached to the western fringe of government property, was a main hub for Special Forces training. Whatever Uther pretended to be, she decided he was more than a mere foot soldier hiding behind the U.S. Army tag.

"Go ahead. Ask," Uther coaxed. "You want to know what I am? I'll tell you. There's no secret. I was one of the Old Guard. Sworn to protect the High Court."

"What happened?" she asked, her mouth gone dry.

Abner paused his game, shifting the blueberry flavored sucker Bert handed out to the other side of his mouth. Nothing good came from dealing with the Old Guard.

"I realized the king and queen were full of shit. Neither wanted the end of their war. There was too much power at stake. I gave up my sword, abandoned my post, and headed into the world of humans. Your kind has always known the potential in a good war. I fought for centuries, from the mountains of India to the fields of France. Wasn't until your American Civil War that I decided to settled down and called this land home."

"That's—" Sara started. Once, his confession would have blown her mind. Now…

"Do you have any idea how many wars your people have fought? Mostly over nothing, in the grand scheme," Uther said. "If only you learned to harness your natural abilities for creation instead of focusing on destruction. You might be something."

"Do you get tired of it?" she asked, ignoring the barb.

"Of what?"

"The fighting."

Uther broke into a smile. "I get tired of your fighting. Some of us are born to do a job. Nah, keeps me young. A good fight keeps me sharp too. You never know where or when that next battle is coming." He shifted in his seat. "Bert, pull over here. We go on foot the rest of the way."

Bert stopped the van before Sara could reply. Clambering out, they all, the sword included, followed Uther down a sandy road blocked with a heavy metal cable. Sara found it difficult to imagine they were safer on foot, but no one bothered questioning the fallen Old Guard. Unused to following blindly, she picked up her pace to come alongside Norman. The gargoyle acknowledged her with a grunt and nothing more.

Whispering, Sara asked, "Norman, what happens if the wolves catch us in the open?"

"We fight."

Her skin was riddled with goosebumps. Every sound in the night amplified. The crunch of boots on sand inspired foul images of salivating werewolves lurking just beyond. Sara felt her stomach tighten. She was trapped between a complete madman sporting a death wish and a horde of monsters wanting to tear her throat out for being in the way. *What if*...

"Norman, what happens if I get bitten?" she asked abruptly.

"You die," Uther chimed in.

"Because of the poison?"

"No, because I'll cut your fucking head off," his answer squashed any doubts of what would happen.

"Oh, pick me!" the sword barked from Abner's back. "I love doing that."

Norman glared back at the gnome, who paled and shrugged. He refocused on her. "Sara, I will not allow anything bad to come to you. You have my word."

Swallowing the lump growing in her throat, she asked, "So being bitten does transform you into one of them?"

He nodded. "From what we have discovered, yes. They carry a gene altering poison from which there is no cure."

"Has any of your kind been turned?"

"No. We are anathema to each other," Norman said.

"Like you shouldn't exist in the same world," she concluded. *Like you all shouldn't exist in mine.*

"I've been building a stockpile for decades now," Uther said as he unlocked the connex and pulled the doors open. "Thankfully the military changes weapon systems slowly. Some of the larger guns are no longer in service, like the 60 over there, but the newer versions fire the same caliber. Nothing tells a puppy to bark like a few hundred rounds of 7.62 to the chest."

Lost, Sara marveled at the endless display of weapons lining the walls, the countless ammunition boxes, rocket launchers, and more she'd never seen before. Far from being an expert, she figured there was enough in front of her to topple a small government. Daniel would enjoy this.

"Stick to the belt feds," Uther told them. "Leave the grenades and the heavy machine guns. We need to be able to move fast and strike hard without being bogged down. The wolves are fast, cunning, and have no qualms about getting into a fight in the middle of everything." He tsked. "No, rocket launchers, Norman."

The gargoyle pulled his hand back from the tube-shaped anti-tank rocket leaning against the metal wall. Lips pursed, he snatched an empty army issue duffel bag instead and opened it. He and Uther began dumping boxes of ammunition. Once the bag was full, Norman took it outside.

Humming, Uther continued plucking weapons, from handguns to a light machine gun. He handed Sara a small wooden crate.

"What's in here?" she asked, fumbling around the dark canisters.

"Smoke," Uther replied as he grabbed a sledgehammer and hefted it over his shoulder. "Ogres are big and dumb, but they're faster than anything once their blood gets hot. We pop a few smoke grenades to give us some cover and we're in and out before they know what we were after."

"I don't like ogres," Bert said.

"That's all it will take?" Sara frowned. "I can't see how stealing one of their children is going to sit well with them."

He paused, as if the thought hadn't occurred to him. "Huh, sounds like their problem, doesn't it? You need to get the sword to the wizard. We need the egg. Simple as that."

Sara followed him out. "Won't they want their egg back?"

"Sure," Uther admitted.

Locking the connex, the Old Guard hefted his bag and ushered them back to the van. The night had grown impossibly dark, closing in around the dim glare of their flashlights. Clouds swept in, concealing the moon. Sara felt choked, stifled under a blanket of oppression. Knowing she needed to latch on to pleasant thoughts, she wondered what Daniel was up to.

All she knew was he'd been sent to New York at the best of Agent Blackmere. Sara liked the quirky old agent despite his rough edges. He bore all the hallmarks of a man who'd been part of the system for too long and found himself languishing under a thin disguise of contempt and caffeine. Without any experience to fall back on, Sara failed to see the appeal of spending countless hours buried beneath a wave of government paperwork, crippling rules and regulations, and the inability to tell anyone about his job. No wonder Blackmere appeared haggard and burned out.

That they had to steal the egg, an ogre's child, twisted her thoughts. No one could say what the wizard would do with the egg, but a volley of images flashed through her mind. As a mother, she wanted nothing more than to abandon the quest and leave the egg alone. Then the rational part took over and Sara accepted the task they were about to attempt. Frustrations settled in. She hated feeling trapped.

Lost in thought, Sara found they were back at the van already. She helped heft the cache into the back, much to the discomfort of Abner, before taking her spot in the passenger seat thanks to Norman's insistence. She silently thanked him, for she didn't see how she'd be able to cope with sitting beside the arrogance Uther exuded. Her hand brushed the waistband of her pants before she folded them on her lap. Armed at last, she felt her chances of survival rise just enough to leave her feeling better. Of course, she still didn't have any ammunition. *Baby steps, Sara. Baby steps.*

It took the better part of forty-five minutes to make their way off post and across Fayetteville. Both Bert and Sara couldn't stop looking out the side mirrors. Their last encounter with the pack left each rattled. Whereas Sara feared for their lives, she heard Bert lamenting the damage to his van. Under his breath he struggled with calculations on replacement parts and repairs. His deep-set eyes pinched, making his already round face appear rounder.

As they drove, Sara turned slightly in her seat to eavesdrop on the planning going on in the back.

"Are you certain there is no other way?"

"Feel free to find one if you can."

"I have no desire to kill a pod of ogres for no reason," Norman replied. "Not for the sake of gods know what this man needs a tribute for."

"We're not going to kill them," Uther argued. "Not if we can help it."

Sara turned fully in her seat to see Norman shifting, his bulk pressing Abner into the back of the van. "How do you plan on breaking into their nest, stealing an egg, and getting away without killing them?"

"That's where the gnome comes in." Uther beamed. "He's already proven his worth by finding and stealing the sword. What's an ogre egg?"

"Me?" Abner's eyes bulged. "I'm not a thief!"

Uther faced him, head cocked. "Really?"

Gulping, Abner sputtered. "Well, I … I mean, I…"

Uther jabbed a crooked finger. "You not only found a sword that has been carefully hidden for hundreds of years, on purpose I might add, but you found a way to best the magic wards protecting it and, through your petty greed, placed us all in danger. Or am I missing something?"

"Fair enough." Abner dropped his head. "But isn't there another way? I barely made it out of the last one alive. Do you have any idea what ogres do to prisoners?"

Uther frowned. "Again, not my problem. You're the thief. This is your arena. If you can't do it, I'm going to have to kill the entire nest. Do you want that on your conscience, gnome?"

Abner didn't reply.

"I didn't think so."

"Abner is correct. He may have stumbled onto the sword, but these are ogres we are talking about," Norman jumped in. "They are violent and indisposed to working with the other races. He is not ready for what you ask."

"You came to me, or did you forget that part, old friend?" Uther fumed. "I'm providing a way forward for the good of us all. Those lycans aren't going to stop coming after you until they are either wiped out or gain the sword. I'm sure Morgen wouldn't mind the small measure of sacrifice I'm asking of you."

Norman folded his arms and leaned back, his face an impassive mask.

Peering over his shoulder, Uther instructed Bert, "Hook a right on Person Street. I'll tell you when to stop."

"You got it." Bert cast a sidelong glance at Sara and asked, "Isn't this fun? Just like old times!"

Fun isn't the word I'd use for any of it. Madness, perhaps. Certainly not fun. "Just great, Bert. Just great. I'll be glad when this is finished."

She watched the city blocks roll by, her mind focused on what these ogres were and what Uther was suggesting. With no answers forthcoming, she felt herself being pulled down into a quagmire that never might have happened if not for Daniel's books. *Damn you and your imagination. This should be you out here, not me.* The first inkling of resentment crept in.

THIRTEEN

Abner Grumman was many things, brave not among them. He'd survived for centuries because of his shrewd sense of caution and his ability to blend in and disappear from prying eyes. If not for his latest impulsivity he might be enjoying a quiet vacation somewhere on the Mexican Riviera and picking a few pockets along the way. Wandering around the shadows in a strange town in search of an ogre egg, of all things, was not his idea of fun. Forget the others sitting in the relative safety of Bert's van, or the pack of bloodthirsty werewolves scouring the countryside because of him. Abner wanted to be anywhere else in the world right now. Unfortunately, one of the hard lessons he'd learned long ago was life seldom cared about individual wants.

Steeling what little remained of his nerve, Abner struggled with slipping back into his natural role. He wanted to do right. He did. Just finding the balance between right and wrong proved difficult. After a string of near disastrous events, Abner decided that he was a victim of circumstance. A pawn in a game far beyond his ability to grasp without bursting a few blood vessels. His knees knocked together. His shoulders shook beneath the loose t-shirt. Sweat beaded on the corners of his eyebrows, refusing to fall.

Guilt gnawed on him. Abner found new conflict alive and well in the depths of his mind. Knowing he alone was responsible for the promise of bringing all the clans to ruin should the lycans gain control of the sword, he felt the first spark of a backbone emerging.

He liked Sara and felt guilty for involving her. The others proved terrifying in their own ways, including the damned sword intent on killing him the moment he let his guard down. He still hadn't figured how that might happen, nor did he want to think about it. Abner decided the best thing for them all was for him to steal the egg and get to the wizard as soon as possible. From there he could cut ties and slip away in what he hoped would be pure confusion. No other alternative proved appealing.

Abner took a series of deep breaths and began the hundred-meter walk to the bridge and the ogre nest below.

"Are you sure he should be going in there alone?" Sara had no idea what to expect, having never heard of or imagined an ogre nest before. Nor did she understand the danger they were in. The only factor of this experience making any sense was the giant bag of guns sitting near her.

Leaning against the van, arms folded and a half-smoked cigar sticking from the corner of his mouth, Uther narrowed his eyes in the direction of the bridge. They'd been careful to park far enough to prevent the ogres from finding them while also giving Abner an escape route should the situation devolve.

"How many gnomes do you know?" he asked without looking at her.

Abner's form slipped out of sight as Sara answered, "Well, none."

He shifted the cigar to the other side of his mouth, a trail of blue-grey smoke following. "Didn't think so. This is what they're good at. Gnomes have been used as scouts, spies, thieves, etc. for as long as any of us can remember. Damned good at it too. He'll be fine." He shrugged. "Or he won't."

"How can you be so casual?" she fussed. "Like him or not, Abner is part of this group. We can't just send him in there to die."

Uther snorted. "Die? The ogres will do far worse to him than that."

"Should he be caught, the matron will likely adopt him as one of their nest. Abner will be forced to live as an ogre until he manages to find a way to escape," Norman clarified before Sara could ask.

She looked up to where the gargoyle perched atop the edge of the van. Despite his indifference, he proved the stonewall upon which she placed her trust to keep her safe. She never imagined they'd be off on an adventure together, nor one so dangerous.

Uther on the other hand gave her chills. The man was a stone-cold killer. There was no measure of comfort or solace from being near him, though she imagined he'd more than pull his weight when it came time for violence.

Then there was the lonesome Bert. The troll was like a shadow of his former self without his brother. She found herself liking him in that big brother kind of way. Massive and brutish, Bert exhibited an easygoing attitude no matter how bad things got.

Confused and amazed in equal measure with her companions, Sara couldn't help but think of Abner again. *We just let him waltz right into it with that stupid gawk of his. At least he left the sword behind.* The thought, unbidden, embarrassed her. Sara thanked the night for concealing her reddening cheeks. She'd never thought of herself first. What mother could? To dismiss Abner in favor of the sword's security tugged on her conscience. Like him or not, he was part of their group.

"He will be fine," Norman commented.

"If he's lucky," Uther added.

Sara frowned before climbing back into the van. The hilt of the sword poked out from under the couch just enough for her to make out the crimson ruby embedded in the metal. She felt the pull, the silent whisper in the forgotten corners of her mind. *Take me. Use me. Together we will conquer the world.* Shuddering, she didn't know what was worse, working with psychopaths or a murderous sword.

An itch struck. Raw, irritating. Abner frowned, unable to dig deep into his shoe to relieve the burning sensation on his instep. Odd such a small thing threatened to give him away. Pressed against the slime covered concrete bridge pillar, the gnome peered into the unnatural darkness cloaking the nest. He'd been in one before, but that was long before the United States officially earned its independence. The land was wild then, untamed and fraught with peril should you step off the beaten path.

The air was rich with a fetid odor. Overpowering, it stank of filth and waste. Few among the clans interacted with ogres. They were crude creatures lacking the required social graces of civilized society. Considered one of the more barbaric races, ogres clung to their outdated way of life. Akin to human gypsies, ogres travelled the land stealing where they could, threatening when necessary. Abner held no ill will toward the lumbering monsters, nor did he have any qualms against stealing from them, though he did consider the theft of an egg extreme.

At no point did he ever recall wondering why or how ogres had eggs instead of live births. As far as he was concerned, they were mammalian. Then again, Abner seldom bothered with deep thoughts clearly over his ability to comprehend. Like most good gnomes, he lived within the constraints of his race and its expectations, for good or bad.

The itch subsided just enough for him to press forward.

The deeper he ventured into the murk the more overpowering the stench became, prompting him to swallow the mouthful of bile threatening to burst free. Say what you will of ogres, but their sense of smell was far superior to any other species on the planet save dragons. Abner stalked along, using his left hand to maintain a fixed point with the concrete. Soon the heavy sounds of several ogres snoring rumbled in his ears. He allowed a thin smile to crawl across his face. Doused in what he deemed the scent of roadkill, Abner began to think he had a chance.

Weaponless, he slipped over the massive boulder marking the entrance to the ogre nest and found himself surrounded by nearly a dozen similar sized objects. They appeared as rocks to the naked eye, but he knew better. Each was the size of a small Volkswagen. All appeared asleep, lost in a dreamscape, if ogres even dreamed. He doubted it, all things considered. Ogres just weren't that bright. A fact he hoped to exploit this night.

Abner slipped in and around the sleeping monsters with relative ease. Centuries of creeping through shadows served him well. He began searching for the center of the nest, the obvious place for an ogre to have its eggs. The soft pad of his steps was accompanied by the gentle rush of the Cape Fear River pushing toward the distant coast, concealing his movements from watchful ears.

He soon found himself in the center of the nest but failed to discover any eggs. Frustration grew. He knew the longer he spent in the nest the greater the odds of being discovered. With time against him, the gnome began to panic. The others hadn't given him a timeline, only the subtle reminder dark powers were stalking them, and time was fleeting at best. Uther's dour warning echoed in his mind. The constant reminder of what failure meant to them all.

Then it dawned on him. Up. The eggs had to be hidden in the perpetual shadows of the top of the piers where the concrete pylons met the bridge. Cursing his momentary ignorance, Abner glanced upward. There, resting along the ledges, was a string of small spherical shapes. Jackpot. He'd found the eggs. Now how was he going to climb up there and grab one and escape without being discovered?

Abner slipped through the nest to the base of the nearest pylon and began searching for a way up. Much the same as the way in, the concrete walls were slick with moss and slime, offering little to no footholds up. He doubled back to the entrance and sought an alternative route—there were none. The only way to go up was by climbing down. Holding his breath as he crawled free of the worst of the stench. Abner doubled back to the trail and headed for the railroad tracks. From there he could easily slip down and snatch one of the eggs.

The threat of a train barreling his way spurred his movements once he was clear of the nest. Abner scrambled over the tar-stained ties, dropping down to peer over the lip. Heights never bothered him, until he was forced to stare down into the rushing waters. His head swooned, threatening to pitch to what promised to be a gruesome demise.

Abner forced the dark thoughts away and began his descent. It was only a few meters to the ledge but without a rope it became far more perilous. The tiny barbs embedded in his fingertips, similar to the ends of a spider's legs, allowed him to grip the smooth concrete in ways no other species in the clans could. Thankful for one advantage, the gnome soon pulled himself down over the lip of the tracks, where he swung for several seconds before reaching out to gain a toehold. Heart thundering in his head, Abner inched his way to the safety of the ledge and attempted to catch his breath.

One problem down, he needed to focus on his climb out. A feat promising to be much more difficult than his infiltration. Abner reached down to touch the nearest egg. It was hard and warm but no larger than a volleyball. Tucking the egg inside his shirt to prevent it from falling, he rubbed his aching palms together and prepared to climb.

That's when all hell broke loose.

FOURTEEN

Abner found himself staring into jeweled eyes the color of burning flames and hate a moment before heavy hands circled his waist, careful not to crush the precious life concealed within his shirt and squeezed. Air left his lungs in one whuff. Spots blurring his vision, the gnome struggled against his captor. Gnomes were no match for an ogre's strength however, and he only managed to secure his capture that much quicker. Veins popped out on his neck and forehead as he slapped on the ogre's forearms.

"Put … me…"

The ogre responded with a roar louder than an oncoming train. Abner felt his ears pop. His hair whipped back as chunks of partially chewed food flew out of the ogre's mouth to strike his face. Abner lost control of his stomach. The contents poured out in a violent spray. Bile caught the ogre in the face, stinging his eyes. Enraged, the ogre loosened his grip to wipe his face. Abner dropped to the ledge and crawled for his life.

A second ogre rose from the night, claws raking the concrete where the gnome just left. Sparks rained down, trailing Abner as he scrambled to the far side of the bridge. His route ended abruptly, leaving him exposed to the wrath of the awakening nest. Frantic, he searched for an escape route that wouldn't result in him breaking his neck, or the egg. Where was the gargoyle when he needed him?

The first ogre regained his composure and barreled after Abner. Left with no room and no time to climb back up to the tracks, Abner pressed his back against the wall and slipped around the corner; a vegetation covered slope was a few meters away. Under normal circumstances he could make the jump with ease. This was anything but normal—Abner didn't have a choice. Staying put meant death and being the main course for an ogre family meal wasn't on his agenda. He took three quick breaths and jumped.

Feeling the swipe of claws rushing through the spot he just left, Abner reached out with both hands to gain a purchase on the foliage. He landed on the balls of his feet, sliding only a few meters before arresting his fall. The ogres were closing in; a glance back showed him three shadowy figures lurching for him. His knowledge of the species proved limited, leaving him wondering if they would pursue him back to the van or remain in the security of the nest. He didn't wait long for an answer.

More ogres rose, milling about in confusion. The largest one, he guessed it was the brood mother, shoved the others aside and made for Abner. He was out of time with nowhere to go. Abner reached for the nearest shrub thick enough to support his weight and latched on for his life. Thorns drove into his flesh. The blackberry bush was overgrown and nasty. It was also the only way up.

Pain shot through his body in waves. Merciless and promising. Abner kept moving. The thunder of footsteps drew closer until the hairs on the back of his neck stood on end. For reasons he failed to comprehend, Abner felt the ogres were toying with him. He was within a few feet from the top when the lone wail of a lycan pierced the night. Trapped between opposing dooms, Abner Grumman whispered a silent prayer. He needed to gain the safety of the van before it was too late.

Princess reached the edge of the railroad bridge first. She didn't know the pack was on the opposite side from her prey. Nor did it matter. She'd caught the scent of the sword stealer. Catching him was paramount. The others remained unimportant to the pack. All that mattered was claiming the sword. She tilted her head back and howled. Her cries were answered by a dozen others.

The hunt was on.

Cracking her knuckles, Princess salivated at the thought of ripping the gnome's throat out and watching him crumble to ash in her hands. Killing elfkind often left her dissatisfied. She needed the feel of cooling flesh and hot blood to satisfy her. Elfkind robbed her of the opportunity, prompting her to consider taking the gnome alive to prolong his torment. First thing first though, she needed the sword. Enough of her pack lay dead along their trail, evoking Gruff's anger. The faster her team moved; the more opportunities opened for her.

Princess crept onto the tracks, crouching down to sniff the air. The gnome was close. His odor contaminated the night air, but there was more. Scents unfamiliar to her. She narrowed her eyes and stared down into the gloom beneath the bridge. Lumbering monsters milled about, as if locked in the depths of confusion. Were they after the gnome as well?

Their size alone told her she couldn't win. Princess recoiled, hurrying back to the edge of the bridge as the rest of the pack caught up. She rolled her shoulders, an old habit helping her focus her thoughts as she prepared for battle. Movement across the river caught her attention. Princess picked out the small figure clawing his way up through a bramble patch and smiled. *Got you!* Howling again, she broke into a run.

Others joined her. Those in wolf form rushed past. The rest matched her stride for stride. Imbued by their combined strength, Princess decided to forgo waiting on Gruff. The pack leader had lost a step of late and that concerned her. His volatile actions left the pack unhinged, operating far from peak. Catching the gnome and claiming the sword for him presented her with the chance to restore order.

She ran harder, the others at her side. They were across the bridge in a matter of heartbeats, scrambling over the edge to be the first to reach the gnome. Princess urged them on. The pack needed to hunt. Needed to kill. Needed a win. She let them go. Not that she could stop them once their blood burned. Lycans were notorious for hot tempers and losing their grasp on reality during the throes of the hunt. Stopping their charge was not only pointless, but dangerous.

Abner made it to the top of the slope by the time the first werewolf leapt down at him. Wincing, he pitched himself forward into the blackberry bush. The wolf soared past him and collided with the ogre matron. Chaos ensued beneath a blanket of snarls and cries of outrage. More wolves rushed down to help their comrade in a whirlwind of lashing claws and slavering fangs.

The matron fell, buried beneath the weight of six werewolves yet fists pummeled the wolves. All thoughts of the gnome were lost in favor of the immediate threat to their nest. Now if he could just find a way to escape.

Princess, saliva drooling from the corners of her mouth, held back. Dark hair sprouted across her face and body. Her limbs were elongated, caught halfway through the transformation. Instinct screamed for her to join her pack. Battle lust gripped them, and they would not stop until a victory or defeat occurred. As much as she enjoyed a quality fight, Princess focused on the gnome.

She looked around, having lost him in the rush. Panic rose. "Where are you, little one? This doesn't need to be difficult. Give me what I want, and it will all be over for you." Her words dripped venom.

"Come out, come out wherever you are," she soothed, creeping closer. "Imagine it. No more looking over your shoulder. No more running. No hiding. Just come to me, gnome. Come and end your misery. Give me the sword."

"Fuck you, doggie."

Uther watched the chaos develop from the concealment of a nearby tree. His hatred for lycans rippled under his skin. As much as he wanted to strike down the female immediately, experience taught him to wait, gather as much battlefield intelligence as possible, and act with unrelenting prejudice. Lycans were tricky predators, capable of turning an ambush through force of numbers. His time as an Old Guard heightened his combat prowess but he was one man against a pack.

Rifle at his side, Uther found himself amused by the recklessness the wolves showed in attacking an ogre nest. Then the female did the unexpected. She hung back and made a fragile attempt at coaxing Abner to her side; Uther snorted and set his weapon down. Creatures like the female lycan deserved a brutal demise. He was going to relish adding her pelt to his wall of trophies.

"Come out, come out wherever you are. Imagine it. No more looking over your shoulder. No more running. No hiding. Just come to me, gnome. Come and end your misery. Give me the sword."

Uther had heard enough. Let the wolves fight it out with the ogres. Win or lose, they weren't coming away with the sword. But should Abner fall into her hands, the game shifted against him.

"Fuck you," he snarled from the night.

The female spun and continued her transformation. The process took seconds. In her place stood a monstrous wolf of the deepest ebon hue streaked with silver along her hind legs. Red eyes glared at Uther, complimented by impossibly long fangs capable of biting a human in half. The Old Guard relished the challenge and emerged from hiding. She snarled with a guttural sound unlike anything he'd heard before.

Spying Abner hiding in the bushes, Uther motioned for the gnome. "Go on, gnome. Get back to the others. I'll handle this."

Looking between the two, Abner decided Uther more than a match for the lycan. He crept from cover, a mass of cuts and open sores, and hurried to get back to the van.

Once Abner was clear, Uther reached behind his back and produced a pair of Roman style gladiuses. Both weapons were honed to unnatural keenness. "Here, puppy, puppy. Let's see about turning you into a blanket, shall we?"

The female roared and leapt.

Uther followed in kind.

"Something big is happening down there," Bert said, his head bobbing.

She didn't want to find out. "Do you think Abner is all right?"

"He has awoken the ogres," Norman said from his perch.

Sara held her tongue. *Of course, he did.* Frustration threatening to unnerve her, she watched the dark for signs of Abner. She feared the worst for him and again questioned why the least qualified to engage in battle had been sent into a certain death situation. She looked around for Uther.

The howls of angry dogs broke the night; Sara froze. The werewolves had caught up to them. She looked up, surprised to find Norman already standing, and in his true form. Dark wings swept out, reminding her of a vulture sunning itself. Only this vulture had fangs. Her heart thundered as he crouched, his head twisting to the right.

Sara reached into her pants for the pistol, forgetting she lacked bullets. Once again relegated obsolete, she backed to the open side panel of the van.

Then she spied the figure rushing toward them. *Abner!* "Look!"

Bert gave his perpetual smile, opening his arms to hug the running gnome the moment he arrived.

Norman had other ideas. He launched into the night sky, racing toward the battle ahead.

Sara stared at the egg in Abner's hands, marveling at all the trouble it caused.

FIFTEEN

They danced in a whirlwind of destruction. Uther's twin blade flashing with blinding speed. The werewolf's claws twisting and turning in the raw attempt at ripping him to shreds. Both breathed heavily. His muscles ached. His mind strained. He hadn't found a way to pierce the lycan's defenses, plunging them into a stalemate. Time was against them.

Uther dropped under a wild swing, narrowly avoiding decapitation from razor-sharp claws. Dropping to a knee, he scooped a handful of sand and rock and flung it into female's face. Snarling, she drew back and exposed herself—Uther lunged for her heart with both swords. A paw clubbed the side of his head in reward and sent him sprawling. His twin blades skittered away.

A cacophony of howls erupted under the bridge. Wolf and ogre dueled in a clash neither wanted nor understood.

The female, maintaining control of her human thinking, used the break in action to shift back into her mortal self. Bruises coated her arms. A slash ran down her left cheek. She crouched, working out the kinks in her neck. "This isn't your fight, guardian," she warned Uther. "Leave me to my prey and we can forget we ever saw one another."

Uther rolled to his knees and reached for the nearest sword. "See, that's going to be a problem. I already gave my word and, not that I'd expect a mutt to know the value in it, my word is unbreakable. You want the gnome; you're going to have to take him from me."

"I was hoping you were going to say that." She shifted back into wolf form and attacked.

Gritting his teeth, small trickles of blood running between them to produce a wild effect, Uther met the charge, dropping into a crouch to catch the weight of the leaping werewolf with a shoulder to her stomach. It took all his strength to use the wolf's weight and momentum against her, pitching her end over end as she passed. Crashing into the tracks, she rolled and came up on all fours. Blood and saliva dripped from her mouth. Hatred filled her eyes as she dipped her head and roared.

Uther grinned, pointed a blade at her and beckoned her with his free hand. His second sword was too far out of reach for him to snatch before she would be upon him. The Old Guard dropped into a low defense and waited.

His taunts proved effective. The female dashed forward with great strides and they clashed again, bodies tumbling. Uther groaned after taking a pair of quick slashes to his ribs. Angered, he stabbed his blade fast three times. The first two missed but the third pierced the wolf's shoulder. She careened away with a yip. Blood flowed in an obscene stain down her fur.

Uther watched her limp back onto the bridge, giving him time to retrieve his second weapon. "Come on, puppy. Is that all you got?" he taunted. Spitting a wad of blood at her, he continued. "You should be in a pound waiting to be put down. I thought your kind were tougher. Meaner. Guess you got robbed of the good genes, huh?"

A howl shattered the night. Ogres stopped their mayhem. Lycans paused to look up.

Rearmed, Uther squinted into the darkness and got his first glimpse of the nightmare heading his way. Standing close to eight feet tall, the lycan strode with the slow confidence of a true leader. Muscles bulged on his arms and legs. A silver mane reached down his back, waving in the stiff breeze. The werewolf stepped to the end of the bridge and halted, rolling his neck.

Uther hesitated. As an Old Guard he fought the worst creatures elfkind had. Never once did he back away from a fight or believe himself inferior to the challenge. But the raw power wafting off the pack leader gave him pause. Uther respected the authority exhibited against him. He also suspected he couldn't defeat the monster one on one. A trio of smaller lycans came up behind the leader, cementing Uther's decision. He needed to retreat. Fast.

Backing away, Uther watched the rest of the pack escape the ogre nest. They were battered and beaten, but not defeated. Uther was in trouble with no way to call for aid. He often wondered what death felt like. The longer he stayed alive the more thoughts of the end crept into his psyche. But thinking of the next life and being in a rush to get there weren't the same thing. Uther enjoyed his life. Enough to not die on a railroad bridge in godforsaken Fayetteville, North Carolina.

The lycan leader pointed at him and the pack burst into howls.

Uther raised his swords and met the challenge with a bestial roar.

They stalked toward one another. Each intent on slaughter. Each certain but one would walk away. The lycan was a mass of hatred. Uther, already tired, was the defender of the righteous.

Ducking under a swing that would have decapitated him, Uther swiped quickly. The lycan proved too fast, jerking his leg back from the questing blade. Rather than clawing, he punched down, clipping Uther in the side of his head and sending him rolling away. The Old Guard fell on his back, wedged between tar covered railroad ties. Pain blossomed through his muscles.

The lycan sensed victory and leapt atop the fallen elf.

Uther was unable to use his swords. Hot saliva dripped onto his face from the lycan's leer. Four paws boxed Uther in. He reversed his grip on the handle and brought the pommel down in the exposed werewolf's toes. The sharpened point broke bone and pierced flesh. Uther knew it wouldn't stop, or slow, his opponent long. He slammed his elbow into the soft flesh of the inner thigh. The lycan retreated just enough for Uther to regain his feet.

The juvenile rhetoric was gone. No more infantile taunts. The only way to defeat this foe was through brute force and sheer willpower. Even that might not prove sufficient. Uther calculated his odds of success and felt an unfamiliar knot form in his stomach. A single drop of blood spilled from the pommel of his sword.

The lycan charged before Uther slipped into a defensive position. Reacting more than thinking, Uther leveled both swords and thrust forward. The lycan twisted his body but not before suffering the sting of steel slicing his flesh. Clumps of stained fur flew from his body, trailed by ropes of blood. Uther followed through, swinging both swords in a move aimed at disemboweling the werewolf before it crashed to the ground—he missed.

He spun, hoping to find the lycan on the ground. Instead, he caught the blur of motion, the stench of hot breath, and the stabbing of claws into his chest as the lycan crashed into him. Uther grunted as the claws stabbed again and again.

Tired of stabbing, the pack leader curled a fist and began pummeling the elf to the cacophony of his pack.

Uther spat a mouthful of blood and closed his eyes. *Damn you Norman for getting me into this mess.*

Norman spent decades at a time without transforming into his natural form. Each time he did came with exhilaration unlike any other. Old memories returned, reminding him of what he was and all he could be again. Launching from the van, feeling the crumple of metal beneath his claws and hearing Bert's lament, Norman became the creature he was always meant to be. Leathery wings swept out, slicing the air without a sound. The sounds of battle grew louder. He flapped harder, letting instincts take over.

With Abner, and the egg, secured in the van, he needed to extract Uther before the lycans caught up to them again. Coming upon the scene of carnage, he realized he was too late. The Old Guard battled the lycan pack leader in the center of the bridge with the werewolf pack arrayed against him. The odds were hopeless, even for Uther.

Norman spied several dark figures lumbering about under the bridge. Ogres.

Sensing their expedition on the brink of failure, he tucked his wings and stretched forth his arms. The lycan had his back to him as he hammered down on the stricken elf, unaware of the presence barreling toward him. The lycan was larger than any Norman had ever seen. A nightmarish specimen capable of killing them all. He tucked his wings and slammed into the beast like a freight train gone off the rails.

With the leader stunned, Norman doubled back and plucked Uther from the ground. He caught a glimpse of the rest of the pack bursting into pursuit, eager to catch him before he escaped. Their howls of fury followed him into the night as he flew higher.

"Put me down, damn it!" Uther huffed.

Norman ignored him and winged back to the van as fast as he could.

"That was undignified," Uther complained as he wiped his sleeves of the dirt and grime accumulated during his battle.

Blood trickled from a score of wounds. His clothes were torn and stained. Bruises, already fading, peppered his face. Sara stared at him in mute horror. How any living creature could survive such punishment was beyond her ability to understand. By all rights, Uther should have died on that bridge. Yet here he sat, undergoing the radical healing transformation only elfkind was capable of.

"You're welcome," Norman replied without turning back.

The van lumbered away from the heart of Fayetteville, but without having a clear direction and only vague purpose, Bert commented about wasting gas to which Sara sighed and the others ignored.

Despite Uther's beating, the mission was a success. Abner sat beside his stolen ogre egg. Bert and Norman watched the roads, checking the mirrors for signs of pursuit. Uther lay sprawled on the couch, a wounded soldier returned from the impossible battlefield. This left Sara feeling without purpose.

She still didn't know why she'd come on this quest. The elf world was no place for humans, especially not ones who remained reluctant to accept its very existence. She wanted to stick her head out the door and scream at the top of her lungs. Anything to vent the frustration and fear welling within. Not that it mattered. The only way to escape this nightmare was by seeing it through. Focusing on the story she would have for Daniel when they both returned home, provided she survived, Sara recentered and found her calm. *Think woman. What would one of his heroes do in this situation?*

"Where are we going?" she asked to break the silence.

When no one answered, Sara stared at the egg, the least confounding item in the van. *What's this guy going to do with it? Make an omelet? I wonder what ogre egg tastes like. Seems a silly thing to risk our lives for.* A mottled assortment of colors, the egg was the size of a small beach ball reminding her of a jawbreaker. Sara hoped it was worth it. She did her best to imagine the egg as little more than a chicken egg. Unfertilized and, well, she let the thought die.

The couch creaked and she turned to face the elf laying on it.

"Wilmington," Uther said without opening his eyes. He shifted positions again and flopped an arm down over his face. "To the battleship."

Norman said, "Bert, get us on 87 heading east."

"You got it, boss," the troll replied. Sara admired the fact that despite the damage to his prized possession and family heirloom, Bert's demeanor was still one of contentment as he gunned the engine.

Victory and defeat toying with them, they drove in silence, leaving what they hoped to be the worst of it behind them. Sara knew from listening to Daniel's ramblings about his stories that it was never the case. No matter how dark the storm appeared, something darker always loomed on the horizon.

Always.

SIXTEEN

Agent Cecile Barnabas pulled her government issued sedan off the interstate and turned the radio down. There was only so much Barry Manilow a woman could take to keep her awake in the middle of the night. The location tracker on her open laptop glowed red, indicating a recent kill in the vegetation lining the road. With the rest of the pack was miles away, hurrying off on their hunt, Cecile suspected what she was about to discover wasn't good.

The road abandoned, she parked and left her car idling as she unclipped the seatbelt, drew her sidearm, pausing to ensure it was loaded and on safe, and exited the vehicle.

She knew she was a far cry from a field agent, despite her desires. Her palms grew slick, prompting concern she might drop her weapon. Cecile suddenly felt trapped by her Kevlar vest. Lightweight and designed to be worn without discomfort, the vests were the latest technology, capable of stopping a 7.62mm round with ease. While she wasn't expecting to be shot, she felt the weight pulling on her.

The car door closed with a click, leaving her alone in the night with the frogs croaking from a nearby pond and an innumerable number of crickets. The crunch of gravel under her heel made her wince as thoughts of boogeymen and worse lurking in the night to pounce on her filled the empty spots in her imagination. Weapon pointed at the ground with her thumb poised to click the safety off and engage any threat, Cecile crept forward.

She entered the scrub grass and small shrubs lining the interstate, slowing to step over a forgotten wire fence no doubt once established to keep livestock from going too far. She didn't know where to look, only that what she sought lay somewhere nearby. Cecile would much rather be chasing down the living pack members, but D.E.S.A. protocols demanded she stop and identify the dead. It dawned on her, as she entered a thin stand of trees, how much easier that would be if werewolves and other, what she considered, nightmare creatures disappeared upon death like the elves. Less messes. Less paperwork.

She found the bodies, rather what remained of them, buried under a screen of broken branches and dead leaves. Cecile holstered her weapon and produced a flashlight—empty eyes stared back at her. She covered her mouth with the back of her free hand as the stench assaulted her nostrils. Whatever killed them was big and powerful, leaving little recognizable. Cecile scanned the remains. One appeared to have had half his face shorn off by the pavement. Another was torn to ribbons. Bone and organs protruded from her wounds. Cecile fought against the burp that would surely leave her vomiting and moved on.

Placing the end of the flashlight in her mouth, she pulled out her phone and began taking pictures of their faces and thumbprints. Cecile recovered the bodies and left having seen enough. Once back in the car she uploaded the images to the agency's mainframe where techs hidden away in the government offices would process and identify the victims. This was not what she imagined fieldwork would be during those endless days of torment trapped in what she considered a cell behind a desk ... At least it offered her a glimpse of what life on the other side might become.

The ping was loud enough in his earbuds to snap Darryl Wallace out of his slumber. Wiping the drool from his chin as he struggled to wake up, embarrassed to admit he'd fallen asleep on duty once again, the tech blinked until his screen came into focus. The blur of ink resolving into letters before a slew of images came in.

"What the fuck," he whispered as he looked through the pictures.

A company man who had no desire to take to the field or do more than his limited experience in IT demanded, Darryl felt his stomach twist at the pictures of ruined bodies and dead addled eyes. The closest he'd ever gotten to witnessing a corpse was during his video game sessions.

He whistled low, leaned back in his chair, and ran a hand through his thinning hair.

"That just ain't right."

Cracking his knuckles, Darryl logged on to the identification portal and uploaded the pictures. The system would provide some answers at least, it always did. He hoped Agent Barnabas might shed a little more light on what was happening. Clicking open his email, Darryl drafted a simple message and hit send. Unable to sit still, he got up and did a short lap around the empty office. Anything to take his mind off what he just saw.

A chime alerted him to the program running in the background. Changing screens, he opened the results sheet and felt his eyes go wide.

Werewolves! Where in the world did werewolves come from? Until now, he'd chosen not to believe the rumors of werewolves, vampires, and ghosts roaming the world. Somethings were too much for his mind to comprehend, even here at D.E.S.A. Elves and dwarves were bad enough. This confirmation opened a new realm of horrible possibilities Darryl wanted nothing to do with. He rechecked his email. Still nothing. Fearing for Agent Barnabas, he struggled with finding a way to give her assistance.

Driving was too far. The distance between DC and North Carolina being too far for him to take an extended break and he preferred the cold comforts of his office. Darryl drummed his fingers in thought. Taking the information straight to his supervisor was out of the question. His hackles were raised with Violet's recent behavior and trust was far from established.

Unable to turn to her and forced to do his job, Darryl struck an idea. He only hoped his contacts were still in place. Otherwise, all he could do was sit by and hope fresh updates came in.

He picked up the desk phone and dialed his Hail Mary. "Hey, Steve. This is Darryl. How you been, man? Good. Good. Hey man, listen, I got a huge favor I need. Yeah, I know. Channels and all that, but we don't have time. There's a field agent in real world danger. You got any drones over eastern North Carolina? I know, but this is life or death, man. C'mon. You gotta have something we can shift to provide overwatch."

He squeezed his eyes shut, pinching the bridge of his nose as Steve rambled a bit. "Cool. You're the man, Steve. Now I owe you one. Yeah, I'll send the coordinates over as soon as I get them. Thanks, man."

Hanging up, Darryl opened another email and began typing. He only hoped Agent Barnabas read it in time. *Werewolves* ...

Gruff bit back a yelp as Good Boy finished stitching the gash on his ribs. Bloody gauze and an empty bottle of rum lay at his feet. His entire body ached. The wounds burned. Were it not for that damned sword of the Old Guard they would have healed already, and the pack would be back on the hunt. But eldritch powers imbued the swords; magics from the old world his kind had no defense against. The wound on his side hurt the worst, leaving him racked in pain he hadn't experienced in years.

"That's it, boss," Good Boy said after smoothing over the last piece of medical tape. "Nothing more I can do for it."

"Hmm," Gruff replied and stood. He wanted to stretch. To force the aches out. Doing so would only serve to rip the fresh stitches and set him back. The alcohol helped, if barely, but nothing proved strong enough to quell his fury. "Princess, I thought I told you not to engage?"

"We didn't have a choice." She raised her head, chin out in defiance as she stalked up to the rest of the pack. Her pants were drenched in drying blood. "We found the gnome on his own and took a chance. We would have had him if not for those damned ogres."

"I don't care about ogres, or excuses." Gruff jabbed a crooked finger at her. "You should have waited until the entire pack was here. The sword would be ours if you had. Ogres or not."

She snarled. "There was no way we could have known about the Old Guard with him. That gargoyle is bad enough. We needed to snatch the gnome before it blew up in our face. I had it under control, Gruff."

A hand curled into a fist, complimenting his glare. Wrestling with conflicting impulses, Gruff held back his wrath. "Our dead and wounded might have a different opinion. Not only that, but we don't know where they're going. Do we?"

She remained defiant. "We'll find them."

"Time is running out, Princess. We need that sword."

Trapped in a web of too many possibilities, Gruff struggled with anticipating which direction their prey fled. Having the main interstate a few miles away presented several avenues of egress the gnome could have taken. He didn't know their destination, nor why they'd linked up with one of the Old Guard. Gruff felt his chances dwindle. If the protectors of the elven kings were involved, his chances of retrieving the sword dwindled exponentially.

Then a cell phone rang; heads turned, looking to Princess as she answered. "Yes?" she paused. "Stay on them. We're on the way."

Gruff cocked his head, waiting.

Princess slid her phone back into her pocket and smiled. "That was Spike. He's found them. They just got on route 87. It looks like they're heading for the coast."

"We've got them," Gruff said under his breath. Louder, he ordered, "Clean up the mess and get on the road. I want that sword before the sun comes up."

The pack burst into action.

Dawn approached. This night, like so many of late, proved challenging. Each nightmare scenario further shrunk the gaps between elfkind and humanity. Throw in a rampaging pack of werewolves and the lid was close to being torn off and carefully guarded secrets exposed for the first time. Morgen, with Alvin at her side, endured similar threats throughout the centuries. Humans were populous creatures insistently sticking their noses where they didn't belong. The most recent threat occurred during the height of World War II when Nazi spies stumbled on an elf enclave during their search for supernatural objects for Herr Hitler.

Morgen convinced her estranged husband to set aside their feud long enough to cast off the Nazis and rescue their people. That truce lasted until the beginning of the Cold War and her kind began playing human games. Confusion and discord always helped keep elfkind in the margins of obscurity. By keeping humans constantly at odds with themselves, the elves found a way to thrive.

And it was all unraveling thanks to one greedy gnome and a sword that never should have been made. Morgen cursed the wizard for his meddling. Despite the aged man's good intentions, the Sword of Grimspire proved a curse from the moment it cooled in the forge. Nothing had been the same since. They'd thought it safely hidden, away from prying eyes and out of thoughts. They were wrong. Never in Morgen's mind did it occur to her one of her own kind would attempt to find and steal it for a profit.

She wanted to deploy the Old Guard to apprehend the gnome and have him tried for treason. A public execution would serve to remind the rank-and-file citizens of who was in charge and what obeying the rules meant for their continued survival. Though filled with disgust after their meeting, Morgen found Abner Grumman as much a victim of circumstance as an ignorant agent of destruction for the elves.

Left with a pair of unenviable choices, the queen of the Dark Elves clasped her hands behind her back and watched the first tendrils of light break through the veil of darkness.

SEVENTEEN

Pain. Everything hurt. He couldn't recall the last time he'd hurt so bad. His vision swam when he opened his eyes, swirling violently. Bones felt broken. The puncture wounds in his stomach continued weeping blood even as his enhanced genetics accelerated the healing process. Not that it mattered, the shame of defeat wrapped around his psyche in a wrathful embrace.

Uther groaned with every bump as the van jostled closer to the shore. His wounds would recover, hopefully in time for their next run in with the lycans. Perhaps then his martial prowess and newfound understanding of who and what he faced might kick in. Despite his pain and self-induced misery, Uther ached for another crack at his newest foe. Thoughts of a lycan pelt decorating his wall dominated his thoughts as he drifted unconscious.

"Is he going to be all right?" Sara asked.

Norman had already switched seats with her as the sun rose. Never a fan of sunrise, the gargoyle simmered in the artificial gloom of the back of the van. He glanced down at the stricken Old Guard in genuine concern. "I have known Uther for many centuries and through countless trials. He will heal, though I have concerns over his mental state."

"Why is that?" Bert chimed in, dropping the flap to prevent the sun from blinding him as they barreled east.

"I do not recall the last time Uther lost in single combat. He, and those like him, prides himself on his ability to dominate the battlespace. This loss is capable of fracturing his psyche."

Sara wondered if elves had support counselors and asked, "Surely he won't let one fight ruin his life." *This is how Daniel reacted when he came home from his last deployment. He didn't talk either.*

The obvious went unstated.

"That is up to him, Sara Thomas. We cannot fight his battles for him. The Old Guard are notoriously independent warriors considered the best of us," Norman explained. "Uther once held a high rank, before choosing exile."

"Do you think he will abandon us?"

Norman shifted in his seat, as if the thought hadn't occurred to him. "I ... do not know."

The prospect of losing their most valuable asset against the werewolves unsettled Sara. *We need all the help we can get and if Norman says Uther is the right man for the job ... Then again, I didn't see Uther fight. None of us has. Well, maybe Abner did but he's clammed up too. What if Norman's friend has lost his edge?* She remembered stories from Daniel's days in the army where soldiers became burned out after a constant string of deployments between Iraq and Afghanistan. How many times had he mentioned one person or another throw in the towel and get out? Why would elves be any different?

Sara admired those who stood to defend their nation and way of life, even as it cost them all in different ways. For most, a four- or six-year stint in the military was enough. Those capable were forced out later at thirty years. She struggled imagining the PTSD bottled up inside someone who picked up the sword for the better part of a thousand years. How dead inside was Uther?

"I don't know how any of you do it, Norman." Her now greasy hair drifted across her face and shoulders when she shook her head. "All the fighting and the violence. Has there ever been a time of peace with the elves?"

"Once, long ago. After the wars with the lycans and those like them we established colonies around the world. We lived. We loved. We laughed. Our society grew, flourishing until the dawn of humanity. The more civilized your species became, the more it needed land and resources, the more we began to diminish. Our time as masters of this planet dwindled and would have expired if not for the quick thinking of Alvin and Morgen.

"They devised a scheme that not only ended our destructive conflict with the humans but afforded us the opportunity to live among you. To learn and help you grow. We have never sought violence. It always finds us, forcing us to react. A conclave of magic users gathered from across the globe and cast the spell to allow us to blend in and live as one of you."

"But why hide if you can affect so much positive change?" she asked.

Norman's eyebrow rose, grey and imposing. "Humans are not a forgiving species."

She failed to imagine a time when elves and dragons ruled the world, stomping alongside dinosaurs, watching the first creatures crawl up out of the oceans. Sara was a woman of faith. She knew there was a higher power out there. She'd felt it countless times. She drew the line with organized religion, however. For her, faith was enough. But now, all she'd been told from childhood seemed incomplete. An entire world existed around her and no one had a clue.

"What happened? Why did the clans fracture?" she asked. Sara felt the tension rise in the van. Bert and Abner remained silent, though they paused to look at Norman with sorrow.

"Like all things your kind touches we found ourselves seduced by greed and the constant desire for more," Norman said. "The king and queen stood on opposite sides of the argument, demanding fealty. The result is what you and your husband have witnessed. We are a fractured people. One I fear doomed to remain so."

The brief majesty of the elves wiped out over the slow course of time left her feeling haunted. Out of everything she'd seen and experienced thus far, that seemed the most tragic.

"Were you there? In the beginning?" she asked.

"After the unification wars. My kind remained in the mountains of what you call Romania for centuries, in seclusion with little or no desire to participate in a greater society," he replied. "It was this unique sovereignty that ultimately proved our demise."

Unsettled, Sara decided to change the subject. "What I don't understand is why those ogres didn't advance like the rest of you. From what you suggest, they are almost like animals rather than sentient beings."

"They choose to revert to their base forms," Norman explained. "Ogres were among the mightiest of us. Their minds were almost as large as their compassion. The schism broke them, and the world has never been the same since. I believe we are all less without their mirth and wisdom. Today, those nests that remain hide from everyone as they are content to eke out an existence far removed from the power struggles consuming us."

"You admire them," she surmised.

"They managed what my kind could not."

"I see ... Why eggs though? Are they cold blooded?"

"That is something beyond my knowledge. Perhaps one of the archivists knows. I can introduce you once this quest is finished."

Unsure whether she wanted to continue being drawn into their world, Sara let the offer pass. They had more immediate concerns. Like how they were going to sneak aboard the USS North Carolina in broad daylight with hundreds of tourists scampering over the decks. One of the main moneymakers in Wilmington, the battleship was a favorite draw of historians, veterans, and the curious.

The van groaned like an old mule, leaving Sara wondering what would catch up to them first as she drifted off to sleep.

Wilmington had always been one of her favorite places. Sara remembered with fondness the seafood place in Carolina Beach where she and Daniel spent their first date. They laughed, ate, had more than enough to drink and, between spending time wandering the nearby aquarium or thumping a dollop of whipped cream on his nose while sharing dessert,

Sara found herself drawn to the army man in ways she never imagined. They both promised to return every year. Life got in the way, as it often did, and she realized she hadn't been there in years. This wasn't the way she wanted to return either.

She yawned and stretched. The rising sun was red and brilliant. She looked at Bert and said, "I think I need to use the restroom."

"Me too!" Abner chirped. He hadn't spoken since his encounter with the ogres, Sara was relieved to hear his voice.

"We don't know where the lycan pack is," Norman cautioned.

Sara cast her best angry mother scowl. "Unless you have an empty bottle back there I can use?"

The gargoyle sighed. "Bert, find the nearest fast-food place. We cannot afford to dally."

"Okay, boss," Bert smiled. The thought of hot food and enticing smell of grease and bacon brought joy to his face.

Relieved and with breakfast in hand, they climbed back in the van and continued on. Wilmington was only a few miles away.

"How do we sneak onto the battleship without being seen?" Sara asked after swallowing a bite of her breakfast sandwich. "I mean, it's not like we blend in. Not with that sword."

"I have a name, stupid."

"I see your point," Norman said. "I suggest leaving Bert and Abner in the van, with Uther for protection. You and I will seek out the elf."

"Will Uther be awake by the time we get there?" she asked.

Uther had remained unconscious since they left the ogres. A fact Sara didn't mind since she failed to find any common ground with the warrior.

"He will. Or he won't."

Abner swallowed a mouthful of a sausage, egg, and cheese sandwich. "Why do I have to stay with him? He doesn't like me."

"He is your best chance at surviving this nightmare of your creation," Norman growled. "We cannot risk taking the sword in public, nor being trapped in the confines of the battleship. The risk to both our quest and civilian life is too great. The lycans are still out there. We need to be cautious."

Thus far they hadn't seen any signs of their hunters, though Norman cautioned they were still on the hunt and were notorious for not stopping until their prey was secured.

"It would help if we knew who we are looking for," Sara commented.

"His name is Orphan Thorne."

Sara peered beyond the gargoyle's mass and was surprised to find Uther sitting up and looking healthier than when Norman dumped him in the van. "You're awake."

"And you haven't shut up since we stopped," he grumbled, rolling his shoulders.

"Haven't lost any of your tongue I see," she quipped.

From what she could see his wounds were healed enough he could move without much discomfort. He did appear itchy as he scratched at his face and arm.

"You're welcome," Norman said.

Pausing mid-stretch, Uther asked, "For what?"

"Saving your life."

"Bullshit. I had him right where I wanted him."

"Idiot," the sword barked from under the couch.

Uther kicked it, much like Sara had wanted to do numerous times, and a satisfying clunk of his boot striking metal echoed around the van. "Quiet before I melt you down and make souvenir ingots out of you."

Abner gulped, eyes wide.

"Try it, pointy ears, and I split your skull in two. Come on. I dare you."

"Who is Orphan Thorne?" Sara asked before tensions erupted further.

"That's not an easy question to answer. Orphan is old, almost ancient. Rumor has it he was the smith who forged the sword under the wizard's direction," Uther explained. "Since then, he's become a legend— a myth you might say. No one has seen him in a lifetime."

"How are we supposed to find him now? And why do you know where he is if he's a myth?" Sara pushed with narrowed eyes.

"I may be exiled, of my own choosing, but I still have my network in place," Uther defended.

"You mean spies," Norman surmised.

Uther shrugged. "Doesn't matter. What does matter is we get to Orphan and give him his tribute so we can find that damned wizard and I can get my hands on that doggy."

"The one who almost killed you," Sara muttered.

"Says you."

"You're the one who came back half dead," she muttered.

"We have one advantage." Norman leaned forward to block their view of each other. "The battleship does not open for a few more hours. No one will be on hand when we arrive."

"The museum must have security," Sara countered. "It won't take long before the police are called."

"That's where I come in. Bert parks the van in a nearby area while you and I slip around the far side of the battleship and sneak aboard."

Sara bobbed her head. "It sounds fine, but time is still against us. From what I remember, the ship is huge. We could spend hours trying to find this guy."

"Relax," Uther threw in. "If the lycans don't get you those gators in the swamp might."

EIGHTEEN

"I don't like this," Bert fretted. "What if them wolves find us while you're gone?"

The van was tucked into the far corner of an empty lot a hundred meters from the battleship's public parking. Sara, doing her best to ignore the increased danger from being exposed, stared across the lot at the grey behemoth moored before them. Saved from the scrapyards in 1960 after a brief life of wartime service in the Pacific, the USS North Carolina found a permanent home in the muddy waters of the Cape Fear River nestled across from downtown Wilmington. At over 700 feet long and bristling with weapons, the battleship soon became a national historic landmark and a tourist destination.

That an elf could hide aboard without detection proved beyond amazing to her. She and Daniel spent the better part of a day exploring the ship a few years back. Two things stuck with her. She didn't trust ladders that were easier to descend backwards than normal ones and she enjoyed bumping her head even less. Still the historical value remained high, something she learned from Daniel's knowledge of military history that he shared with her.

She dug deeper: The museum built a walkway for visitors to view the battleship from all sides, she recalled the swamp on the backside—the side Norman intended to take. Alligators were rare in North Carolina, but a pair lurked in the waters and were often spotted from the rear decks. *Where they there when Daniel and I were last here?* She failed to see any easy way in and, even if they were successful, they'd be trapped once the museum opened.

"Are you ready?" Norman asked, looking at her. "We must be quick."

Why would I be ready? Bottling her nerves and not trusting her voice, Sara nodded.

The gargoyle gave her a queer look before addressing the others, "Bert, ensure the van remains secure. We cannot afford to lose the sword. Uther, are you prepared?"

"Enough." His rifle rested in his lap.

"Abner, the egg if you please." Norman extended a hand.

The gnome dug the egg free from the blanket they'd wrapped it in and gave it to Norman. He looked upon it like a curse and blessing. "Good riddance."

Tucking the egg under an arm, Norman glanced at Sara. "Come. We must not delay."

"Be careful, Sara," Bert cautioned.

They hurried across the parking lot, swinging around the aft end of the massive ship before entering the tall swamp grasses. Sara's heart clutched. She found the sudden fear of being devoured by an alligator more absurd than being killed by werewolves. A chuckle escaped her before she regained control. Norman ignored her, focusing on finding the path through the vegetation.

Before long, though much longer than Sara cared for, they arrived at the backside and stared up at the battleship.

"How do we get up there?" she asked.

"I have wings," he reminded.

She blushed. "Oh, that's right. Sorry."

Norman stopped. A look of concern twisted his granite features. "Are you all right?"

Struggling to keep her embarrassment private, Sara exhaled. "I'm fine. This is all just ... I don't know what I'm doing, Norman. Why did you choose me for this?"

"The others were needed to protect the sword."

The simplicity in his answer was far from reassuring, leaving her with the sensation of uselessness, further proving she didn't belong on this quest. *Oh get a grip already and stop feeling sorry. Like it or not, this is where I am and if doing this means saving my family, well, what choice do I have?*

To her surprise, the gargoyle laid a hand on her shoulder, light and ginger despite his mass. "Sara Thomas, you are a woman of special courage. I would not have brought you if not for your unique qualities. This Orphan Thorne is unknown to me. Having you at my side will undo any sense of confidence he might display."

"Meaning there's no way he's expecting a human," she deduced.

"Indeed. Now, grab onto my waist. We must fly."

She did as instructed, clinging for dear life as Norman unfurled his wings and launched into the air. The flight was fast and direct. She swore she saw the waiting maws of both alligators waiting for her to drop. Her stomach lurched and continued rising before they landed. Legs shaking, she stepped out of Norman's shadow and regained her composure.

"See, easy," he said.

If you say so. "Where to now? This is a big ship."

"The best place to hide is in plain sight," Norman explained. "He will be in a place we least expect."

"It would have been nice if Uther let us in on his secret. What about the bridge? I can't think of anywhere else more obvious."

"Uther often speaks without thought. Orphan Thorne could be anywhere. We shall search there first. If he is not topside, we must go below decks."

The desire to not do that motivating her, Sara followed Norman to the first set of stairs. Their steps echoed across the wood and metal, it was loud and stifling. The sounds were a reminder of the oppression this ship represented to her. She failed to understand how hundreds of sailors could cram into this floating weapon, go to sea for months at a time, risk their lives against who knew what, and enjoy it. Give her the open spaces any day and the serenity of a good cup of coffee with friends over the aggressive nature of this military war machine.

They stopped several times to consult the vague signs leading them deeper into the upper tiers before finding themselves entering the bridge. A far cry from movie depictions, or the fragments she recalled from having been forced to watch, the curved room offered a panoramic view of downtown Wilmington— once you got past the forward gun turrets. Sara admired the view but there was no sign of Orphan Thorne.

"This was a bust," she muttered. "We're never going to find him before the museum opens, Norman."

"There is no choice. We continue searching."

She followed him, winding through rooms filled with desks, radio equipment, and plenty more she failed to label. They descended to the main deck and were rounding the corner between the base of the conning tower and the first gun turret when Norman halted. Sara nearly bumped into him before peering around his bulk to spy the slightest flicker of movement.

Orphan! It had to be.

"Norman, is that…?"

"Shh, we must not alarm him," Norman whispered. "Stay behind me. We don't know what he is capable of."

Sara's excitement faded when she saw the old elf head deeper into the bowels of the ship. She already felt the walls closing in on her, threatening to bury her under the impossible weight of steel and memory. While the military didn't provide much value to her life, she did have a penchant for ghosts and the supernatural. Of course, she never thought she'd be part of her own special. *I watch way too much television. I need to find a better hobby.*

One of the lures of the battleship was its supposed haunting by those who had perished aboard. Sara's heart skipped at the thought of seeking out the specters of the past in the middle of the night. She'd convinced Daniel to tour the haunted prison in Charleston, South Carolina, and the closer Devil's Tramping Ground less than an hour from their house. Both experiences proved exhilarating for her. All Daniel took away from them was a tick bite right between his butt cheeks.

Touching the gun tucked into her pants for peace of mind, Sara crept behind Norman like a vixen from an old film noir detective movie. Any notion she had of sneaking up on the elf was dashed the moment they reached the bottom of the steps depositing them in what had once been the main crew mess.

"Orphan Thorn! We have come bearing tribute and are in need of your services." Norman's booming voice thundered throughout the belly of the ship, making Sara cringe. She caught the rattle of chains somewhere ahead.

At the following silence, a host of possibilities arose as her imagination took over. She envisioned a horde of screaming elves charging from the bowels, swords waving, spears sharp. The ridiculousness of it rattled her and it took all of her willpower to not draw her gun and fire off a few shots.

"Orphan Thorne!" Norman called again.

Sara's hopes sank when again no answer was returned. They were going to have to go deeper into the battleship. Into a space where she did not belong nor want to go.

"Norman—"

Shadows concealing the far end of the mess deepened, swirling in violent patterns. Figures formed. To Sara they looked like menacing beings with open desires to tear them asunder. She slid behind Norman.

"You are not welcome here, gargoyle. Leave me."

Norman stood firm. "Elfkind has need of your services once more."

"They had their opportunities and still shunned me," Orphan replied. "This is no place for you. Or the human at your side."

Sara peered into the gloom but couldn't find the elusive elf. A chill settled over her. The urge to turn and flee grew stronger. If not for Norman, she would have run back to the van and never looked back.

"Enough of your games. We do not have time," Norman roared. "We have the sword of Grimspire with us and must get to the wizard before a pack of lycans finds us and claims it for themselves."

Sara's flesh warmed as the shadows receded. Those haunting figures coalesced into a singular being.

Orphan Thorne stood hunched over, leaning his weight on a dark cane. Stark white hair flowed down over his back, the tips of his ears poking through. He bore deep lines and age spots on his face and hands. The beard creeping down his chest whispered of countless years. He was lithe yet firm. There was fire in his eyes. A passion that inspired her jealousy.

"Lycans?" Orphan asked.

"We have been on the run since last night," Norman confirmed.

"Why do you have the sword?" Orphan pressed. "The damned thing has been the bane of my existence since the monarchy first came to me."

"That is a long tale best uttered on the way."

The elf snorted. "The way to where? The wizard? Sheldon is a prick who cares nothing for the rest of the world. He hasn't left his sanctum in decades. Certainly not to help elfkind. Never trust a wizard. You want my advice? Take the sword and dump in the

Atlantic. Wash your hands of it and go home. The path you're on now leads only to despair."

"We've despaired enough," Sara muttered.

Orphan squinted, studying her face. "What would a human know of suffering?"

Sara resisted the urge to shoot the elf. The thought revolted her, for she'd never been one to resort to violence. "My family has been involved in your world for years, without our consent. Both my husband and I have looked over our shoulders since his first encounter with elves. I didn't ask to be here. I don't want to be here, but I learned a long time ago life doesn't care about what I want. So here I am. Asking for your help so I can go back to my family and my dogs."

Cocking his head, Orphan told Norman, "I like this one. Do you have tribute?"

Norman patted his jacket, light enough to ensure he didn't crack the egg. "I do."

"Good. Come. The museum opens soon, and you don't want to be here when all those humans start scampering over the decks."

Orphan turned and headed deeper into the battleship where Sara's hopes and fears promised to collide.

NINETEEN

Sara realized she was lost after fifteen minutes of shuffling through cramped rooms, descending ladders, and the droning thump of steady footsteps. She spent her time trying to focus on the enigmatic elf leading them deeper into the past. Norman's bulk blocked most of him however, leaving her more frustrated than anything else. Echoes of their hushed conversation blended together. It wasn't long before Sara took to looking over her shoulder, fearing they were about to be ambushed and trapped.

What little she did see inspired conflicted emotions. Orphan appeared ancient on the surface. He walked with a stoop. The constant creak of his bones reminded her of Daniel's knees on cold mornings. Yet despite the obvious ailments and advanced age, Sara deduced much of his manner was camouflage. She felt, more than anything, the old elf remained as lethal as he had been all those centuries ago when war consumed the clans.

How many secrets did these creatures hide buried beneath the detritus of forgotten years? Sara felt their odd majesty, even as they drew her deeper into their world. They were natural survivors, adapting to new situations with seeming ease. She envied them that way, reflecting on her personal challenges throughout her young life. School. Children. Work. Struggling to keep her family afloat during those first few years after Daniel finished his time in the army and couldn't find himself. Were her trials any less than those of the elves? For the first time since Abner dragged himself soaking wet to her door and involved her in his dilemma Sara found herself truly having compassion. There was a sense of immensity now. As if she were fulfilling a part of her destiny.

The next time she looked up, Sara saw they were surrounded by massive artillery shells—Orphan had led them down into the rear magazine. Surrounded by shells almost as tall as she was, Sara felt dwarfed.

"Why are we down this far?" Norman asked.

Orphan waved him off. "Where is the egg?"

As Norman reached inside his jacket, Sara asked, "What are you going to do with it? We nearly lost two of our party retrieving this for you."

"That is my concern." Orphan scowled at her. "What would humans know of ogre eggs? This is not your world, young lady. Best you remain silent until we conclude our affair."

Fuming, she closed her fist and stepped forward. Norman shifted to block her. "She is the wife of Daniel Thomas and my companion. No harm shall befall her, forge master."

The elf paused. "You have powerful friends, Sara Thomas." At her nod, he continued. "Very well. If you must know, the egg holds natural magic. A reservoir of sorts. With the power concealed within, the wizard will be able to send the sword back into hiding where it will remain for eternity. Hopefully."

Sara frowned. The ease with which he answered left her questioning his authenticity. *A magic egg? Seems a little Saturday morning cartoonish to me.* She'd heard more plausible explanations in the books she read to her children when they were little. Even if he was telling the truth, the matter of what happened to the egg remained.

"What happens to it after?" she pressed.

"Eh? The sword? I told you."

"No. The egg."

Orphan scratched his cheek with his index fingernail. "Well, I imagine Sheldon will whisk it back to its family, there being no further need for it."

"You imagine?" She failed to keep the doubt from her tone, causing him to shift awkwardly.

The elf shrugged, a sheepish grin on his face. "It's been a long time since anyone had an audience with the wizard. Have no fear, the egg will not be harmed. It will be back in the nest before you know it, provided you hand it over and let me do what needs to be done before those damned lycans find us."

Sara rolled her eyes even as urgency settled back in its familiar place. "Is the wizard here?"

"No. He is far from the battleship," Orphan admitted.

"Then why did you lead us down here? We have friends waiting in the parking lot with the sword." Her eyes narrowed. "Is this a game to you?"

"Patience, human. I assure you; this is no game. In order to use ensure the egg survives transport I must secure it. My tools are in this powder magazine. Once you cease your incessant questioning, I can retrieve them, and we head back up a few decks where I will send the egg to Sheldon. Is that fine with you?"

Nonplussed, Sara stood her ground. "If this Sheldon isn't here, where is he? How do we reach him? I'm in no mood for games."

"Nor am I," Orphan snapped. "Now, if you please. Give me some peace and quiet and let me do what needs doing. Your questions will all be answered in time."

She allowed Norman to lead her away, giving the elf the time he needed to go deeper into the magazine for his tools. Confusion and frustration clashed in her, and it was all she could do to not lash out at the gargoyle she considered a friend. Forcing her ahead, Norman guided them up one level until they were out of sight.

"I understand your frustrations, Sara Thomas, but your intensity will not force him to speed up," Norman explained. "I have encountered many such elves throughout the years. They believe the rest of us are beneath them and will sour should we question too hard. This Orphan Thorne shows no signs of duplicity. We have no reason to doubt."

"I don't trust him." She crossed her arms and tapped her right foot.

"Then trust me," Norman offered.

Wincing, she closed her eyes and attempted to unjumble her thoughts. They had the egg. They were with the one being on the planet, or so they claimed, who knew the wizard's location. What remained of a pack of werewolves was hot on their heels. Too bad they weren't trainable. She snorted at the thought of a sleeping werewolf curled up on the couch and became homesick. Her dogs were home alone, no doubt making a mess of the place in her absence. She loved her Berners, but they were vindictive, needy creatures when they felt they were being neglected. For the thousandth time she wished Daniel were here instead of her. Sara realized she was better suited to worrying than doing.

"Norman, what are we doing? This is nonsense. Those wolves might already be closing in on Bert and the others. We are wasting our time with no reassurance of reaching our goals. I don't know how much more I can take of this, I really don't."

"You are a brave woman. I have never known another human with your poise or bearing. Let this process play out. Orphan Thorne was once revered among the clans. He will not lead us astray. Not with the fate of the world at stake."

The fate of the world? Thanks for adding that little nudge of pressure. "You're asking a lot from me."

"Yet nowhere near what I expect from the others," he cautioned.

She frowned. Until now, she hadn't seen herself as being separate from the group. Looking away, Sara saw the elder elf leaning against the bulkhead, silently watching them.

Rising to his full height, the gargoyle asked, "Do you have what you need?"

"I could ask the same of you," the elf replied. "Trouble in paradise?"

"That is none of your business."

Grinning, Orphan said, "My mistake. Follow me. The museum's morning staff will be here soon.

The quicker we get the egg to Sheldon the quicker we get to the transport, and I get you out of my life. Just like the gods intended."

"Is that—" A stern look from Norman had Sara falling quiet.

She fell in behind them as they headed up— Orphan led them to the wishing well. A hole bored straight down the battleship's hull where visitors pressed their luck with dreams of fancy. What wishes they hoped to get from an eighty-year-old naval warfare vessel was lost on her. Still, people needed gimmicks. Anything to cling to during trying times. The hole, she noticed, was just wide enough for the egg to fit. Sara watched as Norman lifted the grate, setting it against the nearest wall.

"The egg," Orphan demanded.

Norman gave her a quick look before holding out the egg.

Orphan accepted it with a ginger grasp, setting it on the small towel he'd brought. The forge master unwrapped his leather toolkit and went to work.

His actions were lost on Sara, though she watched with intense curiosity. She suspected the egg was about to be destroyed, especially considering the plan appeared to be to just drop it down the hole and hope for the best.

We are doomed.

A ring of small nails soon circled the egg, reminding her of one of Daniel's favorite horror villains. Give her a good ghost story any day, anything but this. Tiny bolts of electricity danced between them, glowing green and red. Slipping on a pair of worn work gloves, Orphan Thorne lifted the egg over the hole and dropped it.

"What are you doing?" Sara shouted and lunged forward.

To his credit, the elf stepped aside to let her watch the magic imbued within the egg come to life.

A funnel of colors and eldritch powers swirled in tornadic fashion. Instead of falling, the egg drifted on the magical updraft. Sara marveled as a small cloud formed in the base of the wishing well. What happened next she'd struggle to explain for the rest of her life. Magic sparking in pulses, the egg drifted down to the cloud, where a pair of hands stretched forth to snatch it and pull it within. The portal closed with a loud slap. The magic faded, leaving her in a rain of sparks twinkling out of existence.

"Sheldon has what he needs to conceal the sword," Orphan announced. "We should go."

For the first time since agreeing to join the quest, she was speechless. "We?"

Orphan fixed her with an unreadable stare. "Seems I'm invested now. Besides, I feel like stretching my legs."

"Here they come," Bert shouted causing Abner to stir from his place on the couch.

Uther rolled his eyes. "Keep it down. We're not supposed to be here, remember?"

Feigning embarrassment, the troll lowered his arm from where he was pointing. The smile remained. "Hey, who's the old guy?"

"Old guy? They always smell like bad lotion and Old Spice," the sword groaned from beneath it's wrappings.

Peeking out from behind the troll's mass, Abner got his first glimpse of an elf who, in his mind, wanted to kill him. He cowered back inside the van and drew his knees up and buried his head in the hopes Orphan Thorne might ignore him.

Sara and Norman continued forward but Orphan abruptly halted. Sara watched Uther bristle as he reached for one of his swords with a curse. Responding to the challenge, Orphan shed his cane and old man persona, drawing up to his full height. Where he produced his sword from remained a mystery to Sara. *See? I knew he wasn't as harmless as he appeared.*

"You," Orphan hissed. "I should have cut your head off a long time ago."

Uther stepped forward. "You couldn't then. You won't now. I was always the better swordsman, you old bastard."

"Time changes everything, *fallen*," Orphan taunted. "Let's finish this."

"Enough!" Norman bellowed. "We do not have time for a foolish vendetta. Those lycans are still out there, hunting us. We must set aside our differences and get to the wizard."

Uther jabbed his sword at the forge master. "When this is finished, you and me, old man."

"With pleasure."

A motorcycle engine roared from behind them and Sara caught the glint of sunlight reflecting off metal. Her heart sank.

Time was up.

The werewolves had caught up.

TWENTY

Sara stiffened despite noticing the hunter was in human form. She knew, as did the others, where one went the rest of the pack would be close behind.

A fresh wave of desperation broke upon her. *This isn't how this ends.* Something in her snapped as she backed away from the others and crawled into the van, bumping Abner out of the way to retrieve the duffel bag filled with weapons. Rummaging for pistol magazines with the correct ammunition, her face hardened.

Abner popped his head up, the whites of his teeth obscene against the ogre grime coating his face and clothes. "What are you doing?"

"I am sick and tired of this shit, Abner. All of it. I'm done being the victim or the helpless human trapped in this fucking nightmare." Sara slammed the magazine home and chambered a round. "This ends today."

Without waiting for his reply, she hopped back into the parking lot and marched forward. Her bold move caught the others off guard. Using that to her advantage, Sara raised her pistol, clicked the safety off, and began firing at the werewolf leering at them from across the parking lot. Rounds skipped off the concrete, one striking the motorcycle's chrome muffler. Her target balked, dropping into a crouch. As a wolf he might have recovered from any injury. As a man he was good as dead if she hit him.

The others burst into action on either side of her. Norman blurred into his gargoyle form; wings stretched out as he prepared to launch. Uther drew both swords, now glowing a soft gold color, and spat a stream of curses. Only Orphan Thorne remained silent. The ancient elf drew his long sword, planted the tip on the cracked and broken concrete, and waited.

Sara fired the last round, announced by the metallic clicking of an empty magazine, and screamed.

Bert, jolly and non-threatening, came up to take the weapon from her trembling hands. Tears broke free at his kindness. He pulled her into an embrace and let her unleash the torrent of raw emotions.

"You got the doggie, Sara!"

"That little stunt bought us some time, but there is no telling how long before the rest of the pack arrives," Uther growled. "Do we deal with this one or do we flee while we still can?"

Fangs barred; Norman offered a wet growl from the base of his throat. "We cannot endanger human life. They will soon start arriving. I can reach him."

Sara, still in Bert's comforting hold, caught the sounds of a revving engine and the screech of tires—A grey sedan raced into the parking lot and struck the motorcycle a split-second before the rider leapt clear. Bike parts flew under the force of the impact. Smoke steamed from the sedan that drove through the carnage and rolled toward them.

Cecile Barnabas might live to a hundred years old and still wouldn't be able to explain why she decided to speed up. Common sense suggested she slow and avoid the situation. Pushed to the brink of exhaustion, she chalked her poor decision up to the lack of sleep and food. Cecile pulled into the battleship's parking lot and, upon seeing one of her targets in what appeared to be attack mode against a group of others, let instinct take over. She hit the gas and screwed her eyes shut, bracing for impact.

The collision rippled through her stiffened arms, running straight down her spine and into her soul. Cecile winced at the sounds of tearing metal as the motorcycle hit her hood and rolled over the top of the sedan. She'd hit a deer once coming home on a late night and knew the best way to protect herself was by speeding up in the hopes of the deer going over the car instead of into the windshield. She hit the motorcycle with the same principle.

Twin lines of sparks scratched the sedan from the hood to the roof. She imagined both vehicles catching fire and exploding, killing her and the werewolf in a blaze of glory. When the sedan kept going, clearing the wreckage with relative ease, she almost felt disappointed. Opening her eyes again, Cecile couldn't find the rider, but she did see the others, did one of them have wings?, poised on the far side of the parking lot. She headed for them. *How am I going to pay for all this*?

The once pristine government issue sedan screeched to a halt and the driver hopped out like a woman who'd just endured a significant car accident. Sara watched, amazed, as the driver took the time to adjust her obnoxious grey pant suit, flipping the hair away from her face in the process, before walking over to them. The gun in her hand suggested enough, the others got the message. Swords were sheathed.

Norman blurred back into human guise. The situation deescalated without a shot fired. *I might have a new hero*.

"No one move. My name is Agent Barnabas," the woman told them, fumbling with pulling her badge from her inner jacket pocket.

"Fucking DESA," Uther groaned. "Don't you people have more important things to do?"

Cecile blinked, eyes coming together with the quick shake of her head. "This is what we do. Or did you forget the agreement between the government and your clans? Now, someone needs to explain why you are here, in the open, in the middle of a showdown with a werewolf."

Her gaze stayed on Norman.

Sara patted Bert's arm and stepped out of his embrace. "Agent Barnabas, I'm Sara. Thank you for whatever that was back there."

Cecile looked back, a little reluctant to view the carnage she caused. "That was me saving your lives. Do you have any idea the amount of damage you've caused? I've been hunting this pack since last night. You have put too many civilians in harm's way. By rights, I should have you all arrested. This is in direct violation of articles—"

"Are you done?" Uther interrupted. "We've been hunted by those dogs for the better part of the night. We don't need your bureaucrat bullshit. Not now."

"And you are?"

Uther bristled. "No one important."

Cecile narrowed her eyes, lips pursed. "Uh huh, those Old Guard swords on your back suggest otherwise. Who's in charge of this mess?"

Sensing the situation devolving, Sara answered quickly, "No one really. We've been tasked with an important mission. If we fail the implications for the elves and humans are too severe."

"You're not one of them," Cecile concluded as she took in Sara.

"No. I'm just a normal, human woman with a family I desperately want to go home to."

The agent shook her head. "I need to call this in."

"We do not have time for that," Norman told her. "That lycan was but a scout. The others will soon be here. Our quest cannot afford to waste time."

"Just what's so important you feel like breaking the law is justified?" Cecile pressed.

"We are trying to keep the sword of Grimspire from falling into lycan hands and save the world," Norman insisted.

Cecile sighed, her features twisting. "I'm going to need more than that."

"That is all I can tell you," Norman insisted.

"Agent Barnabas, if those werewolves get their hands on the sword, they will claim dominance and the right to rule, plunging both worlds into chaos. We're trying to return the sword to the one who created it and stop the werewolves," Sara added.

"I'm the one who created it," Orphan muttered and jerked his head in the direction of the battleship. "Spend a lifetime creating the impossible and get no recognition for it. None. What good is being an artisan if you're not appreciated? I should have remained in seclusion."

Cecile gestured toward the disgruntled elf and asked, "Is he always like this?"

"I don't know," Sara answered after choosing to keep the barb on the tip of her tongue to herself. "Look, Agent—"

"Cecile. Call me Cecile."

Smiling in that familiar way inspired by false relief, Sara said, "Cecile, we really need to get moving. It's not safe here."

"And just where do you plan on going?"

Good question. Up until now, Orphan hadn't mentioned their destination. Sara turned, altering her tone to prevent the elf from regressing further into anger. "Orphan? Where are we going?"

Huffing, the forge master leveled a glare. "Very well. We are heading to Fort Fischer. I have a boat there. From there, we set sail at nightfall and its, as your kind says, off to see the wizard."

"What wizard? What are you talking about?" Cecile demanded.

Sara understood how the woman felt, for she was finally starting to emerge from that crippling stage. What little she knew of D.E.S.A. told her field agents were stuffy with minimal personality. Hoping to capitalize on their commonality, Sara made her move. "There's a wizard, named Sheldon, somewhere nearby who can hide the sword and save the world from doom. Orphan is the only one who knows where he is."

"This needs to be called in," Cecile insisted, but even as she said it the words took on a heavy undertone.

Sara watched the doubt creep in. "Cecile, please. There isn't any time."

Realizing she still held her pistol, Cecile holstered it. "What am I supposed to do? Sit back and let you scurry away on your secret quest? Hoping what you say isn't true? I have a job to do. Nothing will keep me from it."

"Come with us," Sara said without thinking.

"What?"

"Sara, no!" Norman tried not to shout.

Jerking back, Cecile said, "I agree with them. That's not a good idea."

Sara shook her head. "That doesn't matter. It's the only way to ensure we complete our quest, and you see there is nothing else going on behind your back."

Pacing, the tip of a finger tapping her temple, Cecile stared back at what remained of the motorcycle. A quick glance at her watch had her sighing. "Fine. I follow you. No funny business."

The pressure lifted from Sara's chest. She broke into a smile. Like all good plans, however, it was short lived. No sooner had Cecile given her consent than one of her tires popped off the axel and rolled away.

"Change of plans, looks like I'm riding with you," the agent's tone wallowed in sorrow.

Bert's laughter echoed across the parking lot. He kept chuckling as he climbed back into the driver's seat.

There were some things in life too precious to unravel, Sara thought after seeing the childish joy etched on the troll's face. Laughter was good. It meant they were still alive. She chuckled to herself and climbed in beside him.

"Okay, so where are we going?" Cecile asked with a certain giddiness the others found unsettling.

TWENTY-ONE

"I'll meet you at Fort Fischer at sundown."

Sara remained unclear why Orphan Thorne felt the need to split off from the rest of the group or why he didn't plan on reuniting almost twelve hours from now. They were exposed, vulnerable to continued werewolf attacks and who knew what else. If the previous night was any indicator, they were in for a long day with little guarantee of survival.

Despite his stalwart appearance, she felt Norman's exhaustion in the way his shoulders slumped along with the hollow stare out the windshield. Without the gargoyle she doubted they stood much of a chance of finding the wizard. Even then, Sara couldn't help but worry her troubles would not end if they defeated the werewolf pack. Would her and her family have to move? Go into a form of witness protection from all things supernatural? As absurd as it sounded, Sara feared the worst.

She let her gaze wander through the van. Of them all, only Bert seemed impervious to their situation. His jovial demeanor inspired her just enough to keep going. As if his ignorance whispered all was going to be fine. She was semi-relaxed until she watched Abner's head dip to his chest as sleep claimed him and became angry. This entire fiasco was his fault and, of them all, he had the luxury of going to sleep. Sara struggled with the urge to kick the gnome in his shin.

A soft snort from Uther suggested he shared her thoughts, though his means to an end were far more severe. She tried to study him without drawing his full attention. The sword whispered to each of them, worming into their deepest fears and desires. Sara won her inner battle, avoiding temptation and retaining her humanity. What did it promise Uther? His propensity for violence made him the most formidable opponent in the van. With the sword in hand, he might ascend to become a tyrant. She shuddered as visions of flames and fields of bodies flashed by.

The only one who had no claim on the sword or their quest was the unfortunate government agent. Cecile appeared innocent enough, though Sara doubted the woman was trustworthy. Still, having another human along provided an outlet to vent her frustrations and commiserate on their increasingly desperate situation.

"Cecile, how did you find us?" Sara asked in the hopes of pulling precious nuggets of information.

"That's classified."

"We're a little beyond that by this point, don't you think?" Uther stated.

"He's got a point," Sara said, attempting to smooth it over. "We've been hunted by these things since Abner showed up on my doorstep last night."

Pausing to clear her throat, the agent appeared conflicted before saying, "I was alerted to unauthorized activity. My guess is approximately at the same time as your first encounter. I was dispatched to your house and followed the trail. You've been two steps ahead of me the entire night."

"If you're here, where is the rest of the pack?"

"My guess is somewhere on the road behind us," Cecile speculated. "The one you encountered at the battleship was a scout like you said."

Sara had been around long enough to know when parts of the truth were being withheld. Having children provided valuable real-world experience. Cecile Barnabas might be sincere, but she was also hedging her bets. The agent was hiding something.

As if noticing her look, Cecile shifted the conversation. "The better question is what are we supposed to do for the entire day?" A hint of flush crept up her neck.

"I'm hungry!" Bert chimed in. "We should do breakfast."

"Brilliant," Uther muttered.

Sara frowned at him. "He's got a point. We need to eat and get some rest."

"Did you forget about our pals out there?"

"You have all told me, repeatedly, they won't attack in broad daylight." Sara stood her ground. "What harm is there in slowing just enough to refill?"

"Sara Thomas is correct," Norman declared from the passenger's seat. "We have been hard pressed for many hours. The first stage of our quest is complete. We must regroup and prepare for the next. I fear our greatest test is yet to come."

"Good. It's decided. Bert, find us somewhere to eat." Sara smiled at Uther when he snorted. *Take that. I won this round.*

Bert turned the radio up and rumbled across the river into Wilmington proper before heading south toward Carolina Beach. None of them knew what they were looking for, instead trusting the nose and stomach of the troll driving.

Good Boy heard the engine roar before his hyper senses flared. He dove aside as the car plowed into his motorcycle, narrowly avoiding having his head sliced off by flying shards of heated metal. He hit his shoulder hard, grunting with the bone snapping impact of the compression. A series of snaps from the shoulder to the neck awakened excruciating pain in the lycan and it was all he could do not to cry out. Left arm hanging useless for the time being, Good Boy decided self-preservation more important than delaying his prey long enough for Gruff and the others to arrive.

Rolling to his uninjured side, Good Boy crawled into the ditch between the parking lot and the road, using the depression to funnel his way into the tall grasses before crossing the road and hiding in the trees. He hadn't expected the car and, even before that, realized he'd bitten off more than anticipated by confronting the prey himself. Good Boy had scores to settle with the gargoyle and the Old Guard, but standing before them, a troll, and an ancient elf with way more testosterone than anyone his age had business having, found his chances of victory dwindling to nothing. Then there was the damned woman who shot him. He would take pleasure in killing her, if he lasted that long.

The weight of his pain forced him to sit against a thin pine. Waves of agony pulsated from his shoulder, infecting every part of his torso. Good Boy wiped the tears away. How long had it been since he last cried? Tipping his head back, the rough bark scrapping his flesh, the lycan closed his eyes and steadied his breathing. Calm. Soothing. His thoughts blended into a mirage of darkness. The pain dulled. His breath slowed.

Ruptured tendons and muscles reknit. Blessed with unnatural healing, Good Boy felt the last inkling of pain disappear. He opened his eyes, testing the injured shoulder. It ached, still tender, but the blinding intensity was gone. Full recovery would take some time, at least long enough for the rest of the pack to arrive. He contemplated crafting a story of heroism before deciding against it. Gruff would see through it in an instant. No. Better to be truthful and hope for lenience.

Enough had gone wrong for the pack since their first move on the sword. They'd lost too many friends along the way. Too much family for him. Those names and faces were irreplaceable and worse, depreciated the hunting prowess of the pack. Good Boy wondered if they'd missed their prime opportunity by not taking the gnome immediately after he stole the sword when they were at full strength.

Now he had a formidable array of reinforcements, each capable of demolishing the pack on their own. Right before the crash, Good Boy caught the scent of something he hadn't expected. A human. Wise enough to spot a target of opportunity, the lycan began plotting how to best use her against the others. Should the woman be turned, the pack had a chance. He knew just the right pack member to turn to with the information.

The rumble of the van pulling onto the road made him duck. They wouldn't waste the opportunity to eliminate another pack member, given the chance. Hiding in the scrub brush and tall grasses, Good Boy watched the van lumber away, oblivious to the threat lurking just out of sight. Alone again, except for a lingering cloud of exhaust choking him, the lycan dug his phone out of his pocket and, relieved to find it still operable, made the call that could change their lives.

Or so he hoped.

After crossing the Cape Fear River, the group hooked a right on 421 South. They found a Waffle House not far down the road and pulled in. The cough and stutter of the van when it parked left them questioning who was more tired, them or their vehicle. Norman agreed to remain behind to protect the sword, against the stiff wall of Uther's protests, while the rest went inside and grabbed a quick bite.

The gargoyle watched them enter and file onto a string of seats at the bar. Unlike them, he did not need to eat regularly. Gargoyles were notorious fasters, often used to sitting on their perches for months at a time. Let the others find comfort in a meal. He preferred the quiet solitude.

Norman stood beside the van, stretching the kinks out of his muscles. It had been a long time since he last felt this tired. This sore. His back screamed from the repeated transformations. Knowing rest awaited once the sword was once again concealed, he decided to make a call.

"We have contacted the forge master and are awaiting the next rendezvous," he said after Morgen answered.

"You are certain he will take you to the wizard?" she asked.

"Reasonably." Norman watched a group of motorcycles flash down the road, heading for the beach. He stiffened, fearing the lycans were about to do the unthinkable.

"I don't like this, Norman. We are taking a terrible risk on this. Why are you not moving to the wizard's location now?"

"The lycans caught up with us. Orphan Thorne left once the situation resolved itself. Without him, we have no ability to find the wizard," he explained. His voice dropped low as he contemplated what to say next. "There is more."

"Go on." Her tone suggested she braced for the worst.

"A DESA agent is now with us. She prevented the lycans from assaulting us this morning."

"This complicates matters. How much does she know?"

"Only what we told her. She knows the sword of Grimspire is in play and has been tracking the lycan pack throughout the night. It is my understanding she did not expect to find us," Norman said. "There is no reason to believe the human government is directly involved yet."

Silence. Morgen's quiet had a unique way of unsettling him. Norman, like most gargoyles, prided himself on his unflappable demeanor. He was the wall upon which storms broke. The defender of the clans. A beacon of righteousness. Nothing in his experiences proved as daunting as the queen's silence.

"We must be cautious," she said at last. "DESA must not get their hands on the sword. Do whatever it takes to ensure this, Norman. I am trusting you with the future of our species. Get the sword to the wizard and finish this sordid affair. Before it's too late."

"It will be done." Norman ended the call and slipped his phone back into his jacket.

TWENTY-TWO

A clear crisis of conscience. That was the best way Cecile could describe the emotions ravaging her psyche. As a field agent she spent months in training, learning the different races, their strengths and weaknesses, traits and habits. More exhausting than traumatic, at least until now, she concluded she was in way over her head. Until now these creatures were images on paper. A whisper of possibilities she hadn't encountered. Nothing in her training prepared her for the clash of personalities her new travel companions bristled with.

She knew she needed to report in. Enough had already happened that she dreaded the pending mounds of paperwork awaiting her. Despite what she perceived to be more problems than was worth, Cecile admitted she was having the adventure of a lifetime. How many others could say they chased a pack of werewolves across half the state only to team up with elves, gargoyles, and more? Not that she was permitted to tell anyone. NDA restrictions carried a hefty fine against those caught running their mouths. The paradox infuriated her.

All her life she'd grown up listening to stories from veterans. Her father, a Marine from the Gulf War era, often dragged her and her brother with him to meetings at the VFW, not thinking the wild stories might worm their way into her subconscious. They did and took root. She leapt at the chance to join D.E.S.A., thinking one day she might share her exploits with her father. Little did she know the only way that might happen was by her breaking the law.

Stomach full, she drifted off to sleep after they climbed back into the van. Her last sights were of the impossibly massive shoulders of the gargoyle in the passenger seat.

Sara watched the agent fall asleep. A thousand questions clung to the tip of her tongue. She wanted to know if Cecile had any connection with the operation Daniel had been called away for. If she knew anything to assuage her fears as they plunged deeper into their own misadventures. Nothing good had come from dealing with the shadowy government agency. Or did it?

Begrudgingly, she admitted D.E.S.A. hadn't been involved with their initial debacle a few years ago. Agent Blackmere only arrived at the end. The chaos and confusion stemmed from the internal conflict between the elf clans. This time, it was a rogue pack of werewolves messing with her life. That didn't mean the government wasn't at work being the scenes, pulling strings and keeping tabs. Cecile's sudden arrival was proof enough of that.

What was it then that drove this tangled web of rivaling clans and species fighting to claim dominance of the waking world? Sara wondered if Cecile was part of the problem or a rare example of what doing right by the people should be. Without knowing more, she decided to keep her guard raised. The government specialized in messing up everything it touched. She prayed this quest was the exception. Otherwise …

Bert pulled the van off the main road, into an empty parking lot with a Ferris wheel in the background. Sara knew where they were—the Carolina Beach Boardwalk Amusement Park was a vacationer's paradise. Filled with rides, games, food, and drink, it was the main draw this far down the peninsula. Still a few miles from Fort Fischer, it marked the highlight of beach season. Sara had fond memories of walking along the boardwalk, listening to live music drift over the ocean, and the smell of fresh seafood.

Still early, the park was closed, as were most of the shops and boutique stores designed to entice tourists to visit with their wallets. Sara couldn't pull her eyes from the flock of seagulls squawking over scraps. The clouds were gone. Most of the previous night's rain already dried in the Carolina humidity. Sara longed for the sun's kiss. That supple warmth to invigorate her. She needed to get out of the van, now heady with the stench of body odor and worse, if only for sanity's sake.

"Why are we stopping here?" Uther asked.

Norman looked over his shoulder. "We have the entire day before we are to meet with Orphan Thorne. What else are we supposed to do?"

"Not sightsee," the Old Guard replied.

"He has a point, Norman," Sara added. Though she was contemplating just throwing herself out of the van at this point. "Won't we be too exposed here? I mean, I like a good amusement park as much as anyone, but this feels a bit brazen."

"Perhaps but we have already been through this. Our enemy will not attack in daylight."

"Why is that exactly?" she asked, frowning.

"They can't transform into wolf form," Bert answered, surprising them. The troll met their suspicions with a wry grin and shrug. "What? I watch movies."

"We must consider our options before continuing," Norman added, ignoring him. "There is much to discuss before we meet the wizard."

"You mean like our trust issues?" Sara asked. "The longer we are together the more divided we become." She glanced at the Old Guard elf. "Take Uther's obvious hatred of Orphan Thorne."

"I have my reasons."

"Care to explain?"

Rather than lashing out, Uther opened the side door with a slam and stalked off. Sara watched him go and knew what she needed to do. There was no affinity between them. She doubted the Old Guard considered her as much more than a nuisance. A fly to be swat. She didn't know then what made her follow, only that quiet voice in the corner of her mind that had steered her right for most of her life.

Excusing herself, Sara called, "Uther."

The elf didn't slow.

Breaking into a jog to catch up, Sara said, "Uther. We need to talk."

He stopped and spun, his gaze a mix of hurt and anger. "What is there to talk about, human? You shouldn't be here. This is elf business. Go home. Pretend you never met us and go live your mundane life. We don't need you. Don't want you."

That's it. "You think I asked to become part of this? I couldn't give a flying fuck about your world.

You're fantasy creatures to most of the world. Figments of imagination made popular by movies twenty years ago. The only reason I'm here is because Abner decided to show up at my home last night."

Uther's eyes widened at her anger, and he rocked back. "Doesn't give you the right to interject in elf affairs. I don't care what Norman says."

"The queen," Sara corrected. "Your queen."

Uther paused. "You've met with Morgen?"

"I did. She agreed I needed to see this through, though I doubt we shared the same reasons," Sara said. "Look, I'm not asking you to like me, or any other human for that matter. I'll settle for not arguing until we part ways."

Uther paused, considering the potential advantages to a truce. As a man conditioned to conflict, he admitted to enjoying the thrill of bringing another to the edge of violence. He hadn't expected her to curse. The vulgarity ill-suited her character. He may be many things, but he remained a constant judge of character. His contempt with humanity was blanket. Nothing particular about Sara angered him. Well, nothing more than the fragility of her mortality. Humans were the weakest species on the planet, yet through some inexplicable perversion they dominated all they touched.

"Perhaps," was all he said, waiting to see what she did next.

Exhaling her pent-up breath, Sara felt the pressure leave her chest. It was immediately replaced by the weight of the next problem needing addressing.

"Uther, I need to know something before we continue. The forge master—"

"That's none of your business," he snapped. "Whatever my problem with Orphan Thorne is remains between us. It will not hinder our mission. I assure you."

That was good enough for her. Sara turned to head back to the van; nothing further needed saying.

"Sara, if you need to know, ask Norman."

She stopped and watched him walk away.

Bert stared at the amusement park with longing. He realized he hadn't had much fun since Lou died. The thought of feeling the wind blowing through his hair as the giant wheel picked up speed, staring out over the Atlantic Ocean with an ice cream cone in one hand and a funnel cake in the other, powdered sugar blowing over his face and clothes, reminded him of childhood. Contrary to popular belief, trolls were fun loving, compassionate people. Family centered, they seldom caused trouble.

He missed the old life. Bert lacked the one thing every troll required in life, quality friends. He was the last of his line, save his mother who refused to leave her apartment on Miami Beach. Not that he blamed her, the ocean called to him too. Trolls not being able to swim notwithstanding, why leave it for misadventures that might result in his death? Then again, without Lou he really didn't have much to look forward to in life.

More than once he confronted the alien thought of accepting death. Would it hurt? Would Lou be there waiting on the other side to clap him upside the head?

As amusing as the thought was, Bert decided he appreciated living more than rejoining lost loved ones. Watching Sara trail after Uther tugged at his heart. Lou may be gone, but Bert had adopted a new family. Sure, they didn't get along, and the tension was giving him high blood pressure, but he was willing to lay down his life for each of them. Well, maybe not Uther. Not yet.

He wanted to go out there, follow her in the event Uther did something foolish. The Old Guard's confrontation with Orphan Thorne frightened him. They were impossible forces of nature, locked on a collision course that might take out the entire group if no one intervened. Bert knew where Norman's loyalties were. Abner couldn't do much. That left him. The lone guardian to ensure no harm befell Sara. It was the continuation of his promise to Daniel; one he would die to keep.

Abner Grumman hated life. Hated his position in the group. Gnomes were often frowned upon and typecast into nefarious roles. Granted, most of them deserved it. Abner came from a long line of pickpockets, thieves, and general conmen who occasionally dipped into spy work when times called for it. He shied away from that, choosing to reap the rewards of a target rich environment while the bulk of his competition was away.

Like most gnomes, Abner was successful in his chosen profession. He estimated he'd accumulated, and lost, millions over the course of a lucrative career. But the thrill was gone. He needed bigger. Needed more. That extra was the sword. Instead of fame and glory it brought more trouble than he could handle.

Throw in a group of people willing to steal the sword for their own and leave him to rot, and he felt the pressure building.

While they contemplated their next moves, arguing over alliances and more, Abner struggled against the sword's muttered promises. Every moment he remained near the ancient blade he felt his resolve weaken. The urge to claim the sword and give in to its desires slowly grew. He wanted to feel the power, the strength. To experience the raw fury of a true warrior. Abner didn't know how much longer he could withstand the pressures swirling around him in a corrosive cocoon. He dismissed telling any of them about the sword's influences, doubting any would help.

It wasn't until Sara was heading back that he realized his left boot was pressed against the wrapped sword. Abner jerked his foot away and the thoughts of violence faded to a quiet suggestion lacking the vehemence of a moment ago. Hoping out of the van, he placed his hands on his head and forced down the tears threatening to break free. Nothing made sense. Nothing mattered. He was lost and there was no measure of salvation available to cure his ails.

I'm never stealing another item again. I swear. Just see me through this nightmare and you'll see. Abner Grumman is a man of his word.

TWENTY-THREE

Sara was almost relieved when Cecile pulled her to the side and asked to talk in private. They'd taken turns napping in the back of the van after pulling into the North Carolina Aquarium parking lot adjacent to the Fort Fischer historical park. It was approaching noon. The day heated up as cloud banks rolled offshore. Flights of pelicans swooped down over the waves. Families lounged in the sand. Children played in the water. An ideal day. Or would have been if not for the magic sword and impossible menagerie accompanying her.

They made their way to the small boardwalk in awkward silence. Sara guided them to the old gazebo overlooking the secluded beach where she and Daniel liked to go. At least one thing made sense since Abner crashed into her life. The crash of waves somewhat soothed her. With no way out of her predicament, though she could easily just walk away if need be, Sara's feeling of being trapped worsened by the hour. Every time the spark of thrill in her adventure attempted to take root, a deeper fear slapped it away. She hoped her conversation with Cecile might calm her nerves.

Taking a seat facing the ocean, Sara tilted her head back and enjoyed the cool breeze caressing her face. Weariness spread through every inch of her, mind and body. Despite the cavalcade of worries assaulting her, she felt like she could sleep through the ending of the world right now. If only life were that easy.

"Why can't every day be like this?" she asked, eyes closed.

"Wouldn't that be nice?" Cecile replied. "I could stay here all day. Too bad we don't have the luxury."

Sara agreed. "We never do. Even without the elves to muddle things."

"They do complicate matters. Which is why I felt it best to speak with you directly."

Opening her eyes, Sara wished she'd had the foresight to grab a pair of sunglasses along the way. She squinted. "I don't know any more than you."

"What? No. That's not what I meant. Sara Thomas. Why did the gargoyle feel providing your full name would influence my actions?"

A scream from the beach froze her words in her throat. They looked back to see a pair of young boys playfully dunking each other in the waves. Sara never understood why children screamed when they were playing. Living next to a Montessori, not a day went by when walking the dogs without hearing what sounds like a massacre on the playground. *Did I do that too? I know my kids did.*

Cecile smiled. "The innocence of youth."

"Makes you wonder why we bother growing up," Sara agreed. "You don't know who my husband is I take it."

"Should I?"

It was Sara's turn to smile, the upper hand falling into her lap. "He's the author, Daniel Thomas. And a favorite, it seems, of Thaddeus Blackmere."

Comprehension dawned on the agent, and she let out a low whistle. "You're that Sara Thomas? I had no idea."

"I try not to advertise, but it doesn't keep them from coming to find me, apparently."

"I'm confused. Why are you here instead of your husband?"

Ah, so Blackmere holds his cards close, does he? "He's been pulled away on business. I'm surprised you weren't briefed on it."

"DESA is a big agency. We're seldom briefed in on other operations." Cecile said it too quickly to be convincing.

"Mmhmm."

Shoulders sagging, head lowered, the agent admitted, "This is my first field operation. I'm still not sure how I got here."

"Not sure how you're enjoying a beach day?" Sara chided.

"Well, there is that. I meant how I wound up hunting down a pack of werewolves before running into you," Cecile countered before realizing Sara was playing with her. She shook her head. "Is this sword really as important as you all claim?"

"That's what they tell me. My understanding is whoever controls the sword controls the world. Their world at least." Sara frowned. "Oh, and whatever you do, don't touch the sword."

"Why is that?"

"Because it's a nasty bastard who'd be just as happy killing you as being used in battle."

Cecile's mouth dropped open. "How—"

"It talks." Sara held up her hand. "Vulgar too. That's why we have it wrapped up and tucked under the couch. It's been promising to murder Abner since I met him."

"This is so far out of my league," Cecile admitted before clamping her mouth shut.

Sara felt for the woman, despite her formal training, as her hopes of deferring to the government professional crashed like waves on the shore. The anchor Sara needed hadn't materialized. With nothing to cling to other than a taciturn gargoyle and a bumbling troll still consumed with losing his brother, she feared the only path forward revolved around trusting herself.

As if reading her mind, Cecile asked, "Do you trust any of these creatures?"

"As much as I can. I'm not inviting them to Thanksgiving dinner, but they've kept me alive this far." Sara averted her eyes, still not fully trusting her. "Supposedly we're not far from delivering the sword to this wizard who, if what the others are telling me is correct, will whisk the thing away and prevent an all-out war. Which is a good thing."

Images of rampaging armies of elves and werewolves threatening to tear the world asunder haunted her. Cecile knew she wasn't prepared for this. For any of it. *What was I thinking? Werewolves and elves. I could be working in a bank or something. But no, I thought protecting the world from creatures no one believes in anymore was the way to go. Plus, it is always about saving the world? The world needs to stop needing saving.*

"Everything ok?" Sara asked after Cecile fell silent for too long.

"I don't know how to move forward on this," Cecile admitted with a hushed tone. Nothing in her training compared to being thrown into a real-world situation. "How are you handling it all?"

"Who says I am? The only thing keeping me together is thinking about going home to my family and never seeing any of these people again. I know if I stop to think too hard, I'll fold. That's not something I can afford."

Cecile's head bobbed. "I should get back. I need to report in before my bosses start to worry. The last thing we need is a horde of agents descending on the North Carolina coast."

You got that right. "I'm going to sit here for a while longer. Maybe I can find a little measure of solace before the final push."

"Thank you, Sara Thomas."

Sara watched Cecile walk away. She empathized with the woman. Nothing proved more unsettling than being torn from your comfort zone and dropped into the middle of a waking nightmare with global implications. She snorted as the memory of her mother warning her to make quality decisions in life mocked her. Closing her eyes again, she leaned her head back and folded her arms over her lap. *What would say now, mom?*

An impossible mountain of emotions surged over her, straining to claim dominance, as if settling old scores. For the first time since joining this insanity, Sara allowed them to pass by. She centered her breathing, savoring the sting of salt in the air, and emptied her mind. New possibilities arose. Ones where she became the hero of the story. The thought put a thin smile on her face.

She felt more than saw the shadow fall over her. Smiling, she asked, "Did you change your mind about going back to the van, Cecile?"

"Wrong lady, Sara Thomas."

How Princess stumbled on the prey, whether blind luck or intuition, remained a mystery, but here she was, standing before the lone human of the group. Alone and unprotected. She leered down. Battered and haggard after a long night, the lycan dripped menace. While most of her wounds were recovered, her body remained a mass of bruises and she walked with a limp. Princess stood with hip cocked, the slightest glimpse of her handgun poking from her jacket.

"What makes you so special, human?"

"I've been asking myself the same question all night."

"This isn't your fight."

"I'm not arguing," Sara replied. The veins on her neck popped out, beating a fast tempo. "Who are you?"

Princess waggled a finger at her. "That's not important. All you need to know is the pack is coming. We're going to take the sword and kill you all."

Sara's tempo got faster, and Princess swallowed a growl of pleasure. She loved how nervous the human was. All it took was a little push and Sara would crumble. The werewolf considered toying with her, leaving her on the edge before finally sinking her teeth into the soft part of Sara's neck. Princess leered, sharp teeth poking through.

Sara wanted to scream. To lash out at the woman confronting her. Firing an entire magazine at the other werewolf proved therapeutic, leaving her longing to do it again. "Lady, at this point you can have it," she finally said. "It's done nothing but bring us trouble from the minute it was brought to my house last night."

"Ah, so that was your home where the gargoyle killed my friend," the lycan concluded. "We should burn it down one night."

Sara's fear vanished. Sitting up, she clenched her fists. "You can't do that if you're dead."

"I like you; we can trade threats all day. Time is all you have. But that's not why I'm here. How much do you really know about that sword? Or your companions?"

What are you getting at? "Enough."

"I wonder. I suppose they told you we need the sword to conquer the world? To destroy them once and for all? Something like that?"

Sara narrowed her eyes. "Something like that."

The lycan shifted her weight to the other leg. "Of course they did. If you had any idea how much the elves have fucked this world up, yours and mine, you wouldn't be so fast to trust them. They are deceitful, wicked creatures who harbor a grudge against both of us, blaming us for their downfall. All we want, Sara, is the assurance our kind won't be exterminated thanks to their greed. You don't know them. Elves won't stop unless their enemies are utterly destroyed."

Sara thought back to her meeting with the queen. Morgen stood self-assured and confident, but there was a hidden agenda lacing her words. Woman to woman, Sara refused to trust the queen. Yet for the lycan to throw out subtle accusations, with no expected reciprocity ... "Why are you telling me this?"

The woman moved fast, too fast for a human. Her arms wrapped around her, snatching her in a vice grip. Leaning close, she whispered, "Be careful who you trust. One of them will betray you and bring your little quest to ruin."

Shoved away, Sara watched the lycan slip away with more questions than answers. Their group was already fractured, internal rivalries threatening to tear them apart long before they reached this wizard. Desperation crept in. *Keep calm, Sara. They're not winning yet.*

Circles within circles. Sara once again felt outplayed, as if the others were running rings around her ignorance. The question of who might betray them burrowed deep into the back of her mind. She supposed any of them might turn traitor, for the right price. Herself included. But who? And for what?

Unable to enjoy the beach any longer, Sara stalked back to the van. Sunset was approaching and with it, she prayed, the end of this nightmare ordeal. She missed her dogs. She missed her kids, her home, and her husband. The prospect of a betrayal rattled her, and she feared she might never see any of them again.

TWENTY-FOUR

"Where have you been?" Uther asked as Sara approached the van.

The others stopped their conversations, pausing to look her way. It made her feel more like she didn't belong. The lycan's last words rattled around in her mind: *'One of them will betray you.'* But who?

Shaking her thoughts clear, Sara focused on the more pressing issue. "They've found us."

Norman rose. Bert looked around as if the whole pack was about to leap on him from the nearby trees. Abner withdrew in on himself and lowered his head. Simultaneously, Uther drew his swords and searched for his foe while Cecile pulled her pistol.

"Where?"

"How?"

"Did they approach you?"

Sara held her hands up, closing her eyes to avoid the bombardment of questions. "One of them confronted me on the beach. They've found us and we're out of time. We need to leave."

"And go where? Orphan isn't back yet, and we don't know where to find the wizard," Uther snapped. His muscles rippled beneath his faded Guns N' Roses t-shirt. "We're stuck here for the time being."

Norman frowned. "We are too exposed here. Best we consolidate and find cover. What did the lycan tell you, Sara?"

She fidgeted. "Nothing but threats."

"We have the advantage until the sun sets," Norman said, the slightest hint of suspicion on his stone features.

"That's in less than an hour," Cecile added. "Where is the old elf?"

"He said he will be here. I believe him," the gargoyle reaffirmed.

Doubt in her eyes, Cecile holstered her weapon and asked, "Where can we hide? I've never been here before."

"Neither have I. Couldn't hurt pulling off to the side, use the museum as an egress point," Norman said.

Sara listened to the exchange, noting the tremor of nervousness in Norman that hadn't been there before.

"We stand a better chance on the beach. That way the wolves can only come at us from one direction," Uther disagreed. "I prefer a clean field of fire."

"You can't engage in public, or have you forgotten the accord between the government and your queen?" Cecile fumed. "This is not up for debate."

Glowering, the Old Guard sheathed his swords and slung his rifle over a shoulder before storming off through the parking lot. No one stopped him. His action inspired suspicions in Sara, but without any proof of duplicity she remained silent. The others milled about, trapped in a web of uncertainty. Sara marveled that they'd managed to find success and evade the werewolves, for the most part, without sustaining losses.

"Sara, what time did this Orphan Thorne say he was going to return?" Cecile questioned.

"Nightfall," Norman replied before she could. "There are two hours before dusk."

"That's too long."

"How about we explore? I always liked seeing new things," Bert said with a grin.

To Sara, that was the most genuine thing she'd heard all day.

Fort Fischer was the subtle reminder of a forgotten past situated at the tip of a peninsula on the Carolina coast. History buffs dragged their families to the grass covered battlements to see the Civil War era cannons and anti-ship batteries still in place. Part of a series of coastal fortifications exchanging hands over the course of the war, Fort Fischer was a Confederate strongpoint protecting the port of Wilmington until early 1965 when it fell to Union forces. That defeat helped bring the end of the war by sealing off the last remaining supply route used by Robert E. Lee.

Today it stood as a reminder of what was and a promise of what could never happen again. Sara found it remarkably uninteresting the only time she'd visited, much preferring the animals and fish in the aquarium right up the street. Daniel on the other hand spent most of the day combing through the past, dragging her along. It made for the longest day of her life.

Until now.

The next two hours took an eternity to pass. Uther remained off on his own, presumably hiding in a concealed position pretending to be a sniper. His foul disposition and constant need for disruption rippled through the group. He was the powder keg ready to explode and no one but Norman had the strength to deal with it and that was tenuous at best.

Despite feeling ready to collapse, sleep eluded Sara. Her eyes burned. Her muscles were sore, and her nerves were frayed from one harrowing chase after the next. She kept touching the handgun, though empty, that she had tucked into her waistband.

No one dared to take it away or admonished her for having it. In fact, Uther must have been impressed enough to leave her several replacement magazines on the couch that she found when she got back into the van. She took it for what it was, reluctant acceptance.

Sara looked at each of them. Bert jabbing a finger in his ear with a pinched look on his face. Abner's gaze flitting back and forth. Nervous. Edgy. Cecile fumed under the mounting pressure. Uther never changed. He glowered at any willing to meet his gaze. Norman, arms folded and resolute. *One of them will betray you.* She refused to accept one of them was willing to abandon all principles by helping the enemy. But what if she was wrong? Was she willing to risk her life on it?

With the van parked as close to the main building as possible, she took a small measure of comfort in being able to place their backs against a defensible position. Sara listened to a string of military terms that went right over her head, all flanks and fields of fire, but took comfort in Norman's stalwart attitude. *Let the wolves come and they'll break just like before*.

She was about to try and sleep again when she noticed Bert staring at the cannons in the distant with longing. Sara walked over to him, feeling she owed him from being there when she was ready to break. The troll was sitting atop one of the manmade battlements, running his hand through the grass. A flight of pelicans cruised overhead nearby, chased by the approaching clouds of sunset. The troll looked to be in his element as he hummed softly.

"What song is that?" Sara slipped down beside him and, drawing her knees up, wrapped her arms around them.

"Just something my mother used to sing." Bert's face reddened. "I liked her songs."

Her heart tugged as Sara remembered doing the same for her children when they were still babies. Perhaps motherhood was universal, transcending the boundaries of species. "I used to do the same with my kids," she said, her smile soft and warm. "This is how life is supposed to be."

"Yup," Bert said with a nod. He plucked a blade of grass, pausing to sniff it before placing it between his teeth. "Me an Lou used to take turns singing ma's songs." He paused, picking a handful of grass that he brought to his mouth. "Sara?"

The sunlight felt good on her face, stealing her away to a simpler time. "Yes, Bert?"

"If I die out here, make sure my ashes drift to the ocean," the troll said softly. "I always liked the ocean. Tastes funny though."

She let her initial comment fade on her tongue. Some things just didn't need to be pointed out. "Sure, Bert, but you made a promise not to die on me."

"Oh, I know, I was just planning. Ya know? Thinking ahead and all."

"I know," she whispered. "What do you think about this mess?"

The grass disappeared, ground up between his teeth before being swallowed. "Bout what?"

"All of it. Uther. Orphan Thorne. Our chances of succeeding."

His brow rolled forward, shadowing his already deep-set eyes. "They're not Lou. I don't like them, but they know what they're doing. I think."

Sensing she wasn't going to get any further with this line of questioning, Sara brought up a different subject. "Bert, where do you guys take your names from?"

"What do you mean? I'm Bert."

She pursed her lips. A vague recollection of something Daniel once told her popped up in her mind. He had known a soldier born in Vietnam but who grew up in San Francisco. The man's name was Bob Young. When Daniel pressed about his name, after being told his actual name, Bob replied that his brother had been given the good name, Howard. She frowned, recalling how she had failed to understand the importance of what he was telling her until Daniel explained people coming to the States often changed their names to fit in with society. Clearly the elves were victims of this as well.

Bert. Lou. Abner. Sheldon. Even Norman felt forced. Her mind wandered down a list of fantasy names she remembered hearing or reading through the years. Did any of the elves know they could have taken better names? Ones still popular today? Probably not given Bert's innocent answer.

Deciding she wasn't getting anywhere with that, she patted Bert's forearm and left him to his songs. She feared it was the last measure of peace any of them were going to get until the quest was completed.

Sara found Abner still in the van upon her return. The tv was off and he just stared at the sword with a strange look on his face. He never strayed from the sword, and that worried her. She thought it peculiar an item might have the power to dominate another's thoughts so thoroughly but, being a newcomer to the world of elves, felt out of place bringing it up. For all she knew their world was filled with such items.

Thankful the sword hadn't spoken to her at her arrival, Sara decided to sidle up to Abner and gauge where his head was at. Something about the gnome felt off. Perhaps it was the continued effects of the sword. Perhaps it was the adrenalin fueled adventure his actions produced. Just when she thought he was ready to break and run he found the measure of his courage and continued on. *But for how long? What is the sword showing him?*

"How are you holding up, Abner?" she asked as she reached into the van for a bottle of water. Breakfast was a fading memory, and no one had mentioned getting lunch or dinner. At least her stomach was making a habit of reminding her of her needs. Hungry and thirsty, she knew better than to allow herself to become dehydrated. Fishing out one of Bert's energy bars went a long way in helping her feel like herself.

"Fine," Abner replied. "I'm fine."

"It's ok if you're not," she prodded. "No one else has done as much as you so far. I don't think I'd have the composure you do after all this."

He shrugged without meeting her gaze. "Thank you, but I'm just doing whatever it takes to stay alive." He lowered his voice, adding, "I want to go home, Sara."

You little shit, this is all your fault. Instead, she maintained her façade of calm and said, "We all want to go home, Abner. Soon. This time tomorrow it will all be a memory."

He grunted and hopped outside, digging into his pocket before holding up a cell phone. Only when he spied Sara's quizzical look did he say, "I need to check in with my family. See if they're all right."

Sara let him go despite the suspicion rising.

'One of them will betray you.'

One.

Which one?

Abner stumbled away, phone to his ear.

TWENTY-FIVE

The last fingers of light raced west in the eternal struggle between light and dark. Sara's heart grew heavy. Frogs and insects came to life in the nearby waterways. An owl's hoot reminded her of the bleakness of the moment. The threat returned with the dropping of the curtain of darkness. An uncanny stillness settled over the group, each lost in their own thoughts. Sara stared back up the road, praying she didn't see headlights.

They were at the end of the peninsula with nowhere to go. If the werewolves caught them now, in the open, there would be slaughter. She doubted even Norman's skills would be enough to win them clear and to freedom. Not that she had anywhere to go. Without Orphan Thorne and his vague promises the group was stuck in place. Her hand slipped to the cold pistol grip near her belt buckle.

Uther appeared from the shadows. He hurried across the street, rifle in the ready position. His head swiveled back and forth like he was scanning the surroundings for signs of the enemy. "No sign of the puppies, but there's a boat coming in. Looked like Thorne."

"How can you tell?" Sara asked.

His look suggested he toyed with a multitude of answers to mess with her until Uther patted his rifle. "I put the scope on him."

"So, the forge master was true to his word," Norman said, relief evident in his voice. "We must collect our gear and weapons. Quickly."

They rifled through the van, ensuring to take as much as possible. Soon they were outfitted and heading toward the water by the time Orphan showed his face.

Bert ran his palm lovingly over the hood before moving to Sara's side. She smiled at him before focusing on the water.

"We need to hurry. If we're not in place before midnight, we'll have to wait until tomorrow night." Orphan waved them forward.

Anger welled up, prompting Sara to ask, "Why did we wait this long if that only put us on a tight deadline? Where is this wizard?" At his silence, she demanded, "Why can't anyone give an honest answer?"

The elder elf cocked his head. "My apologies, Sara Thomas. I forget you are not one of us. It has been many of your lifetimes since I last dealt with humans. Though much has changed, our species remain as foreign to each other today as we were centuries ago. Wizards are an eclectic breed, trapped somewhere between elf and human. Theirs is the path of riddles.

"This particular wizard, Sheldon, is fond of schedules. He will not break that for any reason save death. The only time he accepts an audience is at the stroke of midnight. Not a second before, or after." He fell silent with the look of having said more than enough to satisfy human ignorance.

Sara felt otherwise. "That still doesn't say where we are heading."

"North. Sheldon claims Shackleford Banks as his residence. By boat it is about one hundred miles, close to five hours. There is no time to waste."

Glancing at her watch, Sara felt her stomach tighten. It was approaching seven. They were cutting it close.

Orphan headed back to his boat without another word. The elf remained sure of his actions, confident in his approach. Sara grabbed a bag and hurried after him, the others close.

He led them through down a winding sidewalk before crossing into the sand and grass. Their course took but a few minutes to traverse and, upon leaving the tall grasses, dropped them off in front of a sleek boat the color of midnight and angled in a military manner.

Orphan climbed the short ladder into the passenger area and readied the boat. Sara followed, after Norman's insistence. She grabbed what bags and weapons she could lift as they were passed up, stowing them where Orphan pointed. Soon, they were aboard and backing into the ocean. She marveled at the construction of the boat, wondering if it was military issue. Four engines hung off the back. A small lower-level compartment with a bed and toilet was used for storage. Norman insisted Abner go below with the sword and remain there until they made landfall. The gnome's weak protestations fell on deaf ears as Uther slammed the door behind him. Sara stared after him a moment, torn between wanting to stick up for him and locking the door.

Orphan turned the boat north and engaged the engines.

Cecile held her phone up to the sky, frowning when she failed to get any signal. Nothing had gone in her favor since catching up with this group who, in her professional opinion, didn't belong together. She was surprised none of them had killed anyone yet, though a betting woman would put her money on Uther. Since Orphan Thorne returned the Old Guard hadn't taken his miserly gaze off the elf. Whatever caused their hatred threatened to unravel their mission. This group, whatever it chose to call itself, was a powder keg ready to blow.

"You won't get any signal out here," Orphan called out over the whine and hum of the engines as the boat raced north. "I have jamming on. This ship was designed for stealth. The fewer anyone knows where we are the better."

"You think the lycans are out there?" she asked, trying not to look around the rolling waves.

"Perhaps not on the water, but they are relentless on the hunt," Orphan confirmed. "It has been a long time since I last encountered a pack. This one appears more motivated than the others, from what Norman has told me. It would do well to exercise caution from here out."

Cecile looked around, seeing nothing but the faint glow of lights from the shore. She never cared for traveling by boat. The ocean seldom agreed with her. Stomach threatening to rebel as the boat rocked, she moved up beside Orphan. Sea spray caught her face. The cool water at least felt good after sweating for most of the day. "Orphan, I need to know, what is your relationship with Uther? Are we in jeopardy?"

"Of him or us?" the old elf replied with a toothy grin. When he failed to produce a response, he huffed. "Fine, we go back a long way, he and I. Can't say I ever cared for the man. He was always too cocksure and stubborn to listen."

"You had a falling out," she surmised. Why she asked Orphan remained unclear. Call it a gut instinct. Thus far, Uther hadn't shown any sign of warming to her.

Orphan nodded. Water dripped from his long hair. "You could say that. After the last war with the lycans, and the creation of the sword, the queen sent her pets to ensure my forge was permanently shut down. I never figured out why. Shit, it's been so long it doesn't matter now. All I know is Morgen didn't want me making anything else that might be used against us. She proclaimed the sword a danger to all elfkind. By putting me under guard she ensured that was the last.

"Uther and his team showed up at my forge, but I'd already been tipped off. I ambushed them. He and I battled for the better part of a day before I cast a handful of sand in his eyes and snuck off. He's never forgiven me for that. Not that I would either … I fled into exile and stayed there for centuries. I always suspected Morgen knew where I was. Why no one came for me is another matter." He stopped and chewed on the inside of his lip, eyes pinched.

A pair of quick waves slapped the broadside of the boat, producing groans and curses from the passengers.

Cecile, her knuckles bleeding white from the death grip on the crossbar, struggled with that raw feeling in her stomach. "Do you think Uther is going to finish his vendetta?"

At that, the elf gave her a deadpan look. She noticed his teeth for the first time, impossibly white and perfect in every way. She was a little jealous. "Lady, I sure hope so. I've been itching to whoop him for a long time."

Knowing that was all she was getting from the elf, Cecile staggered back to slump down beside Sara. Thankful for the silence, she ran through the scenario. While a great part of it made sense, there remained unanswered questions, each capable of bringing ruin to them all. She knew the legacy of the elves and how often their quests met a dismal end.

The last great adventure in North Carolina resulted in the king's death and his daughter and future son-in-law's incarceration. The carnage spread across half the state. A government chopper had been shot down, crashing into a church. DESA struggled with ensuring the truth didn't get out. Though they avoided civilian casualties, official records said well over three hundred elves and dwarves died that night. And for what? A failed shot at the crown?

The boat continued the quest north to a small island on the North Carolina coast famed for wild horses and a lone lighthouse guiding ships to shore. An island holding secrets older than the foundations of a nation. It was here the fate of all was set to be decided. For Cecile, the game became a matter of who cracked first.

Cecile came from a small family. Growing up on a farm, she learned the lessons of hard work and honesty at a young age. But that life offered nothing for her. She needed more, even if she failed to know how to find it. After a year of lackluster grades in college, Cecile dropped out and signed up for the police academy. It was here she discovered the thrill that continued fueling her. Thriving, she graduated at the head of her class and threw herself into her new job.

A few years later, Cecile made detective and was called out on a peculiar murder case. They responded to the call only to find the scene absent of every material piece of evidence necessary for a murder. Splitting up with her partner, Cecile entered an abandoned warehouse, following the scuff of footprints leading deeper into the building's center. What she discovered blew her mind. There, in the center of the warehouse, battled a pair of sword-wielding madmen.

Cecile watched as one slew the other, but instead of a body falling to the floor, it burst apart in a cascade of ashes. The sword clanged on the concrete. Shock gripped her, refusing to allow her mind to process what she witnessed. Gun all but forgotten, she watched the victor rush off into the night, disappearing forever. When her partner finally found her, Cecile was a blubbering mess.

Not long after, a man dressed in a worn suit, the kind government officials chose for durability over style, with a haggard look of a man who'd seen too much, entered the police station and requested an interview with her. Assuming it was no more than a debriefing from higher, Cecile smoothed her clothing and went in to tell her side of the story without expecting him to believe a word of it. There was no way she could have been prepared for what came next.

Inklings of that first encounter with elfkind tickled her intuition. Beyond Orphan and Uther's open animosity, Cecile failed to find any redeeming quality in the gnome. The gargoyle remained taciturn, indifferent to her. Any thoughts of kinship with Sara dulled by her associations with the others. The only one of their group who appeared harmless was the troll. She felt herself liking the bumbling man in the way she would a lost puppy. Still, something didn't sit right with her. The werewolves were always a step behind, never quite getting close enough to seal the deal and claim the sword. She knew more was at play, but what?

She checked her phone once more.

TWENTY-SIX

"You're certain they're heading north?"

Princess, frowning at being questioned, nodded. "That's what the tracker is showing."

The boat clung a few hundred meters offshore, proceeding on a straight line. Proud as she was, they had no way of discerning where their prey was heading. In her estimation, something was better than nothing: her pack leader wasn't impressed.

"That's great, but how are we supposed to know *where* they're going? We stand to lose the sword altogether," he fumed. "I'm taking an awful risk, Princess."

"You're lucky I got that close to one of them. The right one," she amended. "They almost got Good Boy."

Gruff spared the wolf a glance. Recovered from his wounds but not the indignity of failure, Good Boy lowered his head submissively. Huffing, Gruff returned his focus on her. "What happens when they go where we can't follow?"

"Where would that be? There's no islands out there. No where to hide we can't find them," Princess countered. "Gruff, this is our only chance. We hunt them down and rip them apart. They'll be weak. Ready to fall. I've made sure of that."

He stiffened. "What do you mean?"

"I planted the seeds of doubt. Told the human one of them was going to betray the rest."

"You what?" Gruff raged.

She held up her hands, though refused to back down at his anger. "I did what needed to be done. No one else in this ragged pack has the gift of foresight. I saw an opportunity and took it, for the pack. For you. Who's to say she'll believe me?"

"What if they discover who the traitor is?" he pressed.

"We lose nothing, and they go down one," Princess replied. "Either way, we win."

"Doesn't give me the sword though, does it?" he countered. "Hell, for all we know they will take the damned thing out to sea and dump it in the ocean."

"Why would they give up the one weapon capable of ending our kind forever?" she asked. "Think about it, Gruff. They're taking the sword home."

Rounding on her, Gruff's impressive size towered over Princess with undisguised menace. While applauding her quick thinking, he feared she was growing too bold. Perhaps even harboring aspirations of making a play for pack leader. Challenges to authority weren't uncommon among the packs. Most often met with violence, they left a string of corpses around the world. Some succeeded. Most failed.

Gruff respected Princess for a schemer but knew any shot she had at usurping him came through trickery, not brute force. The time was going, he decided, when he was going to have to make a lesson of her for the others.

"How can you know that?" he demanded. "What games are you playing, Princess?"

"I spoke with our inside man," she replied with a blank look. "He told me enough about their plan, there can be no mistake. They are taking the sword back to the wizard in the hopes of hiding it away forever."

"Hmm, didn't happen to tell you where this wizard is, did he?"

"He didn't know," she admitted.

"Didn't know or wouldn't tell you?" His suspicions roused; Gruff needed more to fully commit the pack to a single course of action. They'd met with one defeat after the next since tracking the gnome to the human's house. Too many were gone, leaving him weakened when strength was needed most. He felt the rising discontent among the others, making the statement he intended to make with Princess more important. But not yet. Now was not the time. He needed to get the sword first, then punish the necessary people.

"He said they weren't told. Something about waiting for an orphan to return," she drawled out. Princess turned her head a fraction, tilting it as she narrowed her eyes. "What's going on?"

"Nothing. We need to move," he brushed her off. *Damn it. I need to be more careful before she gets a sniff at what I'm planning. Cunning bitch is already too clever for her own good.* He faced the rest of the pack. "Get on your bikes. We head north. Princess, you and Good Boy take point."

Howling, the lycans tossed their cigarettes, knocked back the rest of their beers, and cranked up their motorcycles.

Darryl didn't sleep well. He stumbled through a quick meal before showering and trying to relax watching the morning shows. It never did the trick, but then again, he didn't watch them for any provided value. They served as background noise as he played his video games before getting a few hours of sleep. Working nightshift was grounding him down. The psychological detriment proved far more taxing than anything physical. He wasn't sure what made him request it when he was first hired. Perhaps it was the promise of additional pay, perhaps the perceived solitude. It didn't matter anymore.

Working for the largest clandestine government agency in the world had plenty of benefits. Being able to do so without interacting with many others one of them. Darryl always considered himself a loner. Best suited to talking to himself than sitting in large meetings filled with bristling tension and too many opinions. No thank you. Give him a cubicle without a window in the middle of the night with only a skeleton crew any day.

Little did he understand what he was asking for. The first few years were fine. Darryl enjoyed coming to work and diving into the clandestine world of elves and dwarves. Fascinated by how a completely separate society existed within the constraints of humanity, he absorbed every detail of the elves, no matter how obscure or nuanced.

In the beginning, Darryl loved his job.

Then came Violet Meyers.

His world ground to a halt after her appointment to department supervisor. She refused to tell anyone how she wound up in the forgotten ward, but the few others Darryl befriended did their research and discovered Violet was a disgraced field agent. Her current position was a punishment. A career killer. And they suffered for it. Violet drove her minions with the ruthlessness of a woman scorned. Every contemptable quality cinema portrayed all wrapped up in one vile human being.

So, Darryl spent his downtime staring up at the ceiling wishing sleep would come wipe his troubled thoughts away. Sleep, being the fickle mistress it was, amped up the pain instead. He couldn't get Agent Cecile Barnabas out of his mind. She was in real danger, and he was the only one providing a lifeline to safety. At least he was until she stopped responding to him. Knowing she was tangling with a pack of werewolves rattled him. Knowing Violet Meyers stood ready to double cross him, threw extra fuel on the fire.

Dressing, eating a quick meal, and grabbing his keys, Darryl hurried back to work. Hoping to see an email or message from Agent Barnabas waiting for him was equally exhilarating and terrifying. He became consumed with knowing she was fine, that nothing a mangy pack of werewolves had to throw at her was enough to stop a D.E.S.A. field agent from completing her assignment.

Darryl swiped his access card and entered the office—

Violet Meyers was waiting for him. Her arms folded, one foot tapping. Darryl cringed. The last thing he needed was scrutiny from the one woman no one wanted to work with. Her stern glare threatened to freeze him in place. Swallowing what little good attitude he brought to work, Darryl attempted to pass her, silently praying she didn't stop him.

"Mr. Wallace, a word" she snapped.

"I'm not late, Ms. Meyers," he protested.

"This has nothing to do with being late or not," she replied. "The situation you reported to me last night has developed. I need you in my office. Now." She spun, the clicking of her heels trailing behind.

Stunned, Darryl watched her go. If she needed him in her office, what was she doing by the security station? He shook his head. Sometimes things just didn't make sense. Giving the guard at the desk a shrug, which was returned in kind, Darryl loped after his supervisor, praying he wasn't in trouble.

Seated behind her desk, Violet Meyers waited for Darryl to enter. She'd already subsumed authority from the day shift manager. Not that it took much. A wry smile, the hint of leg, and the allusion of more happening after drinks and the married man was puddy in her hands. Other higher ups were intimidated into following her instructions. That left one problem— Darryl Wallace. The man's lonely innocence proved the only hurdle to her designs. The sooner she dispatched him, or swayed him to her cause, the better. First thing first, she needed up to date tactical data from the agent in the field.

The knock drew her focus. She gestured Darryl to the chair opposite her.

Sitting awkwardly, he waited for her to speak.

Violet studied the man, searching for any exploitable weakness. She clicked her tongue on the roof of her mouth, pleased with his startled reaction.

"The situation in North Carolina is devolving. I need to know where our agent is and what her plan for neutralizing the lycans is and I need to know immediately," she launched without pause. "What do you know?"

Clearly caught off guard, Darryl blinked rapidly. "Ah, well, the last I report I saw was Agent Barnabas was closing in on the werewo…er lycans somewhere outside of Wilmington. We changed shifts and I haven't been brought up to speed on any new developments, ma'am."

"As of nineteen hundred hours Agent Barnabas officially disappeared from the grid," she revealed, drawing him in. "We have had no contact from her in two hours. This is unacceptable. I expect positive identification immediately, Mr. Wallace. Do whatever it takes. We must have eyes on our field agent. Am I clear?"

Darryl swallowed. "I'll do my best. You have my word."

"I expect nothing less." She flashed him her best smile and pointed at the door.

Watching him go, Violet ran through the list of assets available to her office should they deem the situation out of control. Agency policies were strict, especially regarding lycans and other less than savory species out for blood. Should it come to it, she'd rain hellfire down on them all. Burning every last creature out of existence. In the name of humanity, naturally.

TWENTY-SEVEN

They landed with thirty minutes to spare. Orphan drove the boat into the reeds alongside a hidden dock to a chorus of groans and warning cries. The old elf chuckled as he wheeled his boat in with the expertise of a man who'd performed the act too many times. Cutting the engines, he barked at Norman to tie the boat off. The others, still in shock from their near collision with the dock, collected their gear, ensuring to outfit with as many weapons and ammo as possible. When Abner attempted to pass the sword off to anyone else, he was met with anger. No one wanted to risk the sword's ire this late in the quest.

Sara felt for the gnome, despite his meddling having created the problem. She watched the misery in his eyes, the way he carried himself, deepen by the hour. How much could one person be expected to take before breaking? She reached out for him, only for Abner to shake her off with a tired glare. Sara adjusted the pack on her back, keeping the weight high on her shoulders like Daniel taught her, and followed the others down the short wooden path.

They wound through sand, water, and grass before hitting the soft beach. Sara heard the snort of a horse and froze, fearing they'd been discovered. Sara slowed her breathing, surprised to find her pistol in her hands when she reopened her eyes. That's when she remembered the wild horses.

Shackleford Banks was famous for two things. Holding one of the state's many lighthouses and a small herd of wild horses. It was one of the many attractions she had yet to visit thanks to the many demands of raising and providing for a family. Now that she was here, Sara wished Daniel was with her. He'd been mentioning going to the lighthouse for the better part of a decade. It felt wrong being here without him.

Stepping out from behind Bert, who moved in front of her, Sara got her first look at the island. Dark shapes moved at the edge of sight—the horses. In the background stood the lighthouse. A warning beacon for approaching ships, it was their destination and the promise of finishing their quest and finally being free of the werewolf menace. Sara felt hope surge, threatening to distract her when she needed her wits sharp.

"We must hurry. Time is almost up," Norman unnecessarily announced. "Orphan, where is the wizard?"

Wiping his lower lip with a thumb, Orphan Thorne gestured with his head. "The lighthouse."

"Is there a way to contact him? Let him know we're here?"

"He knows."

The answer felt bitter. Like a sore mysteriously appearing on her somewhere. Sara's face twisted and she stopped walking. "If he knows we're coming, why did we park on the other side of the island?"

"Land," Orphan corrected.

"I don't care!" she snapped. "The point is we have to walk all the way over there with what, thirty minutes left? It doesn't make sense. None of this does."

Norman halted midstride to respond to her concerns. "Sara, one does not question the will of wizards. They are a fickle bunch prone to brash actions when their feelings are hurt."

"Maybe it's time somebody did," she fumed. "Let's get this over with. I want to go home." Still, Sara found it difficult to focus on the task at hand. The ability to care about the outcome diminished with each step inland. The males gave her space; only Cecile marched at her side in silent commiseration.

The lighthouse beckoned. A subtle vibration channeled through the ground and into her bones. She didn't understand how an inanimate object could generate power. Brick and stone, the lighthouse dated back to pre-Civil War days. Knowing what she did, Sara questioned who really built it and if there had been an elvish influence from the beginning. She'd been exposed to so much these past two days nothing seemed impossible. Questions danced on the tip of her tongue but when she opened her mouth, a "shh" from Uther kept them there. He hadn't spoken since leaving the mainland. A glance at Cecile offered no condolence either. Despite being surrounded by a host of capable warriors she'd come to know and appreciate to some extent, Sara felt alone, much like the heroes in Daniel's books.

Abner felt exhausted. The sword wore heavy on his back. His steps grew leaden. It took every ounce of energy to keep going, to not throw down the sword and head back to the boat. He'd done what the queen commanded. Seen the sword safely to the wizard. Enough was enough.

"I knew you were a weak little bitch from the moment you stole me."

"I'm not listening to you," Abner whispered and shook his head.

"Of course you are. It's all you can do. All you think about. Why don't you just give in already? Make me happy once in this miserable relationship, gnome."

Abner squeezed his eyes shut. "No. I'm not listening. Shut up. Just shut up. These people are my…"

"Your what? Friends?" The sword scoffed. "Face reality, Abner. Not a single one of them would give their life to save yours. You saw what happened when they sent you into that ogre nest. Left you to die. Abandoned you when you needed them most. Take me, Abner. Let me strike them down and end your misery for good. Do this for me. I beg of you. Perhaps then I'll slit your throat nice and quick. No suffering."

"I hate you!" Abner shouted, unable to handle the taunts any longer. "I fucking hate you!"

The sword laughed, a hissing mockery of a sound scratching down Abner's spine. "That's the spirit. Ah, Abner, you and I are about to create a masterpiece of slaughter."

"Quiet back there. Are you trying to give us away?" Uther snapped at him.

Abner shot him a glare, unaware that anyone had heard the conversation. "It wasn't me. It's this damned sword."

Uther snorted. "Of course it is, idiot. Figured you'd have guessed by now. That's what the sword does. It twists your mind until you don't know right from wrong. Makes you want to use it, unleash its power on the world. Do that and we all die."

"That's the point, Old Guard," the sword mocked.

Uther paused, suddenly conflicted by the desire to claim the sword for himself and hand it over to the wizard. Heart pounding, his fingers trembled. "That's enough from you. With a little luck, Sheldon will melt you down forever."

"Fool. You think I'm terrestrial?"

Having no answer and unsure what the sword meant, Uther kept walking. Flesh and blood he could fight. This was supernatural. Anathema to his skillset and training. Still a brief flash of desire surged through his blood. *Take the sword. Slay the lycans. Claim the throne.* His hands clenched, aches spreading through his bones. Like that, the images of victory dissolved, leaving him once more in the quiet of the night with naught but the buzz of mosquitos for companionship.

"Keep moving. We're running out of time," he ordered.

Uther waited until Abner staggered by before picking up the trail position. He'd traded in his sniper rifle for an automatic, trusting the killing power should they walk into an ambush, that or Sheldon proved unreliable at this hour. *Wizards. What were we thinking? Can't trust a wizard any more than you can a goblin.*

Norman listened to the argument developing behind him. He knew the strengths and weaknesses in each race. Most were resilient, enough to overcome the potential nightmare unfolding. He also knew each of them had been tempted by the sword at various points throughout their journey, especially the closer they got to finding the wizard. Thus far, each had remained strong. He couldn't trust that to continue in their present state. Curiously, he had not once felt the acidic temptations the sword of Grimspire spewed. Perhaps his kind was immune to the magic? He didn't dare question. Not now.

"Your people are falling apart," Orphan mused to him as he cut a clear course to the lighthouse.

"They have done well to fend off the primal urges of your creation."

Orphan stiffened, missing a step before continuing. "Remember gargoyle, I but created the tool. It was the wizard who imbued with magic. It was the weapon we needed at the time."

"There should have been another way," Norman countered. "You trapped us, tied our fates to the sword forever more."

"I did what was asked of me."

"And in doing so damned us all."

"Perhaps," Orphan said. "That is not for any of us to decide. Do not let the foolish debate of right and wrong occlude your purpose, Norman Guilt."

The gargoyle stiffened, if such was possible. *Would that I had an army of my kin to settle this day. Perhaps there would be no more wars.*

"The only deception being played is your sword. The queen is most displeased with the current state of affairs," Norman insisted. "This mission cannot fail."

"You can remind *her highness* it was at her behest I forged the damned thing in the first place,"

Orphan spat. "You think I wanted that to be my legacy? Not only did it ruin my life, when I tried to destroy it before handing it over, she sent her Old Guard hounds after me."

It all fell into place for Norman: Uther must have been one of the Old Guard sent to claim the sword. Their battle resulted in Orphan going into hiding and Uther's demotion and subsequent removal from the Old Guard. To harbor such animosity for so long seemed foolish in his eyes. As straightforward as they came, Norman felt the two should have been forced into a small, locked room and not allowed to leave until they solved their differences. It worked in the past. No reason to think it wouldn't now.

"We cannot live in the past, Orphan. The only way to succeed and prevent the lycans from stealing the sword is by working together."

"Aye, I agree. But once we return the sword from whence it came, he and I shall have a reckoning," Orphan vowed.

"As you will," Norman agreed, knowing it was beyond his control.

From her place a few steps behind the gargoyle, Cecile grew concerned. She'd heard too much from both sides and feared a darkness was rising, threatening to swallow them with little regard to the future. By all rights she should have stopped the group, claimed jurisdiction, and summoned assistance from higher ups. This was a dangerous moment, one capable of slipping out of control in the blink of an eye. Conflicted by the need to do her job and to help Sara see her mission through to completion, Cecile walked on unsteady legs.

Unprepared for any of it, she found her first combat operation a far cry from the simulations run in training back at the academy. Imposter syndrome bubbled in her stomach. The only way to prove she belonged was by standing her ground, relying on her training, and praying they stayed on target. Anything less…

"Look, the lighthouse." Orphan's announcement broke her train of thought.

They huddled together, staring up in awe at the pale green light swirling inside the glass high above.

"That's not natural," Sara gasped, feeling the vibrations running up her legs from the ground.

"That, Sara Thomas, is the wizard Sheldon," Norman explained.

Forming a semi-circle, they pulled up and watched the clouds of power swirling atop the lighthouse. There was simple majesty in it, a relic of a forgotten time when wonder dominated the world. She almost felt… she didn't know exactly.

Bert scratched his jaw and hummed. "Now that's some shit, to be sure."

Sara broke into laughter. No truer words had ever been spoken.

Focused on the display of magic, none spotted the multiple pairs of yellow eyes reflecting back at them from the tall grasses.

TWENTY-EIGHT

Thirteen figures burst from cover to surround them. Dripping venom and staggering on impossibly twisted legs, they had no faces, no definition other than the perception of bottled hatred born from a madman's gaze. Standing over ten feet, their elongated arms ended with barbed claws. A chorus of moans poured from their bodies, riding the wind like impending doom. They waved in the breeze, reminding Sara of trees about to die. She almost retched when the wave of putrefied flesh and debris filled her nostrils.

"What is this?" she gasped, struggling not to vomit.

"Dryads!" Orphan hissed as he drew his sword. "Put your guns away. They are of no use here."

Grunting, Uther shoved his machine gun into Sara's hands and drew his swords in one motion. They sang leaving the scabbards, each blade glowing pale yellow in the crisp night. He wore no grin or show of emotion, only the cold determination of one marching to potential demise. Sara watched the Old Guard roll his shoulders in anticipation and bend his legs, lowering his center of gravity and strengthening his balance. They may not see eye to eye, but she was glad they were on the same side. Provided he wasn't the traitor the werewolf warned of.

"None have been seen in this country for hundreds of years." Norman sized up the closest pair.

Even with his mass and strength, he doubted he could manage to tackle more than one before the others slashed him to ribbons. "Bert, protect Sara and Agent Barnabas."

"What about me?" Abner squeaked.

Uther looked back at the trembling gnome. "You have the sword, shithead. Now might be a good time to use it."

Abner quaked where he stood before sneaking beside Sara and into Bert's shadow.

"We should get back on the boat," Cecile suggested. She hadn't felt this helpless before in her life. Armed with nothing but a service issue pistol and one magazine, she had nothing capable of stopping one of the tree monsters. But neither was trusting her security to a troll a better option. She needed to fight, to prove herself in the field, even if she fell. Going to the grave knowing Cecile Barnabas had what it took to wear the badge was reward enough. At least that's what she told herself. Anything to steady her frazzled nerves.

Cecile drew a steadying breath and was dismayed to find it not working. Nothing in her training even touched on the impossible creatures coming to kill them. *My first mission and I have elves, werewolves, disgraced Old Guard, and whatever the hell these tree things are. I'm going to be a legend, if I survive. A warning if not.* She raised her pistol, ready to fight.

The circle constricted. The dryads moved as one, lurching a single, ponderous step inward. Sand, grass, and dirt kicked up. The ground trembled, groaning as if wounded.

Orphan waved the others back, into a tighter circle. A veteran of countless wars, he'd never fought such a beast. What knowledge he held came from texts from the Middle Ages when every brush of wind or odd shadow was the Devil come to claim souls.

"They shouldn't be here," he mused, shifting his stance from one dryad to the closest on his right. "Some trickery is at play. I can feel it in my bones."

"Those trees are going to be feasting on your bones if you don't snap to," Uther warned.

Gone was the pretense of a disgraced elf in exile. In its place stood a proud warrior searching for a way out of their nightmare. The anxious jump in his right leg promised action, threatening to throw the entire clearing into chaos. Uther liked chaos. All things became possible when the rigid was thrown off balance. Desperate to reclaim the advantage, he broke into a growl from the base of his throat.

"Don't," Orphan warned. "We don't know how they will react."

"I'll tell you. That one in front of me is going to be chopped in half. The rest can deal with the fallout," Uther vowed.

"Fool. What if this is a test?"

Uther paused, rocking back on his heels. "What nonsense is that? A test for what?"

"The wizard. We know their unsavory natures. Quick to chicanery when it suits their whims," Orphan explained. "This could well be a test to see if we are worthy of his audience."

"Then he needs to show himself real quick. I'm tired of the fucking games, Orphan," Uther roared. "All I want is a fair fight."

The dryads shook, trees in a hurricane. Debris fell from their bodies, maggots and worse wiggling away after hitting the sand. A horse whinnied in the night. Atop the lighthouse, the clouds of green magic seeped from the glass, forming a widening circle over the island and bathing all in an eerie green glow.

"What's happening?" Sara felt the pause, as if the world stopped spinning for the span of a single heartbeat. Sweat trickled down her back despite the cool tang in the air. She didn't realize she was holding her breath until the dryads attacked. They stormed into the tiny group before her mind caught up with what her eyes showed her. Claws curled into fists, smashing into the ground. Uther and Orphan roared ancient battle cries and met the assault with the fury of seasoned veterans.

"Everybody wants to be a hero," Sara muttered.

At her side, Norman blurred into his natural form and launched at the nearest dryad. He was caught by a pair of limbs across the chest and swept out over the island.

Bert roared, but it was for show. The troll hadn't lost his temper in so long he feared he'd never find it again. When the dryad crashed into him, thinking to bowl him over to claim Sara cowering in his shadow, it was met with rock and stone. Bert absorbed the attack and began pummeling the creature with massive fists. His actions, while preventing their immediate demise, left the women, and Abner, unprotected from the dryads closing from behind. *Not today, tree thing! This is for Lou!* Bert fought like a troll possessed.

"Run!" Cecile screamed.

She and Sara broke in the same direction. The rush of wind as claws scraped the air where they'd been standing shoved them forward. They stumbled before breaking into a sprint, making it a few paces before being snatched off their feet and ripped back. Sara screamed. Cecile fumed, kicking and punching to no avail. A dryad had them, twisting its grip to ensure neither escaped. Her clothes ripped. Cecile felt the trickle of hot blood spilling down her arm. Face red from straining, Cecile felt powerless in the dryad's clutches. She wanted to cry.

In the chaos, Abner found himself alone. With eyes so wide his face felt like splitting, he watched his companions engaging the dryads with little or no effect. His hand twitched with the unnatural desire to draw the sword.

"Now's the time, Abner. Set aside your fears and become the man you were meant to be."

"No. Not like this," Abner whined.

The sword fell silent, judging him.

A calm fell over the gnome when one of the women screamed. Abner's heartbeat slowed. His breathing normalized. His limbs stopped trembling. He knew what needed to be done, for them, for himself. He looked at the others a final time, weighing the pros and cons of what he was about to do. They hated him.

They all did. He knew it. The sword told him so. What difference did it make if they died tonight? As long as he lived, nothing else mattered.

Breaking into a feral grin, Abner Grumman adjusted the sword on his back and stepped away from the battle. His giggle was quiet at first before turning deep, maniacal.

He walked right into the waiting arms of the lycans.

Norman picked himself up from the wet ground, sand and grass coating his wings and clogging his eyes. Enraged, the gargoyle shook his wings and surveyed the battlefield. One dryad was down, hacked in half at Uther's feet. Bert was entangled with another, wrapped in wooden limbs as he beat the tree into the ground. At the front, Orphan wielded his sword with unmatched skill. His eyes fell on the humans, both caught in a dryad's clutches.

He took the dryad above the shoulders in a bone jarring crunch. Norman felt something snap just before intense pain rippled through his body, he held on.

Stunned, the dryad dropped the women as it was driven into the sand.

Blood trickling from his mouth, Norman growled, "Get out of here!"

Sara picked herself up from all fours and, having the awareness to snatch Cecile by the collar, dragged them both clear. Supernatural sounds penetrated them, piercing flesh and sinew. Silent screams echoed in their minds. Survival instinct kicked in and Sara ran for her life, Cecile on her heels.

It wasn't until they were clear of the immediate threat she stopped, hands on her knees and gasping for breath, and looked around. Tears stung her eyes from exertion. Sara took into the scene playing out and noticed one person was missing.

"Where's Abner?"

Cecile shook the weeds from her hair, cursing under her breath about not tying it back. Worse, she'd lost her pistol somewhere in the fray, leaving them both unprotected should the dryads discover them. At Sara's question, she squinted, failing to spy the diminutive gnome. Or the sword.

"We need to find him," Sara said.

"Go back into that?" Cecile's courage abandoned her. Any pretense of being a field agent, competent and capable of handling dire situations dissolved in a flare of wasted illusion. She belonged behind a desk. Of that there was no doubt. She hung her head, the shame consuming her. Escape and call back to headquarters for help. That's what she needed to do.

Pain blossomed across her upper chest, and she looked up in shock to see Sara drawing back for another swing. "What the hell?"

Sara, her hand curled into a fist, snapped, "We don't have time to feel sorry for ourselves. Not tonight. I want to go home, and you want to prove yourself. Now stop the pity party and help me find Abner. Without him this is all for nothing."

Blinking, Cecile bobbed her head as her thoughts cleared. *I needed that, but I'll be damned if I let her know.* She was still in the fight.

Back to back, the four remaining group members were ragged caricatures of themselves. Cuts and bruises covered their bodies. Broken bones struggled to reknit before the next onslaught. Clothes were torn, muscles weary. Their strength sapped, what little they had left would be sore pressed when the remaining dryads renewed the attack.

"This isn't how I expected to go out," Uther panted.

Orphan dropped the tip of his sword, sucking in a breath. "Our story isn't finished yet. You and I still have a score to settle, Old Guard."

Uther smiled.

Norman furled his wings and dropped to a knee. "We have given a good accounting this night. I am honored to have stood beside you."

"Yeah, what he said," Bert echoed. A nasty gash ran down his right arm, bleeding freely in wide sheets of bright crimson.

"What's this? We're not dead yet," Orphan admonished. "We've already taken down three of these monsters. What's ten more?"

On cue, the dryads reared to full height and threw their arms in the air. Lightning stuck, brought down through the green cloud hovering above them. Smoke and fire swirled, slivers of magic and power coagulating into a defined shape.

They braced for the end...

...What they got was far from it.

Stepping from the storm came a short man in pale blue robes. The tips of his fingers barely poked from the fanned sleeves. His legs swished as he walked, the fabric clinging to his muscles. Bald with naught by thick, silver eyebrows on his head, he halted inside the ring of dryads. A snap of his fingers and the trees disappeared as if they'd never been.

The man grinned, satisfied he still had the touch, and settled his stern gaze on the heroes. "Elf. Gargoyle. Troll. An unexpected collection on my doorstep. But one thing is missing. Tell me, Orphan Thorne, where is my sword?"

TWENTY-NINE

Gruff's fingers curled around Abner's neck with enough force to pop the gnome's head off. The lycan took immense pleasure in the act. Too many of his pack were gone. They'd spent the better part of a week hunting Abner down, trailing him across the state and leaving a swath of destruction and failure in passing.

But now, this night, Gruff stood at the precipice of victory.

He glared at Abner, the thought of crunching half his face dancing in his mind. Gruff found nothing special in the gnome. Small and unremarkable in every way, yet somehow he succeeded where countless others, Gruff included, failed. The irony was not lost on the pack leader. *One little snap and it would be all over. Just like that.*

"You've been a bad little gnome," Gruff scolded.

Face turning purple from lack of oxygen, Abner beat on Gruff's forearm weakly. "You have the sword. Let me go."

"No, I don't think I will. You've cost me too much. I'm either going to kill you or keep you for a pet."

"He played his part, Gruff," Princess injected.

Standing a step behind him, she had her hips cocked, arms crossed. The dry look on her face told him enough. "Feeling cocky about yourself, aren't you?"

Princess' scowl deepened. "I did what was required of me. You wanted the sword. I made it happen. For you. For the pack."

"Hmm, the pack," he echoed. "No aspirations to become alpha?"

She saw no point in lying. Others died for less. "Who doesn't?" At his growl, she added, "Now's not my time, Gruff."

"That's right. It's not. Your place is behind me. Always. Now let me decide what to do with my toy here." He shook Abner for emphasis and the gnome squawked. "See how much fun he can be?"

"Just kill him already," Princess urged. "He's no use to us broken."

Suspicious, Gruff tossed Abner to the ground with a grunt and spun on her. "What are you driving at? What does this gnome mean to you?"

She shook her head, avoiding the quesiton. "I don't have the stomach for games."

Gruff stepped closer. His breath hot on her neck. "How did you turn him?"

Convincing Abner it was in his best interests to hand over the sword and betray his companions hadn't been difficult. He needed an out. She provided it. The rest fell to the details. And those she wasn't willing to share.

"I saw an opportunity and took it," she lied.

"When?" he pressed, eyes narrowed.

"Back at the bridge. There was a moment where neither of us were accounted for. I caught him and gave him an offer he couldn't refuse."

That much was true. She skipped the promise of violence and the illusion Abner would be forgotten once the sword was in their hands. Princess also left out her personal designs on the sword and claiming dominance of the pack.

"Perhaps you'd like to know the sweet nothings I whispered before he wet himself," she taunted. "You know how effective I am."

Unsatisfied with her response, yet uncertain how to prove she was lying, Gruff turned his attention to the rest of the pack. None of their faces betrayed them, or her. The way they stood, glaring back at him with silent threats of violence in their eyes, spoke volumes. Gruff stepped back and threw his arms out in challenge.

"I don't like what I'm seeing," he announced. "Why is that do you think, Princess?"

"Not my place to say, Gruff."

He snorted. "Haven't I delivered what I promised? We have the sword! The only thing preventing us from taking over the world. That leaves just one thing left to do."

The sounds of battle erupted behind them when lightning crashed. Their hair stood on end. Several transformed into wolf forms, wheeling about to face the threat. Gruff watched his pack prepare for battle and stretched a claw out for the gnome.

Princess stared at the sky as it shifted through hues of green. Unnatural. Something wicked was coming. She felt it. Her blood stuttered in her veins. Her heartbeat became irregular. A threat pressed on her conscience, but from where? Scanning the night, she failed to spy any living creature.

"We should leave," she was surprised at the sound of her voice.

"Not yet," Gruff remarked. "We got scores to settle."

Princess flung her arm toward the disturbance. "We can't fight whatever that is! Are you mad?"

"We got the sword," he reminded. "How much more do we need? I'm done playing second fiddle to these elves. Time's come for the packs to show their worth. You with me or do I need to start culling the ranks?"

Several dropped their heads. One or two shifted stances, not enough to provide challenge though. Princess seethed inside, knowing her best chance at usurping the pack was now gone. Faster, younger, she had the martial skillset to defeat him, but she needed the sword. The only way to get that was by killing Abner and pulling it from his corpse.

Through all the madness of the night, the gnome still clutched the sword like a dying family member, refusing to let go even after fulfilling his end of the bargain. She marveled at how such a creature managed to live so long without running afoul of those he crossed.

The green cloud vanished suddenly, leaving them in near total darkness. A wolf howled, the dire call of warning to all within earshot. Confused, the others milled around Gruff in search of guidance. But without a proper target, the werewolves remained immobilized.

Slinking closer while the others were distracted, she knelt beside the gnome. "Abner, give me the sword. I promise to let you go."

"Why should I trust you?" he hissed. "You've already betrayed me once."

He had a point. But then, she never promised he'd live through this. "Fine words from a traitor. What do you think your friends will do once they realize you delivered the sword to us? Will they kill you outright or drag you back to their queen for a lifetime of misery and torture before you are forgotten in a cell, lost to all time and space? I've heard the stories of Morgen's rage. She is far worse than anything I might do. Give me the sword and slink away in the night, back to where you belong. Your part in this can end. Now."

Abner discovered he was regretting his decisions. Made from fear and the unwavering desire for self-preservation, he allowed her poisoned words to corrupt an already fragile mental constitution. Abner thought that by giving them the sword he might atone for his crimes. The quiet rant she just delivered showed him the error of his thoughts. Lycans were not to be trusted. Ever. Instincts warned that should he succumb and give Princess the sword, she would kill him outright and unleash a tidal wave of carnage in both worlds. With him as the catalyst.

"Give me the fucking sword, gnome," she demanded. "I won't ask again."

He blanched, uncharacteristically holding his ground.

"That's right," Gruff said from behind. "You'll be too dead to do so."

Princess half turned, attempting to rise when Gruff barreled into her, transforming as he did. She yelped as he tackled her to the ground and allowed her wolf to take over. Claws, fangs, and fur sprouted between them. Gruff bit down on her shoulder and spat out a mouthful of flesh and fur. Infuriated, Princess retaliated.

The rest of the pack surrounded them.

A first gunshot erupted, quickly followed by a hundred more.

On the opposite side of the island, in a small RV park overlooking the sand, an old man woke to the sounds of gunfire. A yawn and scratch of his chest later, he popped up in bed. Glancing down to see his wife fast asleep and cursing how the woman never woke up for anything, he climbed over her and slipped into his robe. The old man crept through his camper as quiet as possible, stopping to ensure the kids were safe and asleep. At the foot of their beds was the family lab, an old companion who had seen too much and kept a great many secrets behind her greying face.

No stranger to gunfire, the old man made a pitstop in the bathroom to relieve himself and cursed again. Getting old was no fun. A quick wash of the hands and he continued stealing through the camper, stopping to grab the shotgun he kept under the couch. The old man ensured it was loaded and headed outside.

Crisp night air driven in from the ocean made his breath catch and a slight gust of wind was enough to kick open his robe. Scowling, he retied the robe and peered through the gloom of his immediate surroundings.

His boat rocked in the gentle lapping against the dock. A handful of other campers and small houses, little more than huts, filled his field of vision. Friends and acquaintances he'd made over the years of coming down to the beach for a weekend getaway. A trash can overflowing with empty bottles and cans stood beside the remains of a campfire. He snorted at the red-hot embers still glowing. How many times had his friends chided him for leaving the fire roaring while he staggered off to bed?

With no immediate threats that he could see, no creeper looking for an easy score, the old man shook his head. Paranoia was another lovely gift of age. He didn't sleep well these days and found a way to worry about things he dare not mention. He was doubting he'd actually heard gunfire when he spied the green glow over the other side of the island.

He'd been around the world thanks to a stint in the Navy a few decades ago and had seen the aurora borealis firsthand on a northern tour in the sub, but this was unlike anything he'd ever seen. Twin lightning bolts startled him, knocking him off his feet. The shotgun hit the sand butt first. Thank God he hadn't clicked the safety off or there'd be hell to pay when everyone came outside wondering what was going on.

Grimacing as pain lanced through his back, the old man watched the green light die. That's when they came—six figures in drenched uniforms. They stalked up from the shore. Face paint camouflaged their hands and faces, turning them into heavily armed nightmares. Weapons tucked into their shoulders and night vision goggles disrupting the outline of their silhouettes, they moved with utter surety, not once sparing a glance at him as they passed through the campsite.

He watched them until they disappeared into the night, knowing they were heading for trouble. What sort of trouble remained to be seen, and the old man decided he wanted nothing to do with it. In the morning, knowing better than to wake the wife up this late at night with what she no doubt would think a drunken concocted story, he intended on packing up the family and the dog and hightailing it back west.

Vacation over. Period.

Then the night exploded in gunfire. Scrambling to his feet, the old man burst into his camper and shouted, "Get up! We're leaving!"

THIRTY

Sara searched to no avail. There was no sign of Abner or the sword.

With the dryad threat gone, at least she hoped, she dared to venture more than a few steps from Bert and the others. Darkness gripped the land, refusing to allow her more than a few meters of vision before swallowing all into the cold nothingness of the unknown. Frustrated, she raised her hands to her mouth.

"Don't," Norman warned, appearing at her side. "You don't know what's out there."

Whirling in confusion and anger, Sara snapped, "We have to find him! He has the sword."

"We will. I can see better than any of us at night," Norman assured her. "Let me do a sweep before we foolishly give in to temptation."

Rebuked, Sara crossed her arms and fell silent. Being a hero was harder than she thought. That and the sting of Abner's betrayal bit deep.

"Ah, a gnome," the wizard said. "I always figured it would be one of them to find the sword. Pesky creatures, if you ask me."

"You're the reason this is happening?" Sara fumed.

A bushy eyebrow rose. "Sheldon, at your service."

Rolling her eyes, Sara prepared to unleash a torrent on him. "Why you—"

Orphan stepped between them. "Wizard, the gnome has the sword but there is a pack of lycans out there hunting for it. We are not safe here."

"Forge master. How good to see you after all these years." Sheldon smiled. "I didn't expect to find you among this group."

"Trust me, I don't want to be here," the elf confirmed. "We have a problem."

"I believe you, but without the sword on hand there is little I can do. Are these lycans close?"

"We don't know. Last we saw of them was back at the battleship. I can only assume they are still on the trail," Orphan explained.

"I can take care of that." Sheldon closed his eyes and raised his palms to the sky. Uttering an ancient incantation, he cast out questing vapors of magic, trailing vermillion streams up and away. Sara was distracted by it until she saw his face pale. "Your wolves are here, on the island."

"How?" Uther gasped. "We left by boat."

Squeezing his eyes tighter, Sheldon replied, "They tracked you. One of you is marked."

Shit. Sara rummaged through her pockets as dread rose. Her fingers brushed against a foreign object. *Please, no.* The object was no larger than a button, circular and cold metal. It looked like a watch battery that she had to get once for Daniel. She bit her bottom lip and faced them. "I think I know how."

"What is that?" Bert asked, his face twisted in confusion when she held it out in her palm.

"A tracking device." Uther snorted. "When did they slip that on you?"

Swallowing the lump choking her, Sara found herself trembling. "I've never seen that before."

Even Norman stiffened. The circle around her constricted. She felt the anger seething. The betrayal, innocent enough on her part, awakened their mistrust. Sara had never felt so small in all her life.

Cecile snatched the tracker to inspect it. "I got nothing," she confirmed. "Whoever gave them this tech is beyond DESA."

Sheldon snapped his fingers and the device disappeared, leaving only guilt and humiliation in Sara. *'One of you will betray the others.'* The words haunted her, prompting her to doubt herself. *Am I the traitor? Was it me all along*? "One of the lycans found me on the beach. I should have told you but I...I'm sorry," she offered, even though the words felt hollow.

Norman went to stand by her side. "I believe you, but that does not excuse you keeping this from us. What did the lycan tell you?"

"She tried to convince me to work with them," Sara struggled to recall the conversation. "She also said one of you will betray the whole group." She closed her eyes against the burning of tears. "I guess that was me."

"No. There is another," Sheldon intoned, surprising her.

"Abner." Uther's statement was one of surety. Vehemence. Clenching a fist, he added, "He must have slipped it in your pocket when you weren't looking. I knew I should have killed him when I had the chance."

"What would that have solved? The lycans have been one step behind us the entire way. Now they are in front of us. With or without Abner, it matters not.

They would have found their way here eventually." Norman frowned. "Abner is neither problem nor solution. Regardless, he has the sword. It is a fair assumption he is delivering it to the lycans as we speak."

"We must stop him before it's too late," Cecile interjected. "We cannot allow lycan dominance." She wanted to say more but her thoughts fizzled under the strain of dire thoughts colliding at once. The worst of them stemmed from knowing the total collapse of elf society would come under her watch. The implications staggered her. *How am I going to report this*?

"Agreed. Our best bet is to split up into teams. We can cover more ground, faster," Uther said. His tone left little room for debate. He shot the wizard a knowing look. "Unless you can snap those waterlogged fingers and produce our wayward friend?"

Sheldon shook his head. "You know magic doesn't work like that."

"Of course not." Uther sheathed his swords in favor of his weapon. "Bert, keep Sara safe. Agent lady, you're with me. Norman, take him."

If Orphan or Cecile took offense, they didn't show it. No one voiced objections as they paired up. Weapons and ammo checks took a matter of moments.

Through it all, no one questioned what the wizard planned on doing while they scoured the island. Sara found it odd, but given the previous displays of power, felt better having him sidelined. The thought of being turned to slush from magic threatened to rob what little strength she had left. "What could possibly go wrong?"

"Are we ready?" At their nods, Uther briefed, "Sweep the island and return to the lighthouse. The objective is the sword. Nothing else matters."

"What about Abner?" Sara piped up. Even after the truth of treason was revealed she found it difficult to abandon him altogether.

He fixed her with a deadpan look. "You find the sword, you radio for backup. If the lycans are here, we'll need to fight them together. Let's move."

Uther hefted his rifle and made it one step before six red lasers centered on his chest.

"Targets acquired. Painting now."

The six commandos knelt in the waist high grass, waiting for the command to open fire. Wet, cold, and tired, they wanted nothing more than to complete their mission and return to base. The last second deployment, thanks to a lead generated from D.E.S.A. headquarters, marked the first time in months the special unit was called into action. Threat mitigation protocols were in effect. Collateral damage was authorized, if necessary. None of the men taking aim at the hodge podge of elves and trolls had been in a situation where they'd taken elfkind life, though all were prepared to do what was called for to ensure containment and de-escalation.

"Go on my mark. No one fires," the squad sergeant ordered. "Ready, mark."

As one, they rose and stalked into the open, their weapons trained on what they deemed the greatest threat.

"Weapons down. Hands up," the sergeant ordered.

He wasn't sure what to expect, certainly not what met him. The elf with twin swords poking over his shoulders immediately lowered his rifle and held out his empty hands. Following his example, the others did the same. All but the lumbering brute who held no weapon at all.

"My name is Sergeant Hasko. Who's in charge here?"

A female, human, slipped to the front. "I am. Agent Cecile Barnabas."

Hasko hesitated. "You're agency?"

She nodded, slowly producing her badge from her inner jacket pocket. "Hasko? Jim Hasko?"

His rifle lowered a fraction. His mission briefing didn't correlate with the action on the ground. "That's correct."

Swallowing, Cecile tucked her badge away and smiled. "Jim, it's me, Cecile. We were in the same weapons handling course back at the academy."

"Thought I recognized your name. What's the situation? My orders didn't mention any field agents."

"The situation is critical." Cecile went on to explain the important facts, from the sword to the rogue werewolves operating on the island.

"My team came from the east. There was no sign of the targets." His face darkened at the misdirection in his orders.

"Sergeant, time is of the essence," one of the males of the group suggested. His rumbling voice carried over the field, grating on nerves and making more than one of the commandos flinch.

Hasko stared back at the hulking figure, spying the wingtips and massive claws on his feet. Having never seen such a creature, he suddenly doubted the efficiency of his small arms.

The howl of a lone wolf broke the tension. His team braced themselves, expecting an onslaught of ravaging werewolves. When no threat materialized, Hasko realized they were in for a long night. Home had never felt further away.

"Right. We move," Hasko agreed. "I assume you have a plan?"

Cecile nodded. "Three teams of two. Sweep the island and collect on the lighthouse."

"Works for me. I'll take my team up the center." Without waiting for their agreement, Hasko spun and took his team back into the night and the lurking danger just out of sight. "This just got interesting. Should be fun. See you when it's done."

Thrilled with the unexpected reinforcements, Cecile suddenly felt renewed hope. D.E.S.A. commando teams were among the highest trained veterans in the world. Pulled from special forces from multiple services and nations, they were the greatest asset of any government. Cecile marveled at their tenacity and dedication to professionalism. Each had a rack of ribbons threatening to crawl up and over their shoulders from repeated combat deployments to the worst places on earth. In their current capacity, most had already deployed to contain species humanity was deemed incapable of comprehending.

Cecile was thrilled at seeing Jim Hasko again. She'd spent long hours fantasizing over the man several years ago, never thinking to cross paths again. Yet here he was. On the same beach on the same night. Were it not for the werewolves threatening to burn everything to the ground, she might have summoned her courage and asked him out.

"What?" she asked, feeling an intense stare on her back. "Can't a woman dream?"

"Not when it can get us both killed," Uther replied. "Let's go. I want first crack at that gnome."

"You mean the wolves," she countered.

"Them too."

Sara clung to Bert like he was the last lifeboat on the Titanic. Neither were suited for combat, though she'd seen Bert's rage in action and knew he was strong enough to handle whatever was thrown at them. Satisfied with partnering with him, she hoped the others survived the night. Turmoil followed them like summer thunderstorms, each instance getting worse. Now, at the end of the road, they were faced with life or death. Sara didn't know what the others felt, but she was terrified.

Bert lumbered ahead, unsteady in both purpose and desire. He liked Abner, then again, he liked almost everyone since his brother's passing. The recent turn of events soured his mood. Trolls being fiercely loyal, he struggled with reconciling Abner's treason, even while understanding it was true to form. The gnome didn't concern him much however, it was the looming threat of the lycans terrifying him. After all, a man only had so much rage to spend. His first concern was keeping Sara alive. The rest, he figured, would sort itself out.

Norman gave Sara a final look before they disappeared in the night. He disapproved of Uther's selections. Putting Uther and Orphan Thorne together would have been their most effective combat team, if they managed to stay away from each other's throats long enough to reclaim the sword. That did little to ease his pain from failing to follow through on his promise to Sara. He'd watched her for years now, since that fateful night Cassandra attempted to murder her in her bathroom. Though their species shouldn't mix, Sara was the closest thing to family he had.

And he was walking away when she needed him most.

THIRTY-ONE

Falling back on her training, and at this point that's all it was, Cecile stalked a step behind and to the side of Uther. The Old Guard veteran moved with purpose across the combination of sand and dirt. Every movement precise. He stalked more than walked. Shoulders forward, slumped a fraction to absorb any potential rifle recoil upon engagement. The man whispered lethality in ways she failed to comprehend. No amount of agency training measured up to the standards of a man with thousands of years of martial experience. She found the ease in which he moved and behaved enticing. *He's what I want to be*. The admission stunned her, for some dreams seldom came true.

Hurrying after the Old Guard, the crunch of rock and shells under foot, Cecile scanned the immediate surroundings. They were heading off the beach and into the grass. Visibility reduced to an arm span, robbing her of the one advantage she had. Her heart rate rising, Cecile gripped her long rifle tighter. She began tapping her index finger above the magazine well, a nervous tick dating back to her first time running through the search and clear drills back at the academy.

If Uther shared her hesitancy, he didn't show it. Everything about the elf spoke confidence. The twin swords on his back hummed, prompting her to question if every elf sword was imbued with magic, or foul tempers. Or maybe she was just imagining it. Uther kept his rifle high, the butt tucked into his shoulder; the mark of a true warrior. A veteran. Cecile watched him with awe, and it was all she could do to keep her mind from wandering down roads of fantasy and fancy, the sort that got people killed. Lost in thought, she narrowly avoided bumping into him as he pulled up and crouched to a low firing position.

"What is it?" she whispered.

"Shhh," he hissed back, not facing her.

Cecile's stomach twisted, the way it did before every harrowing situation she'd ever faced. She noticed the area had grown still. No insects or frogs. Not even the sound of waves lapping the distant shore. Her eyes closed as her index finger slipped into the trigger guard; her thumb depressed the safety button. A breeze kicked up, rustling the grass. She forced her eyes open, swiveling her rifle back and forth across her sector of fire while carefully avoiding flagging Uther.

The Old Guard spun, faster than her eyes tracked. Moving in a blur, Uther had his rifle ready. She felt, rather than saw, his desire to open fire. To unleash hell on whatever approached. The discipline exhibited proved remarkable. Cecile knew she would have already given in to her nerves had she been on point. Her heart thundered in her ears. *Thump. Thump. Thump.* Cecile trembled, the strain of holding her rifle in one position for too long growing.

A noise grew: the plod of footsteps approaching. Cecile frowned. Her limited knowledge of werewolves suggested they were near perfect predators but, because of their weight, had a heavy footprint. Whatever was coming upon them wasn't a wolf. It couldn't be. The threat burst from cover a heartbeat later. She squeezed the trigger, even as Uther knocked her aim high. Tears of adrenalin clouding her vision, Cecile stared down at the possum now scurrying back into the safety of the grass.

"You just gave our position away," Uther snarled.

"I..." Cecile closed her mouth, knowing anything she said was little more than an empty excuse, and admission of failure.

She shrank from his unspoken frustrations, despite her best efforts at remaining strong. Rebuked, Cecile exhaled her moment of weakness and recentered her focus. She was a professional. The moment she dreamed of was finally upon her and, allowing a moment's grace, she'd be damned if anyone robbed her of it.

"Let's move." Her voice shifted from shaky to confident.

Uther blinked. His tongue poked against his cheek as if he was about to say something. Grunting instead, the Old Guard resumed moving.

Pride flushed Cecile. Not only had she stood up to a heavily armed menace, she earned a measure of approval. The last bit might have been pushing it, but she clung to it like a life ring.

Then the night erupted in howls, snarls, and no small measure of gunfire. *Shit*.

The decision wasn't hard. In fact, it proved the opposite. The need for decisive force drove them. Victory by crushing a blow. Anything less resulted in mission failure. Sergeant Hasko waited long enough for his team to get ready, the light machine gun in the center. From the last man in line, a series of touches on the shoulder of the man to the left told Hasko they were set. He closed his eyes, muttered a quick prayer, and counted down from five.

The squad went into action on one. Rising, they drew beads on targets and opened fire with the fury of the gods. Hasko watched lines of tracers slashing across the night to burrow into the werewolves. The burp of the machine gun as the gunner found his target overpowered the others. A hundred rounds pumped into the night. Blood, fur, and gouts of flesh flew. Screams followed. A wolf turned, ready to pounce. Seeing the shift, the gunner adjusted fire and was rewarded by the red line pummeling the wolf in the head and shoulders. He kept firing until the drum emptied. By then it didn't matter. The werewolf was dead, most of its head pulverized.

Hasko began the advance. His squad followed. Every other man dropped their empty mags simultaneously. The others provided a base of fire until the first group reloaded and resumed the assault. Hasko and his second group followed suit until all had fresh magazines. Step by step, they drove the stunned werewolves back.

Several spun away. Two more died where they stood. Nerves left them twitching in the blood drenched sands. Only two ignored the team. They battled in the center of the broken ring. Titanic monsters incapable of rationale. Hasko stared impassionately, for each was wounded in a dozen places. How either remained on their feet was a mystery. He'd seen a handful of creatures suffer similar punishment over the course of his career, but never anything like this.

Distracted, he almost failed to spot the attacking werewolf bounding over the corpse of a friend. Claws extended, the creature pushed off with impossible strength. Muscles rippled from neck to hind legs. Saliva and blood drooled from its mouth. Less than a meter from its target, a barrage of small arms fire knocked the wolf off course. It sailed past the closest commando, tilting on its side before crashing into the grass. The squad shifted fire, ensuring the werewolf stayed down. With the wolf still twitching, bleeding from a hundred bullet wounds, Hasko drew his combat knife, silver edged and razor sharp, and plunged it into the stricken wolf's heart. The werewolf died with a whimper. Hasko watched until the hate left its eyes.

"Back in position," he ordered. "We're not done yet."

Men hurried to comply and resumed the assault through the objective area. But by now no werewolves remained. The survivors scattered, even the two so intent on killing each other. Sweat covering his head under the tactical helmet, Hasko wiped his forehead with the back of his sleeve.

"Evans, get facial tags on the dead. Everyone else refresh your ammo. Agent Barnabas is going to need a little help before this night is through," Hasko ordered.

Only after the last bullet was fired did he take time to breath and replay the frantic two minutes of their assault. Three enemy killed in action. Zero friendly casualties. He estimated another eight werewolves were loose on the island.

"Don't shoot!"

Hasko spun, rifle already training on the target. He paused, not expecting what stepped into view.

Abner Grumman often heard humans talk about seeing their lives flash before their eyes. He passed it off to exaggeration, a trait they were far too prone to indulge in and left it at that. Never once in his long existence did he imagine he'd find himself in such a position.

Abner cowered as Gruff and Princess battled. Others howled and cheered. In the confusion, the gnome discovered he was untended—until the battling wolves crashed and nearly rolled on top of him. Abner squawked and dove aside before getting crushed. Another lycan snatched him by the shoulder as the circle around the leaders grew tighter. Claws punctured his flesh, doubling him over in waves of pain. Tears spilling down his cheeks, Abner struggled to break free, but the grip proved too firm.

"Stop moving, imp," the lycan warned. "Princess says you live, but I don't care. It's been a long time since I killed a gnome."

Defeated, Abner hung his head and watched the lycans battle for pack supremacy.

Princess was younger, lighter, and faster. Cunning and naturally manipulative, she lacked the pure venom Gruff brought. The pack leader slashed down Princess' flank. Red claws dripping, Gruff kicked his second in the face, catching her jaw with a bone snapping crunch. She flew backward with a yelp. *Not so confident now, are we?* Sensing victory, Gruff pursued. He knew, as did she, any reprieve, the slightest change to regroup or catch his breath, might prove his undoing. He needed to dispatch her with authority, leaving no doubts in the rest of the pack as to who the true leader was.

He pummeled Princess where she lay, breaking bones and tearing flesh. She fought back, as much as she could. Still pinned, she lashed out with her hind leg and was rewarded with her dew claw slashing Gruff's tendon. Howling, he reared back and gave her the opportunity to slink clear. This was a true challenge worthy of his time.

Gruff closed his eyes while his tendon repaired itself. It had been generations since the last fool made a run for alpha. The nonsense from two nights ago barely registered, in his opinion. Princess had heart but lacked the natural violence a true leader required. He relished the opportunity to kill her and purge the ranks. It was past time they rebuilt, especially with what he had in mind now that the sword was in his possession.

Flexing his claws, he readied for her assault. Princess was on him in the blink of an eye. Deciding she needed a lesson in humility, he unleashed a punishing series of body blows. Princess ducked as a fist crashed into her kidney and caught him in the throat as he followed through with the shot.

Abner watched it all after being cast to the ground a second time. His lycan captor stood on his back, pinning him face down in the sand. The sword of Grimspire lay not far off. Within reach if Abner was given the chance … He wasn't. Surprisingly, no one seemed interested in claiming the sword for themselves.

Cruelty in every heartbeat, the lycan pressed down harder. "Nah, you're not going anywhere, gnome," he leered. "I got a bone to pick with you. Your friends almost killed me back at that battleship. Now's time for payback."

Squirming to no avail, Abner opened his mouth to retort—

The clearing erupted in a hail of gunfire before the first word left his tongue. Abner screamed as the lycan atop him was shredded. Blood and gore dripped onto the gnome in a torrent. He didn't stop screaming until what remained of the lycan toppled sideways. Free and able to breathe again, the gnome gathered his wits enough to slink into the grass.

The sword was gone.

THIRTY-TWO

"I don't like this. Nope. Not one bit," Bert grumbled as he slashed a path through the grass.

Sara felt his glower. The troll was good natured, but she'd seen enough to know a simmering rage lurked just beneath the surface. If ever a time for Bert to go full Hulk mode, she figured it was now. They'd been beaten down, shot at, and hounded. If she was furious (she was) then she knew Bert seethed. As much as she wanted to coax him to go ahead and lose control, Sara felt the moment would either come or it wouldn't. Elfkind was nothing if not trapped by its traditions.

They hurried without direction. Abner and the sword were out there, somewhere in the night and with him stalked a pack of bloodthirsty werewolves. Part of her refused to believe Abner was the traitor. That all his fear and cowering was naught but a ruse at their expense. What did he hope to gain from it? Sara fumed as she walked, desperate to unravel the missing link even while questioning what was it all for?

She took it personally. How could she not? Abner trusted her to see him to safety and it pulled at her motherly nature, playing on her already frazzled emotions. His betrayal was a stab in the back. She wanted to snatch the gnome by the throat and choke the confession out of him.

"I wanna pound him to a pulp," Bert said, as if reading her mind. "I let him play my video games, Sara! No one gets to do that."

"I know, Bert. He fooled us all," she replied, the words choking her. "We must find him first, before those werewolves do. If they haven't already."

"I don't like them wolves either," he snapped. "They smell so bad when they get wet."

Sara broke into a giggle, unable to prevent it from turning into full blown laughter. The image of one of the pack shaking after being bathed was too amusing to ignore, she struggled to regain composure. Bert soon joined in; his rumbling laughs akin to a deep bellow.

Distracted, they failed to spot the werewolf until it leapt on Bert.

Sara shouted, fumbling with her pistol despite the weapon's safety being off. She watched as beast and troll grappled, helpless without a clear field of fire. Remembering what little Daniel tried to teach her, Sara tore her gaze from the battle to scan the surroundings. If another wolf be close by, they were dead.

Bert huffed as the air was driven from his lungs. He blanched at the stench of wet dog smothering him. The werewolf wrapped its arms and legs around the troll and squeezed. It took effort, but the troll jerked his arms free from the embrace in time to catch the wolf's lower jaw as it snapped for his neck. Eyes wide, Bert shoved the head back with as much strength as he could muster. The wolf fought back, determined not to let its prey escape.

Fangs clamped down on his fingertips; Bert reared back in pain before slamming his head forward, cracking the wolf's jaws. Teeth and spittle flew. It was enough, just, for Bert to break free and begin his counterattack. The troll lumbered into the wounded werewolf. Rage blossomed. Indignity for old wrongs suffered. Bert saw his brother cheering him on. Saw Sara waiting to be killed. His friends. His family. Bert attacked.

Sara turned at the sharp sound of agony, surprised to find her friend attempting to rip the werewolf's head apart ala King Kong.

Bert bled from a dozen cuts, slashes turned his clothes to tatters. Blood ran freely down his arms and legs. She swore one of his fingers was shorter. Ignoring his injuries, Bert succeeded in snapping the lower jaw until it dangled against the werewolf's chest. He tossed the body down, content with his deeds. Sara felt the blood drain from her face at the carnage.

The beast was twitching. Some fight remained, or the brain hadn't caught up with the body yet. Regardless, she knew what she needed to do.

Sara walked up to the wounded beast; pistol pointed at its head. Their eyes locked. She saw the agony and desperation in its eyes, begging her to do it. Closing her eyes, she pulled the trigger. Sara swore she heard a sigh as the last breath left the werewolf's lungs. An unbearable weight settled over her, threatening to drag her down.

"It's ok, Sara," Bert whispered.

"I've never killed anything before," she said before breaking into sobs.

She stared at the weapon in her hands. The killing instrument. Was this how Daniel felt during his first deployment? Did it get easier? Or was she bound to this sensation of guilt for the rest of her life. She handed the pistol to Bert.

She'd had enough.

Norman Guilt had never been the sort to give in to base emotions. Gargoyles were notorious thinkers, tacticians, and strategists, often making the best battlefield leaders. For one to rush into action without weighing the pros and cons of any situation suggested poor upbringing. His father raised him right, at least he liked to think so. Throughout his centuries of stewardship overlooking changing cityscapes, he sat, and he thought. The one inescapable conclusion he repeatedly arrived at was his kind should have never gotten involved with the elves.

They were their own worst enemies. A hindrance to the future. Through their shortsightedness other races rose from the night. Oh, there was always some claim to the throne in play. Most seldom carried over from a thought. This time was different. With the king dead, and Morgen the one running the show, leastwise until a new leader of the light clans could be chosen, the lycans sensed their time had at last come. Norman wondered if having Abner steal the sword had always been part of the deal, if the gnome double-crossed the lycans as he had the group. No amount of treachery was beyond a gnome after all.

He hoped he stumbled upon Abner before the others, knowing he alone had the fortitude to hold back and hear the gnome's side of the story before handing him over to face the queen's justice. Norman performed many roles, executioner not among them. His sense of duty made him leery. The others were quick to strike. Eager for blood. He'd seen it too many times. Elves were dangerous creatures. They wouldn't hesitate to kill the gnome and be done with it.

Hindering his search efforts was the forgotten forge master, Orphan Thorne. Taciturn beyond measure, which was saying something to a gargoyle, the elf hadn't spoken a word since the group split up. Nor was Norman able to read his expression. Frustration boiled, threatening to pull the gargoyle out of his comfort zone.

He heard battle raging across the island. The sheer amount of gunfire suggested the D.E.S.A. commandos had made contact and were unleashing their punishment on the lycans. Norman felt nothing for either faction. Both were proven detriments to his wellbeing. The fewer in the way between him and returning to his roost, with Sara alive, the better. Orphan Thorne failed to see it the same.

"We should converge with the humans," he suggested. "They are no match for a lycan pack."

Norman questioned what the elf knew about commandos, having exiled himself long before the agency's creation. Having abandoned the elves centuries ago, Orphan turned his back on all matters of state. Was he still beholden by the signed accords? Forced to abide by rules and regulations all but strangling the clans. Norman needed answers if he was to trust the elf responsible for creating the single deadliest weapon in their storied history.

"Abner is our primary focus," he insisted. "We are bound by rules, Orphan."

"Forced upon us by humans with little to no concept of what it means to live forever," Orphan countered. "Why must we live by their rules? Elfkind deserves more. Demands more. We were the stewards of this planet long before they evolved from apes."

"Your argument is obsolete," Norman replied, suddenly unsure what game the ancient elf played. "The accords have been established and we are bound to them. Whatever you are proposing will result in our sanctioning."

"Bah! When did we ever need humans? They are a nuisance best ignored and set aside while better men and women restore order to this broken world."

"That is not for us to decide. We…"

Norman stopped mid-sentence to blur into his natural state, with wings swept behind, the gargoyle crouched.

Three lycans ran for them.

Orphan Thorne launched into the attack, catching the first lycan unawares with a crippling slash across her chest down to her waist. Her scream echoed, prompting the others to stop their flight and wheel about to meet the threat.

Norman gave the forge master room to swing his cruel sword. Lifting into the night sky, the gargoyle extended his claws for the nearest lycan. Large and covered in midnight black fur, the beast bristled with muscle and claws, more than a match for an already tired Norman. Attempting to lift them into the sky, where he could drop the lycan, Norman struggled. The beast weighed far too much. They crashed into the water along the shore.

Norman let his prey go in a desperate attempt to regain his footing. The lycan was faster. It moved, throwing the gargoyle back under a series of hammer blows to the neck and chest. A claw raked down, slashing through his leather-like wing. Norman roared, curling a fist and smashing the lycan's face. The force of the blow sent the beast reeling in a spray of blood and water.

Tucking his wings back, Norman splashed toward his foe, knowing he had met his match. There being no substitute for brute force, gargoyle and lycan clashed in knee high water. A flock of egrets burst from their nests as the violence came too close. Turtles scurried away at their feet, desperate to keep from being crushed. Norman exchanged blows with his foe. Neither gave way.

Blood dripped from Orphan's sword, running down the blade to coat his knuckles in crimson. He hadn't fought another in a lifetime. The exhilaration flowed through his veins. He hacked and slashed, spinning against the wounded lycan in a dazzling display of martial prowess. The lycan never had a chance. She died as his blade took her head. It sailed away; a surprised look etched upon her face as the corpse fell with a splash.

He pivoted on the remaining lycan. The beast, prepared more than its companions had been, stayed outside of arm's reach. Orphan drew his sword back, prepared to strike. The lycan never gave him the chance. A yelp turned their heads. The second lycan died with Norman's fist buried in its chest. Seeing the gargoyle rip his fist free, the last lycan turned tail and fled.

"Leave him, he did not have the sword," Orphan said when the gargoyle went to follow. He knelt to wipe his sword on the dead lycan's chest. "The sword is paramount. Not the body count."

Chest heaving, Norman shook his hand.

"Can you fly?" Orphan asked in dismay.

"No. My wing is damaged," Norman admitted. "We must continue on foot."

Orphan nodded. "Good. I prefer a fair fight. Let's go to the sound of the guns, shall we?"

THIRTY-THREE

Cecile emptied her magazine into the werewolf. The sound of gunfire deafening, she winced with each shot. Unused to the violence of action, she continued squeezing the trigger long after running out of rounds. For its part, the werewolf shuddered under each impact before turning its head to leer at her with bloodstained teeth. Cecile shivered, dropping her empty magazine and fumbling for another.

The werewolf raced toward her. Sand and water kicked up in its wake. Cecile felt the waves of hatred pulsing off the creature, nauseating her as it thundered closer. She dropped the magazine—

A flash to her right. A scream. She stared at the severed limb flopping in the sand.

Uther began dismantling the werewolf with the uncanny precision. His blades sang. Ropes of blood splashed the grass in obscene patterns. Grunting, the Old Guard plunged his blades into the dying beast's heart.

Tearing his blades free, Uther asked, "Are you injured?"

Shock held her tongue. Cecile shook her head despite a small measure of doubt. Tears threatened but she remained steadfast.

"Good. We need to keep moving. I don't know how many more of these things are out there and we need that sword."

Why isn't that damned wizard helping? This is his island. Where did he go?

Stirred at his words, Cecile said, "Wait, I can find that out!" She slung her rifle over her back the way she'd seen too many soldiers in movies do and pulled out her cell phone.

"What the fuck are you doing, lady? We don't have time to make a call," he hissed.

"The tracking app. I can use it to tell us where the werewolves are and how many are left," she fired back. She turned away before the Old Guard could spy her trembling hands.

Rather than spit a sharp rebuke, Uther cleaned his blades before sheathing them and picking up his rifle. He checked the magazine, ensuring he had enough for the next engagement. He liked to give the impression of a man always on the go, refusing to remain static in combat situations. Simple movements and sharp commands quelled any doubters and established his authority. In truth, Uther was tired of leading. Tired of being the banner others flocked to when the hour grew darkest.

His years in exile afforded him the opportunity for reflection. What he found disturbed him in more ways than he felt comfortable admitting. Warfare consumed him. He'd lost a piece of himself somewhere throughout the course of his career. And for what? To join forces with a handful of ragged humans and misfits against an unworthy foe capable of killing them all? His soul yearned for more. The man inside, beaten back into the protective cocoon he'd so carefully woven to prevent the effects of causing so much damage, yearned to be free. To feel the fresh wind blow across his face without threat or worry. As much as he longed to step away and be forgotten, he feared it was far too late for that.

Cecile's eyes lit up under the bright light of her screen. Mouthing words he couldn't make out, he moved closer to glimpse her screen. Most of the tracking dots on Shattuck Island had gone red. They were spread across the better part of a kilometer and moving in different directions. With the only way onto the island by boat, they were cut off. Unless…

"Well?" Uther demanded, not sure what he was seeing. The inaction gnawed at him.

"There's only four left," she replied. "Looks like they are running wherever they think they can escape."

"That's good news."

"It should be." Cecile's tone made him clutch his rifle tighter. "But one is heading for a boat. If it gets off island with the sword this will all have been for naught."

Uther calculated, forming a plan. "How far to the boat?"

"Looks like a few hundred meters."

"Let's go. We head to intercept. Let the others handle the rest."

Sheldon preferred a life in the shadows where he could practice his magic and attempt to do good for the world. For the past few centuries, he'd done just that. He sat and watched as mankind grew more determined to self-destruct. Not that he had a problem with that. Humans were a simple species, more concerned with base greed and placing value on ignorant objects. How many wars were sparked over land or perceived wealth? Sickened by it, Sheldon watched as the elves fell prey to similar conceits.

So, he adopted a 'let the world burn' philosophy. Which had been going well until the gnome unearthed his most hated creation and brought both civilizations to the brink of annihilation. The fools on the island didn't know it. How could they? Each was consumed with finding the sword for personal reasons. He alone knew what needed doing, but until he had the sword in his possession there was little he could do.

"Curse that gnome!" Sheldon huffed to the darkness.

The others were gone. Spread across the island in their desperate bid to hunt down the lycans and restore a modicum of normalcy. Peace, he understood, was the great lie. Far too many cultures, races, and species occupied the world for there to ever be true peace. He doubted they could find a way to get along even if faced with the threat of an alien invasion. Not that he believed in such. Some thoughts were a bridge too far. Even for him.

Tucking his hands into the ridiculously large sleeves of his robes, Sheldon strode back to his tower. The lone voice of reason in a world gone made. He refused to get involved. Violence begot violence, perpetuating the never-ending cycle. The only way to break that cycle, in his esteemed estimation, was by stepping aside and letting matters play out. The elves would either succeed or they wouldn't. There was no other option.

Gunfire shredded the night calm. He kept walking. "Humans and their guns. Almost as bad as dwarves."

Sheldon began whistling an old tune as he walked. Anything to take his mind off the carnage devastating what had been a sanctuary for him for years. He supposed he needed to find a new home. Somewhere far away, and with a better climate. The North Carolina humidity was murder on his skin. Thoughts swirling around potential destinations, Sheldon stepped through the portal to his inner sanctum. He'd had enough adventure for one night. Much yet needed to be done before this night was through.

Working for the most secret agency in a government shrouded in secrecy came with immeasurable benefits. None of which involved prolonged firefights with werewolves. Since being accepted to D.E.S.A.'s commando battalion Sergeant Hasko witnessed too much that, from his point of view, shouldn't exist. Creatures torn from the pages of literature and off the big screen were not only real, but they were also existential threats to humanity's development. If the general population knew what he did there would be open revolts.

Their prey this night was the thing of nightmares. He wished he'd had the foresight to bring additional forces, but the vague orders failed to detail the real threat. Hasko intended on leaving a scathing after action review once they returned to base, but first thing's first he needed an accurate headcount of his people and an estimate of how many remaining threats were loose on the island.

"Jones! Get me eyes in the sky," he barked.

Jones dropped his pack and rummaged through it for the drone. It took minutes for him to prep the sleek, black plastic and launch. With the bird in the air, Jones hurried over to Hasko with the viewer. They studied the image in real time, silently counting the trail of bodies littered about. At last, Hasko had seen enough.

"Bring it down," he ordered. To the others he said, "Listen up! Intel shows three remaining live targets. Two are headed for the docks. The third is lingering seventy-five meters due east. Alpha team with me. We're going after the squirters. Bravo, handle the remaining threat and collapse back on the dock. Questions?"

"What about this one?"

Hasko followed the soldier pointing at their captive and groaned. The gnome. He'd almost forgotten about him. *Shit. I don't have time for prisoners.* "Cut him loose. He can burden someone else," he replied. "This one's not our problem."

Abner rubbed his chaffed wrists, glaring up at the humans.

"Sorry, bud," he added in afterthought.

"Not right," Abner mumbled under his breath after he was left behind. "Come back! Don't leave me alone."

The wind echoed his pleas, strangled and broken as it evaporated. Abner caught strange sounds filtering back. The wild horses were gone. Likely as far away from the battle as possible. His friends, no, they were never friends, were off in search of the lycans and, if he was any sort of judge, eagerly searching for him and the sword. Gnomes weren't known for handling stressful situations of solitude with grace despite their penchant for criminal frivolity.

Abner frowned, unsure how to proceed or where to go. Returning to Norman and the others was out of the question. His betrayal put them all in danger. No doubt Uther and Orphan would take his head at the first opportunity given the chance. Bert might offer protection, but he was one person and the sort who went along with the flow. Trusting humans was less than desirable. He knew Sara pretended to care for him, but her loyalties lay elsewhere. Turning him over to Norman was her cleanest option. He shuddered at the implication.

Abner shook the conflicting thoughts away and settled on the only course of action that didn't result in his demise. He set off in the hopes of escape and a chance to reset his life.

"Stop right there, Gruff. We have business to finish." Princess raged at her former pack leader.

She knew they were done. If any of the others survived, they would be fleeing for a safe haven. That left her and Gruff. He was almost at the boat and freedom. With the sword. Determined not to let him get away, Princess cast aside her personal safety. She needed this confrontation. After years of cowering behind his lead, the time had come to step into her own.

Gruff halted, one foot on the dock, and turned. Slow. Deliberate. Hatred poured from his eyes. His wounds were healed, leaving scars and bloodstains. The sword on his back hummed in delight, the sound unnatural to her. "This is our last chance, Princess. One last ride to kill the queen and reclaim our place at the top of the food chain."

"Not until I get my due," she insisted. "We're not done." The sound of humans approaching suggested otherwise but she held her ground.

"I think we are. If I don't leave now, we all fail."

She struggled with the urge to transform and attack. That animal instinct to sink her fangs into his throat and taste his blood. Princess had waited so long, but retained enough composure to recognize the pack was finished. Surviving the night was all that mattered. Escape the island and hunt Gruff down. Become the queen.

The humans were getting closer. The boat pulled away, leaving her ashore.

She turned and ran. A final reckoning with Gruff would come, but not this night.

THIRTY-FOUR

Abner searched the surroundings before stepping into the open. Failing to spy any lycans or, worse, human commandos, his heart slowed. Orphan's boat lay directly ahead, with no sign of anyone. He knew better than to let his excitement get the best of him. So much had gone wrong over the past few months he wasn't leaving anything up to chance. Stalking across the open area, the gnome slipped onto the boat and, giving a backward glance, headed to the controls. It was only then he realized he had no idea how to operate a boat.

The buttons and gauges stared back at him, mocking his ignorance. Abner frowned. Waves lapped against the hull, sloshing a simple rhythm. It was the snap that drew his attention. Abner whipped about, wishing he had a weapon. He spotted nothing. The boat rocking, Abner hurried back to his futile attempt at starting the boat. The cloud cover broke enough to allow hints of moonlight down, bathing the island in an eerie amalgamation of shadow and light.

Frustrated, Abner began flipping switches. He swore he heard laughter. "Whose there? Show yourself. I have a gun."

Stupid! I have a gun. Who says that?

A breeze answered. Judgmental. Mocking.

Abner turned back to the control panel, his actions furious now. A snap of a branch, just out of sight, drew his focus. His left foot began bouncing, gaining momentum until it threatened to tip him over. Abner squeezed back the tears threatening to break free. He slapped the wheel until his hand hurt. "Start, damnit. Why don't you start?"

"Abner."

He froze. He knew that voice. Abner gripped the wheel with both hands and closed his eyes. Dozens of creatures were loose on the island and the last one he wanted to see again had found him.

Trapped, he shuddered. "Go away. I did what you wanted. You have the sword. Leave me alone," his voice was but a whisper.

"Oh Abner, that's not how this works," Princess stepped into view. "You see, Gruff was right. We should have killed you a long time ago. You've caused us more than a little trouble, gnome."

"I did what you wanted!" he repeated, slamming his eyes closed.

"You set us up," she snapped. "My pack is dead. Murdered by your friends, because of you. I'm here to settle a score."

"Whe-where's Gruff?" he asked, fresh fear choking him.

"Don't you worry about that," Princess said. "He's off to take care of his own business. Mine is with you. Before this night is done, I'm going to tear your throat out and watch you die. Even if it's the last thing I do."

Exhaling the breath choking him, Abner forced himself to open his eyes as he threw his arms out to the sides, palms open. "Do it. Get it over with. I've done nothing right. Ever. My whole life has been a lie. I'm a disgrace to my people, my family, and now my friends. Kill me and end this misery," he pleaded. *I'm tired. Oh, so tired of it all.*

Abner watched as hair sprouted over Princess' right arm. Her hand elongated, fingers turned into claws. "This isn't going to be quick. I promise you. I am going to enjoy tearing you apart."

Death stalked closer one slow, ponderous step at a time. He wanted to close his eyes. Wanted to turn and jump into the ocean and let the currents sweep him away. He didn't. He stood there, arms still outstretched, and watched his doom approach.

Princess' head exploded before he heard the shot. Blood, bone, and brain matter fanned out. Smoke poured from the hole. Abner vomited over the side of the boat. He heard Princess' body collapse and heavy boots scuffing to a halt.

"There you are, you little shit."

Abner wished Princess had done it. Anything was better than suffering the wrath of the elves.

Uther and Cecile stepped towards him.

"That's it. The island is clear."

Hasko removed his helmet, running a hand through the thinning crewcut. The others milled about, rechecking their gear and grabbing a snack. They stood in a group, talking quietly among each other while giving the others a side eye. With the mission complete, there was naught to do but await pickup.

"One lycan is unaccounted for," Norman told him.

Hasko shook his head. "My team counted the bodies. They're all dead."

"No, he's right," Cecile added. "Their leader is missing."

"One rogue werewolf isn't a threat. Let him go. We've done what we can here for." Hasko folded his map and tucked it into his utility vest.

Cecile flushed. "There's ah, one more problem. This werewolf has the sword."

"So?" Hasko failed to see the point.

"He's heading for the queen."

"Fuck. Do you know what this means, Cecile?" Hasko asked as the implications set in. "There's no way we can get back to Raleigh before him. He had a head start and we're waiting for pickup by boat." At her grimace he took a deep breath and shook his head.

"But you can't just let him kill her!" Cecile protested. "She's the key to this whole mess. The queen must live."

"There's nothing I can do. We have our orders." He glanced at his men. "I'm sorry. I am, but you know how the agency works. My hands are tied."

His tone softened. No field commander worthy of the name abandoned orders to risk operative lives and careers for emotional decisions. Hasko liked Cecile, but she was an agent under a different command. By the time the request ran through official channels whatever gambit the wolf was playing would be finished. He caught the roar of engines drawing near. Time was up.

"Cecile, we have to go. Our ride is here. I wish we could do more." He placed a hand on her shoulder and gave her a gentle squeeze. To his men, he said, "Ruck up and hit the beach."

The commando team filed toward their transport, clapping each other on the backs and sharing their enthusiasm for completing a difficult assignment.

Hasko waited until the last man was gone before offering a clipped nod to those still watching, his gaze lingering on Cecile a moment too long before he turned away.

"Jim, wait," Cecile's call paused him midstride. "How did you know to come here? I never called for backup."

He turned with a smile. "Home office deployed us. You have an angel watching over you. Stay safe, Agent Barnabas." Hasko offered a lazy wave over his shoulder and hurried to catch up with his team.

"Typical humans," Uther snorted from his seat on a tree stump.

Sara frowned. "Earlier you were complaining about how we didn't need them. Now you're sad to see them go?"

He shrugged. "I'm entitled to my opinions. Doesn't change the fact we're stuck here while the lycan is hauling off to the queen."

Cecile searched and failed to find a way to stop the disaster she saw approaching. She threw her hands up. "What do we do now? Even if we got off this island in time there's no way Bert's van can drive fast enough to get us to Raleigh before that werewolf."

"Hey!" Bert fussed.

Sara patted his arm with a chuckle. "She didn't mean anything by it. Cecile's right. We might as well start a fire and make s'mores. This little adventure has been for nothing."

"I knew I should have ignored you." Orphan Thorne grunted at Sara's glare. "I'm taking my boat and going home. Anyone want to join me?"

"Is there no other way off this island?" Sara asked.

He shook his head. "Nope. No road coming in. No road going out. Looks like I'm your only ride."

"Is my van all right? It's been a long night and I'm worried about it, Sara," Bert said. His forehead sloped over the rest of his face, made larger by his frown and pinched eyes. "It's all I got left."

"I'm sure your van is fine, Bert," she soothed. "It's too far south for us to get to it and get back to Morgen in time though. That's all."

"Oh," he said, clearly not understanding.

"What do you have to say, big guy?" Uther asked.

Norman stood, arms crossed, watching the commando boat shove off. He admired the commandos for their grit and valor but failed to understand them abandoning the quest at this critical juncture. Elfkind was about to collapse and D.E.S.A. appeared to want nothing to do with the inner politics.

"My duty lies to the queen. With my wing damaged I cannot fly. I have failed." He turned to face them, pain and dejection in his crystalline eyes. "We have failed."

Sara rose from the large rock she caught her breath on, moving to their center. "Even if he kills Morgen, we still have an obligation to take him down, or out, or whatever you say. We can't give up now. Don't you see? We've come so far. We have to stop the werewolf and get the sword back. We owe it to ourselves."

"I still have his tracker online," Cecile added. "We'll know exactly where he's going."

"I'm done hunting doggies, lady," Uther said. "Get your DESA boys back and you take care of it. Your government seems to have claim over us anyway."

"That's not true," Cecile protested. The sting of what she took as betrayal from Hasko and the others broke through.

"Seems like it to me. Otherwise, you'd have let me take the gnome's head like I split that lycan's."

Abner stood, glaring. "Do it. Kill me and get it over with! I'm tired of saying sorry. Kill me already! You know you want to. You've wanted to since the moment you saw me."

Uther, an amused look lighting up his face, commented, "He's not wrong."

"Justice will be served, but not until we have retrieved the sword." Norman went to stand beside the gnome. "Our mission is not over."

"It is for me, Norman. I'm going back to Fayetteville and forgetting all about this," Uther announced.

Instead of arguing, the gargoyle remained silent. Enough had already been said.

The thunderclap knocked all but Norman off their feet. As the swirl of dust settled, they were surprised to find the wizard standing among them. His jovial face was twisted by concern. Sheldon looked to each of them, as if taking measure before saying, "I may be able to help, but it will not be pleasant."

"Where were you when the lycan was stealing the sword?" Uther's voice bore a sharp edge. "Could have used a wizard."

Heads nodded. Angry curses were muttered.

Sheldon ignored him. "I can open a portal taking you to where you wish. It won't stay open long, and your journey will only be as clear as the image in your minds. I cannot follow." Sara opened her mouth, but the wizard was already speaking, "No, do not ask why. There are some secrets we must keep. Now, where shall I be sending you?"

Norman moved first. "We are going to the throne room."

"But I've never been there!" Cecile protested.

Sheldon gave her a conspiratorial wink. "Leave that to me, my dear."

Slapping his hands together, Sheldon began the incantation. His eyes rolled over white. Spittle dribbled from his mouth. Space and time fractured. Reality distorted. A hole opened up. Norman nodded his thanks to the wizard and snatched Abner by the collar before dragging him through. Sara, Bert, and Cecile followed.

Sara stopped at the edge of the portal. "Are you coming, tough guy?"

Uther rubbed his chin to conceal the grin. Going back to the queen didn't enthuse him, but it might be his only chance of finally being released from his prison. "Fuck it. Why not? There's still one more wolf left to kill."

The portal closed behind them, leaving Sheldon alone with Orphan Thorne.

"I thought they were never going to leave."

Orphan nodded, staring at the empty space where the portal had been. He yawned, stretching the kinks out. "What do you have to eat around here? I'm starved."

Alone for the first time in decades, Gruff leaned forward and cranked the engine. Wind blew his hair as he roared down the highway. Tonight, he planned on killing the queen and claiming his rightful place in the world.

"You're going to be like all the rest you know."

"Eh? Quiet, sword. You'll drink your share of blood soon enough," Gruff snapped.

"Oh yes. Yes I will."

Gruff drove faster. Time was against him. Tonight, the end of the elves was about to begin.

THIRTY-FIVE

The sword of Grimspire stabbed between the glass doors, slicing down to split the lock. Leering, Gruff sheathed the sword and gently pushed the door open. He waited for an alarm—none sounded. The ignorance of humans never failed to amuse him. He shoved the doors wide and strode into the Wells Fargo Building. With naught but the orange glow of streetlights and a pair of red exit signs to guide him, the werewolf strode cautiously down the hall.

The click of doors closing accented his footsteps. No doubt the queen of the elves had layers of security. He turned a corner and wasn't disappointed. Three figures detached from the shadows, swelling in size and shape. Gruff watched, unimpressed. Moving to the center of the lobby, his right hand dropped to the sword's hilt. A hissing sound echoed deep in his bones. Gruff drew the sword and waited.

Centuries old, the golems were the voiceless defenders of the throne. A last line of defense should all others fail. Made of clay brought from the shores of the Sea of Galilee long before the coming of Christ, they had yet to allow a threat to pass. Gruff didn't care about their history. He needed to get by them and slay Morgen before any more of those pointy eared bastards arrived.

"It's about fucking time someone knew how to use me," the sword hissed. "Kill them all and then I'm going to rip your throat out, wolf."

"First thing's first," Gruff replied. The fur on his neck rose.

He attacked in a blur. The sword sang through the air. Sparks flew with each blow. The golems retaliated. Their hammer fists swung and pounded, desperate to smash the threat and return to the forgotten shadows. A blow clipped Gruff's shoulder, sending him sprawling in the grip of deep pain. The insult aroused his hostility. He rolled, coming up on all fours. Rather than plunging back on the offensive, he waited.

The first golem lurched forward. Gruff rolled forward, coming up between the golem's legs. He hacked and slashed across the backs of both legs and the creature collapsed in a pile of dust as it hit the tile. The werewolf laughed, spurred on by success and the power in the sword, and attacked the remaining defenders.

Morgen paced. Dawn was not far off, bringing the promise of a new day filled with hopes, broken promises, and the end of dreams. Her mind swirled around the news from New York. Xander and her estranged daughter were reported dead, though she suspected the truth was a far cry from the government's explanation. With one problem solved, she ordered the Old Guard to arrest the prime minister for his role in the debacle. A storm followed, but one she found manageable considering the avoidance of crisis.

Since her husband's death, Morgen found her grasp on the clans slipping away. She remained far from panic, despite the walls closing in. Word from the coast soured her mood but she was out of options. A warning alarm told her the golems were attempting to stop an intruder from entering her sanctum. Darkness threatened elfkind and, in this singular moment, she felt powerless to stop it. The ding of the elevator reaching her floor chimed.

She stiffened.

Gruff braced as the elevator doors opened, expecting an onslaught of defenders. Silence greeted him. Thrown off by the lack of security in the heart of the elven kingdom, he stepped into the hallway and waited. He knew elves were notorious tricksters. Sword poised before him, the wolf slowed his breathing, staving off the disappointment threatening to unravel him. Age tempered his thoughts. The idea of slaying the queen while in human form enticed him far more than it would have decades earlier.

He wanted a fight. Needed one. The golems did little but raise his ire. To be met with naught but emptiness evoked a simmering fury long used to keep him at the head of the pack. The others might be gone, but he knew he'd have no trouble raising an army with the sword. Muscles rippling with anticipation, Gruff took his first step into the heart of the queen's realm. Enough playing.

A soft orange glow beckoned. It was the only light on the floor. He made no sound as he stalked forward. No trail of his passing. An empty desk sat on his left before he stepped into the main greeting room. A curved staircase swept upward before him, revealing the heart of Raleigh's skyline through the double story windows behind it. What appeared to be a closed restaurant was on his right, beside a hallway winding deeper into the building interior. A second hall went left.

Gruff sniffed. The air stank of elves and humans, confusing his senses. Having never set foot in the building before tonight, he had no idea where to look. Instincts took over. He took the left hall, sweeping through meeting and dining rooms already set for tomorrow. Empty room after empty room laughed at him, mocking him. With the left half of the floor secure, Gruff hurried back to the other side. He found only locked doors and small meeting spaces, all empty.

Frustration grew, though his mind knew the queen was near. One floor to go. Gruff crept up the stairs, ignoring the view. Upon reaching the top floor he dropped into a crouch. The stench of elves grew stronger. He broke into a grin. He was close. Resisting the urge to taunt his opponent, for trapped as she may be, Morgen was a formidable foe, Gruff stepped into a large room swathed in pure darkness.

"Got you, bitch," he hissed under his breath.

A small light clicked on, shining in his eyes. Gruff froze. "Who is that?" he demanded. "Show yourself before I—"

"Kill me? Chop off my head with your toy sword?"

The voice, female, mocked him. Gruff felt his anger surge. The desire to do precisely what the voice said grew. He had so much to pay the elves back for. The faces of his dead pack haunted him as his failures. Elves and gargoyles wreaked havoc on his mind, reflections of a stifled dream. Here, now, he stood upon the cusp of victory. Ascendence.

"Don't tempt me with a good time," he barked. The sword laughed in his hands. "Come face me and let's get this over with. You've been queen long enough."

More lights clicked on, revealing the entirety of the room for the first time. Gruff twisted his head, throwing a hand up to protect his eyes as his night vision was robbed in a flash of brilliance. Blinking rapidly, he discovered a host of figures arrayed against him. There, by the light switch nearest the exit, was the gnome.

"Idiot, you should have killed him when he had the chance," the sword taunted.

"Shut up," Gruff growled, unsure how his foes arrived here before him. "Gnome! I'm coming for you."

Abner gulped and shrank in on himself.

Standing beside Norman Guilt, Morgen frowned. "Come now, lycan. He's already caused enough harm to us both. Abner will be punished, but not by the likes of you." When he growled again, she sighed. "I'm the one you want, no? Face me and be done with this farce. I have far more important matters to attend to."

"I'm going to savor taking your throne. Maybe I'll keep you alive as a pet once I claim my rightful place," Gruff teased. He found himself impressed with her stature in the face of certain death. *Regal to the end.*

Movement behind drew his attention. He set eyes on the fallen Old Guard, blocking his escape with a pair of swords glowing yellow.

"You didn't think we were just going to let you in without a proper welcome, did you?"

"We don't need to do this," Morgen called, a sliver of compassion in her words. "I'm giving you one opportunity to set down the sword and walk away. None of my people will stop you, nor shall they persecute you after. You will be left to your people. You have my word."

Gruff spat after running his tongue over the insides of his lower teeth. "I think I'll take my chances here. I've already beaten the best of you. The others will die quick enough, just like you murdered my pack."

Morgen stiffened. "This is your last chance. I'll not offer another. My mercy does not extend far, *lycan*. Set down the sword and leave."

Gruff's gaze shifted to each of them. The gargoyle stood, massive and impossible to read. Beside him, the two human females. Useless. Weak. Both struggled not to fidget. Then there was the queen who proved all he'd heard over the years. Tall, resolute. She was the combination of past and future promise. A majesty in more than title—killing her would be a true pleasure for him.

"Nah." The word echoed throughout the room with grim finality.

"Now it's a party!" the sword laughed.

Clutching the sword a little tighter, Gruff whirled and sprung on the Old Guard.

Uther expected the assault and stepped back to absorb Gruff's charge. Swords flashed, clanging in sparks and the screech of steel. They were evenly matched, with a slight advantage going to the lycan in size and strength. Still, Uther was hard-pressed to keep the sword of Grimspire from striking a fatal wound. He caught Abner streaking off as the fighting drew near, leaving the open floor to the two warriors.

Unable to break the assault, Uther weaved. He struck high with his right hand, sweeping the left across Gruff's midsection. The lycan proved too fast. Gruff dropped low, transforming into wolf form under the blows. He bowled Uther off his feet and rumbled past, rising with sword in hand.

The Old Guard drew deep breaths. Tired and sore from the action on Shattuck Island, he was at the end of his limits. Yet failure was not an option: kill the lycan and reclaim his life. He strode toward the towering lycan, launching a series of strikes. His blades moved faster than the eye, morphing into an endless swath of silver with murderous intent. Still the lycan matched him blow for blow.

"It could have been you holding me, *elf*! Now I get to kill you!"

Uther grimaced and redoubled his efforts. He wished the sword had a face so he could break it. Neither side gained advantage. The sword of Grimspire laughed manically with each wing and thrust, adding madness to the scene. Uther's blades hummed with power. They had been confined for too long, forgotten and ignored. The Old Guard broke into a feral grin, at last feeling like his old self. He struck. They clashed with blinding speed. Blades nicked. Steel dulled.

Then Gruff scored the first hit and blood flowed.

A tiny cut, mere inches long and superficial, lanced across the top of Uther's thigh. The elf winced and leapt back before a backswing could remove the leg. Elves might regenerate wounds faster than humans, but no amount of magic had figured out how to regrow limbs. Uther grew wary. He recalculated his attack methods and paused. The lycan proved more cunning than anticipated. Cunning, but not immune to making mistakes—Uther owed him.

Gruff roared in challenge; sword high above his head. Base instincts spurred his actions when he lashed out, kicking Uther in the chest and sending him sprawling. Both of Uther's swords clanged away, out of reach and leaving him defenseless. A gasp from Sara drew his attention. Weaponless, he stood straighter in defiance.

"Enough of this." Morgen scowled. "Norman, finish this."

Blurring into gargoyle form, Norman rushed at the battling duo.

"This is madness!" Sara shouted.

Morgen fixed her with a grin. "Isn't it?"

THIRTY-SIX

Sara's eyes widened as she covered her ears to keep out the deafening roar. The werewolf was the largest she'd seen. A true monster in every regard. Armed with the sword of Grimspire, the monster kicked Uther into the wall with bone breaking force. The elf fell unconscious. Sara watched as Norman sped across the gap, only to twist away before the werewolf cut him in half. Norman continued into the open area before arresting his course and doubling back... Gruff roared as he beat back every assault, whether from sword, claw or magic.

Swing around from behind, Norman struck. The werewolf was faster. He slashed down Norman's chest, sending him careening into the wall. Uther leapt and took a claw to the ribs. At Sara's side, Cecile drew her pistol and emptied the magazine. Bullets bounced off the sword, only a handful striking flesh. The werewolf didn't slow. He barreled toward the queen.

Sara watched Morgen from the corner of her eye. If the queen of the dark elves was frightened, she didn't show it. She braced, ready to meet the charge. A hint of sliver dropped from one of her sleeves. The dagger was curved, ancient. Nothing capable of stopping the werewolf. Then again, madness gripped the world and Morgen was top inmate at the asylum.

"Look out!" Sara shouted and knocked Morgen out of Gruff's path a moment before the sword came slashing down.

Carpet shredded. The sword bit deep into the floor.

Gruff howled in rage and snapped forward—Norman drove into him from behind. They collapsed in a heap of talons and claws. The sword of Grimspire knocked free. Both ignored the weapon, so intent on slaying the other. Norman's talons raked down Gruff's back, tearing clumps of blood mottled fur loose. The werewolf responded by kicking back with a hind leg on the top of Norman's thigh. The gargoyle roared in pain and fell back.

Everything happened in slow motion.

From across the room, Uther had regained consciousness, collected his weapons, and screamed ancient battle cries as he charged back into the fight. Gunfire rang out after Cecile reloaded. Haze from the gunpowder drifted in a small cloud, choking the air. Sara felt the rush of air blowing by, followed by a wave of nausea and she doubled over.

A hand snatched her by the arm, jerking her around until she stared into the enraged queen's eyes.

"Never touch me again," the queen hissed and shoved her away.

Before she formed a reply, Sara watched Morgen storm toward the battle, dagger in hand. The first slivers of dawn broke to the east. The queen's mouth moved but Sara was unable to hear.

Helpless she watched on. *I dare you to come up with a better finale, Daniel. This is nuts.*

Norman absorbed a pair of body blows to the sternum and reeled back. Gruff, refusing to give him room to move, pulled him close and began hammering the gargoyle's kidneys. Blood flew from Norman's mouth. He all but doubled over under the repeated abuse. Gruff punched the gargoyle in the throat, dropping him to his knees. Spinning Norman around, Gruff grabbed him by the wings and pulled. The snapping of bones was louder than Norman's scream.

"NOOOO!" Sara screamed.

The werewolf turned, leering. He kicked Norman to the ground and left him there, as he reverted to human form.

The queen moved and the lycan grinned, motioning her closer.

A blur to the right hammered Gruff, driving twin blades into his chest. He pitched back, his step faltering as the ancient steel plunged deep through organ and bone.

Tears streamed down Sara's face, gaze on Norman. Something broke within her.

"Sara. It's going—"

Sara shoved Cecile away. Fury raged on her face, twisting her features. She stopped and picked up the sword of Grimspire.

"It's about fucking time," the sword said. "Let's kill this thing."

Raw power surged through her, filling every pore and vessel with energy threatening to split her skin. Startled, Sara laughed, feeling invincible in the face of overwhelming odds. The sword sang in her hands.

The werewolf didn't see her coming, absorbed in his fight with Uther. Uther slashed one of Gruff's legs to the bone and swing upward to hack off one of the werewolf's hands.

Weakened and losing blood, Gruff still punched Uther in the face, knocking out teeth. He crawled after the elf when he shifted away.

"Hey, asshole," Sara snapped.

Gruff turned, eyes widening as she drew the sword back and swung with every ounce of strength in her body. The blade sank into his neck, cleaving through bone and flesh to rip out the other side. Gruff's body dropped one way; his head rolled the other.

Sara stood over the corpse in victory, raising the sword high overhead and roaring. Hot blood ran over her hand dripping down her arm to splash on the carpet. Power electrified her. She felt strong. With a thought she could reach out and claim the elf throne for herself. Terrible and strong as the shifting of the world.

Everyone halted.

Cecile stood with mouth agape. Uther hobbled to stand between Sara and Morgen, ready to kill Sara if need be. Or die trying. Rushed footsteps came from the elevators. Queen's guards and more hurrying to defend their ruler. Abner cowered in a quiet corner, arms wrapped around his knees.

"Put down the sword, Sara Thomas," Morgen stated and cleared her throat.

Blinded by rage, and the violent whispers of the sword, Sara took a step toward the queen. She gestured to the body at her feet. "He is no longer a threat—I am. Do you know how easy it would be to kill you all and end your secret reign? To save my kind from your depredations and careless games? This world doesn't need a queen. With this sword I can cleanse the world for generations to come."

"Yessssss."

Morgen's jaw set.

"Uh, Sara, what are you doing?" Cecile asked. "This isn't you. You're not a killer. Just put the sword down and we can fix all this."

Turning, Sara pointed the sword at her. "Why? So, you can have it? Take it back to your precious DESA? I don't think so. The sword is *mine*. No one wields it but me and I choose to wield it now!"

"Come on then. Let's see what kind of claws the little kitten has," Morgen taunted, brandishing the dagger before her.

"No, please God no," Cecile muttered.

Sara clenched the sword, ready to charge. She longed to teach the haughty queen, the architect of so much trauma, a lesson.

"Sara Thomas," a weak voice begged, "do not give in to the temptation of the sword. It will … it will destroy you and all you hold dear."

She looked down to see Norman reaching for her ankle. Sara paused. Reflections of her true self shining in his eyes. "Norman!"

The sword whispered in her mind: *Kill him. He only wants to hold you back. Kill him now and stop his lies. You and I are all that matters. Use me to fulfill your destiny. Become the queen slayer and claim the throne.*

She blinked and moved away from his outstretched hand. *I* ... Norman was the one friend she had among the elves. The voice of reason she needed to find balance through the confusion. Yet he presented himself as an enemy. A foe standing between her and becoming the woman she always dreamed of.

Do it. Kill him. Now.

"Sara," Norman said quietly, grabbing her attention from the sword. His hand dropped, slapping the carpet as his eyes closed.

Now. While he's weak.

Sara shook her head. "Get out of my head!"

Use me. I beg you.

Tilting her head back, Sara screamed. A wave of emotions broke upon her.

I can't. I'm sorry. She collapsed, the sword falling from her hand. Days of stress poured free, crashing upon the emptiness of realization. She fought the urge to curl into a ball and forget the world. She'd seen too much. Done too much. And her soul suffered for it. She looked at Gruff's remains and gagged. *I'm never reading another one of Daniel's books again. I swear it.*

Cecile was the first one to her, wrapping her in a hug. "Shh, it's all right. You did it. You bested the sword. The threat is gone. It's over, Sara."

"Not quite," Morgen said.

The queen of the dark elves stood before them, her face an unreadable mask. She surveyed the room. Blood stained the carpet in several places. A few tables were broken. The lycan had become human again in death. Weak. Insignificant now.

Close by, Norman lay on death's door. Uther was on one knee, struggling to catch his breath as his healing powers kicked in. They were among the best she had. Losing either, despite Uther's self-imposed exile, concerned her. Huddled alone and trembling in the corner beneath a flipped table cowered Abner. She locked eyes with him and knew then he understood all that had befallen them was the direct result of his greed. The gnome turned away.

The humans proved the lone surprise of the night. She changed her opinion of them, seeing them for what they were, formidable allies in an endless war. How best to tell Sara so remained elusive.

At last Morgen's gaze fell on the cause of their trouble. The fabled sword of Grimspire. Venting curses and oaths in every elvish tongue, the sword appeared no more than a piece of angry steel. Whatever hold it had upon them was broken. Cast aside with Sara's rejection. Powerless, the only bit lay in the twisted personality locked within.

"Old Guard, secure the sword," Morgen commanded.

Uther rose and, on shaky legs, hobbled over to retrieve the weapon. When he returned, he handed it to her and said, "I am no longer Old Guard."

"Against my better judgment, your rank and position will be reinstated if you so choose," Morgen explained. "For deeds of conspicuous gallantry this night."

"Thank you, your majesty, but I have much thinking to do before I will give an answer," Uther replied. The faintest hint of a smile crept onto his face.

Morgen accepted the sword in disgust. The vile thing had caused too much pain and heartbreak over the years. She decided she needed to have a word with the wizard. "Aislinn! Bring my phone."

Stifling her sobs, Sara wiped her face. "What did you mean not quite?"

"The sword remains a threat so long as it is loose. It must be delivered to the wizard Sheldon and returned from whence it came. There is no other way." Morgen paused. "I do not expect you to continue with this quest. You have done more than enough. More than I had a right to ask."

Sara's cheeks flushed crimson. "If it's all the same to you, I think I'd like to see this through the end. I owe myself that much."

The queen's eyes lit up, giving Sara pause. The entire adventure she wanted nothing more than to go home and be forgotten. Now, given the opportunity, she passed it up.

"Indeed." Morgen turned to Cecile. "I trust DESA has a vested interest in seeing this matter closed as well?"

"We do," Cecile confirmed, letting her arms unwrap from Sara's hunched form.

Nodding, Morgen focused back on the Old Guard. "Uther, are you fit enough to escort these ladies and the sword back to the wizard?"

"I am."

"Good. I must get my people in here to clean up before the humans arrive for their work shifts. Use the portal. It will take you directly to Sheldon. Do inform him I am most displeased with him and that I shall be visiting very soon."

Uther nodded and took back the sword.

"What about Norman?" Sara felt a fresh round of tears rise as she stared at him. The gargoyle was broken, beaten, and on the edge of death. And for what? A hollow victory in an endless cycle? It didn't make sense. None of it did. "He...I wouldn't be here without him."

"He will recover, though I fear he may never fly again. A shame. He was one of my best," Morgen admitted without emotion. "And one quite fond of you, Sara Thomas. You shall see him again. Go now, finish this quest and return home. You have earned my respect."

Morgen watched the trio limp away, leaving her with the gnome. "As for you, you little shit, we have much business to discuss. In my office. Now!"

Abner squawked and ran to where she pointed.

Morgen stood in place until her crew swept in to clean the room and take Norman Guilt to the infirmary.

THIRTY-SEVEN

Sara tilted her head back and closed her eyes, luxuriating in the warmth of a new day caressing her face. Three days of the impossible transformed her, even while leaving her feeling depleted. The sun rejuvenated her in ways she could never understand and ways she would forever appreciate. The smell of salt in the air took her back to better times when she and her husband would spend days on the beach before having their children. This trip proved far different from anything she had done before. *Can't wait to tell you about this, wherever you are. I hope you're safe.*

Nearby were the others huddled in a group as Sheldon began a long-forgotten ritual. At his side was the forge master, Orphan Thorne, slightly angered at having his card game disturbed. Despite his reluctance to continue working with the main group, the ancient elf was the only one capable of performing the task required.

A flight of pelicans raced by, ignorant of the deeds of elves and men.

"It is time," Sheldon announced.

Opening her eyes, Sara saw the wizard raise his arms to the sky, palms open. Magic swirled in a kaleidoscope of colors seeping from his fingertips. The colors blended in a funnel stretching for the tallest point of the lighthouse. Sara watched in awe. Butterflies rose from the grasses, flitting about the wizard. Birds swooped in to fill the trees, chirping up a storm. Behind them, standing on the shore, the wild horses stopped to watch.

Sara felt, more than heard, a slight song in the air. It pulled at her heart, awakening a peace she hadn't felt in a long time. Her mind and soul settled, calmed by pure bliss. Several butterflies of a hundred colors landed on her shoulders.

Orphan Thorne unwrapped the sword of Grimspire, now subdued and without the sting it once held, and raised it above his head. Tendrils of magic reached down, curling around the tempered steel. The ground vibrated as Orphan released the weapon and stepped back.

They watched the magic lifting the sword higher, concealing it beneath waves of near blinding color. A soft pop and it all disappeared.

The sword was gone.

"That's it? We couldn't have done this from the start?" Sara asked.

"It is done," Sheldon announced with a tight smile. An oppression lifted. New life swarmed back into the land and all was well.

Sara sat back with a smile. She had endured what few humans ever had. Feeling wiser and more experienced, she felt one with the new dawn. The heavy doubts from the past few days were gone, replaced by confidence in her ability to withstand the worst life had to throw at her. She felt ...renewed. *Time to go home*.

Cecile pulled her gaze from the last remnant of color dancing on the air. "Where did you send it?"

"Why would I reveal that?" Sheldon was genuinely surprised, and Sara rolled her eyes.

He'd changed into faded yellow robes with red accents before performing the spell. Despite the flair, he remained the same dour wizard they'd encountered the night before. Sara realized the older the creature was, the less inclined it was to deal with new situations. Wizard. Elf. Human. It didn't matter. The problem with age proved common across the board. She certainly hadn't wanted anything to do with the situation, yet here she was at the end.

"Shouldn't I know?" Cecile asked, pursing her lips. Yet he had a point. They'd run the gauntlet to the end, at the cusp of the fall of elves because Abner Grumman found the sword. Revealing where Sheldon sent it only served to lay the foundation for it to happen all over down the road and open the prospect of lying to her supervisors in Washington.

"No," Sheldon said flatly.

"Fair enough," she replied. "The better question is do we need to worry about it?"

"Oh, not for some time I imagine. Certainly not before your grandchildren are old," Sheldon said. "The sword of Grimspire is no longer in play. Should it become endangered again, I will be left with the unfortunate task of destroying it forever."

Cecile and Sara exchanged a private glance.

"Come the day, wizard," Orphan said with a nod. He headed for the shore where his boat awaited.

Uther watched the elf go, eyes narrowing as he contemplated running a sword through his back. Their animosity fueled him, keeping him warm on cold winter nights. Even though, The Old Guard discovered one inescapable truth preventing him from attacking. He was tired, mentally and physically. The war with the lycans left him drained and, despite the healing magics Sheldon spread during the ritual, he remained depleted.

"Another time," he called out.

Orphan continued walking but raised a hand in a slow wave of acknowledgement before disappearing around the bend.

"Whose going to keep me young now?" Uther rubbed his jaw, lost in thought.

"Bye!" Bert chirped.

The hum of boat engines cranking up was the last they heard of the forge master. Sheldon raised his eyebrows, silently questioning them why they were still on his island.

Sara caught his look and cleared her throat. "I guess we should be going too."

"That would be nice, yes."

Cecile slipped her sunglasses on and offered her hand. Sheldon stared at it without moving. She dropped her hand and stepped back, a smile creeping across her face. "Wizard, thank you for your assistance in the matter. The government is appreciative of your services."

"Indeed," Sheldon replied.

"What do we do now?" Sara asked. "Magic transported us back to the island … We have no way home."

"I fail to see how that is my problem."

Frowning, she placed her hands on her hips. "It's your problem because we can't leave. Unless you have room in your little hidden tower and prefer some company, it's in your best interest to send us home."

Sheldon scowled. He was about to respond when Bert interrupted, "Oh, but what about my van? It's still down at the army fort."

Having no desire for another ride in Bert's pride and joy, Sara said, "Perhaps you could send us in our separate directions? I've done enough sightseeing for a while."

"Aww." Bert hung his head.

Sara opened her mouth but was interrupted.

Uther clapped him on the back. "That's all right, big guy. I'll ride with you." He ignored Sara's smile to add, "Besides, I'm heading to Fayetteville."

"Not Raleigh?" Cecile asked.

"No. I'm not interested in Morgen's offer. Leastwise not yet. I like being on my own. No one bothers me. Or they didn't until you people came along," Uther explained casting Sara a look. "Besides, I need a vacation."

Sara couldn't fault his thinking. She needed a vacation too. Hopefully Daniel would be home by the time she returned. She'd had enough adventure for the time being. Time to go home and be a wife and mother again. Without knowing why, she hugged Uther. He stiffened before returning the gesture.

"You have proven yourself, Sara Thomas. It has been a pleasure," Uther told her. "Wizard, send us back to Bert's van."

Sheldon snapped his fingers and Uther and Bert slowly faded before vanishing. Sara didn't know why, but she felt a piece of her was now gone.

Impatient to be alone, Sheldon asked, "Any particular requests? Or can I just send you back to Raleigh and be done with this? I have work to do."

What sort of work would a recluse have waiting? From what I've seen you haven't been too fond of getting your hands dirty. What changed? Sara hummed. "Raleigh is fine. We can figure out how to get home from there."

"As you wish."

Sara nodded her thanks before turning to Cecile. "I don't know where to begin…"

"You don't have to," Cecile replied. "We were looking after each other. The way things should be. It was a pleasure meeting you, Sara. Your husband is a legend at DESA."

She snorted. *Of course he is.* "Yeah, he should have been here. Not me. Daniel would have done a better job."

Cecile beamed. "Would he? You proved you have what it takes. If you ever need a job, call."

Sara returned the smile. It had been a long time since she felt individual validation. She went to embrace Cecile, but the agent faded away with a wave.

Looking down, Sara saw her own legs losing definition. Sara felt nothing. She was transparent from the waist down before she asked the wizard a final question. "Wait! What did you need the ogre egg for?"

Sheldon's blank stare was the last thing she saw.

He didn't answer.

Wind swirled and a bright flash deposited Sheldon in his inner sanctum. He strolled through racks of unopened scrolls, textbooks, and various lab equipment. A fire warmed his old bones. The smell of coffee laced the air. He hadn't allowed a visitor in centuries but kept his chambers in immaculate condition just in case. Never one for a mess, or to waste precious time cleaning, Sheldon had automated brooms and mops on constant duty.

He stepped around a mop and bucket, pausing to scratch the baby griffon's chin in passing. The creature mewled, craning its neck in enjoyment. Sheldon preferred creatures over elfkind. There was much to learn and no drama. He'd had enough to last him the rest of his life. He hoped he'd done enough to ensure the world remained safe for the rest of eternity.

Sheldon forced the thoughts away and took up a worn chair. The red fabric stretched up from the seat to the dark wooden back capped with caricatures of dragons. He settled in and stared at the table. A glass of wine sat beside a book, dominated by the ornate chessboard taking up the center of the table. Several pieces were in play. A game stretching back decades. There, in the chair across from him, waited his opponent. The ogre egg rocked, changing colors at his arrival.

Sheldon chuckled. "Soon, my friend, we can resume our game. Be warned, I've been studying. You won't find me so easy to beat this time."

Darryl Williams punched his timecard and headed for the breakroom to grab a cup of coffee before heading to his desk. He hadn't slept much since the events in North Carolina began. Worry over a woman he'd never met fueled his paranoia in ways he'd never imagined. Every agency employee understood the job came with a measure of risk, what job didn't, but Darryl's tenure had been as plain as a wall without a painting. He wove his way through the endless blue cubicle maze and plopped down in his chair. The hum of his computer starting almost drowned out the approaching footsteps. He didn't look up, already knowing who it was.

"Hey, Steve," he said as he inserted his ID card in the keyboard and typed in his password. "How's it going?"

"You didn't hear?"

Darryl perked up. "Hear what? I just got in."

"She's gone!" Steve announced, his voice taking a decided munchkin tone. He appeared to be ready to break into song and dance.

Darryl always wondered why the munchkins had a choreographed song and dance rehearsed for when one of the witches died but who could he bring that conversation up with? "Who? What do you mean gone? What happened?"

"Rumor has it Violet got a promotion for sending in a strike team to solve the Carolina problem. I don't know about that, but I do know her office is cleaned out. Nametape off the door." He chuckled. "Ding-dong the witch is dead, my friend."

"Don't," Darryl playfully warned before continuing. "Gone huh? I guess she got what she wanted after all."

"Thanks to you," Steve agreed. "Her promotion wouldn't have been possible without your groundwork. Good job, buddy. You saved us all!"

Steve skipped away with a cheerful whistle, leaving Darryl in shock. He hadn't tried to make Violet look good. In fact, it was quite the opposite. He hated working for her and wouldn't have gone to her if there was any other option for helping Agent Cecile Barnabas. Frustrated by the consequences of his actions, Darryl leaned back in his chair and rubbed his eyes with his palms.

Over. It was over. Violet Meyers was gone. The threat in North Carolina ended. His eyes flew wide as he realized that meant Cecile was home again and unharmed.

He broke into a wide smile. "I guess I did some good after all."

EPILOGUE

Sara collapsed on the couch and let out a long sigh. She sank into the worn cushions, tilting her head back and closing her eyes. For the first time in almost three days, she felt no pressure. Truly. The kids weren't scheduled to return for another few hours, no doubt lamenting the end of the long weekend vacation with Aunt Amanda. The idea of being alone had never sounded better. Unfortunately, the dogs had other ideas. They howled and barked in joy with her return. Tails wagged. Fur flew in tiny clouds. The male bumped into her repeatedly with what was affectionately termed the Berner bump. She'd never been happier.

It didn't take long for her to drift off to sleep. She couldn't recall the last time she'd been up for so long. Hours later Sara woke up to find the sun setting and a pair of dogs anxiously awaiting their dinner. Her stomach growled as a reminder. Wiping the crud from her eyes, Sara stretched and headed to the kitchen. The dogs followed. She scratched behind their ears and rubbed their heads the whole way.

The house was immaculate, not at all the way she left it. Berners shed more than any dog she'd ever known. Owners joked they had two shedding seasons, January to June and July to December. No matter where she looked, she failed to find a single hair. When she stared at the dogs they stared back.

"Impressive," she whistled. "Who did they get to clean up after you monsters?"

Tails wagged.

The click of the front door unlocking tore the dog's away from the promise of full bellies. They raced to the door, barking and howling with glee. Sara smiled despite the noise. She started pulling out ingredients for dinner.

Daniel stepped into the kitchen a moment later, after being bombarded by a pair of excited dogs. Setting his bag down by the couch, he slipped around the island and came up behind Sara to embrace her with a hug and a kiss on her neck.

"Miss me?"

"More than you know," she replied with a smile.

"What's for dinner? I'm starving."

She playfully shoved him back with an elbow. "I'll let you know when I figure it out. I just got home myself."

"Oh yeah? Where'd you go?"

She tensed. "Oh, you know. Taking care of this and that."

"Sounds better than me. You wouldn't believe the things I've seen and done these last few days," Daniel said. Exhaustion weighed his tone down. "I don't know how I'll ever explain it to you. You just wouldn't believe me."

A chime sounded on her phone. Sara paused, looking at a text from Norman stating he was going to be fine after all.

Setting the phone down, Sara faced her husband. "Try me. It couldn't have been as bad as beheading a werewolf."

"Well, there were ghosts and … huh?"

Grabbing his hand, Sara led him back into the living room. "Daniel, we have so much to talk about. I just might have an idea for your next book."

END

Daniel and Sara will return soon in

Of Elves and Men!

Check out these other great series
by
Christian Warren Freed

It is a troubled time, for the old gods are returning and they want the universe back…

Under the rigid guidance of the Conclave, the seven hundred known worlds carve out a new empire with the compassion and wisdom the gods once offered. But a terrible secret, known only to the most powerful, threatens to undo three millennia of progress. The gods are not dead at all. They merely sleep. And they are being hunted.

Senior Inquisitor Tolde Breed is sent to the planet Crimeat to investigate the escape of one of the deadliest beings in the history of the universe: Amongeratix, one of the fabled THREE, sons of the god-king. Tolde arrives on a world where heresy breeds insurrection and war is only a matter of time. Aided by Sister Abigail of the Order of Blood Witches, and a company of Prekhauten Guards, Tolde hurries to find Amongeratix and return him to Conclave custody before he can restart his reign of terror.

What he doesn't know is that the Three are already operating on Crimeat.

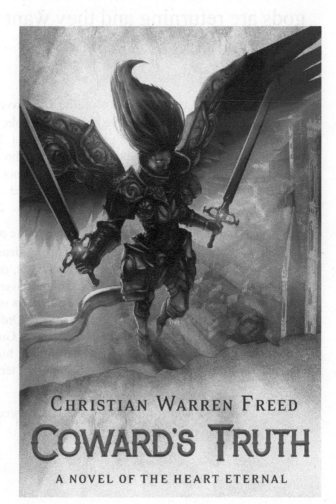

CHRISTIAN WARREN FREED

COWARD'S TRUTH

A NOVEL OF THE HEART ETERNAL

Stranded on a gunpowder age planet, a makeshift squad of space marines must do whatever it takes to survive long enough to be rescued.

They were supposed to be going home. Then the enemy found them. Sergeant Hohn managed to piece together ten fellow soldiers from their doomed ship. Not the best or brightest, the squad crashes on a forgotten world where gods and monsters rule.

Nestled in the heart of the great desert is the Heart Eternal. The city of Ghendis Ghadanaban has been the jewel of all peoples for millennia. But with its reputation comes danger. The city awakens to the murder of their god-king. A desperate crew is assembled to escort the fallen god's essence to the fabled mountain of Rhorrmere where he may be reborn and return to save the city from certain doom.

Time stands against all, for the powers of darkness have gathered. Can Hohn and his people survive long enough for their rescue? Will the god-king be reborn before it's too late?

Find out in the first chapter of the Heart Eternal Saga, a sci-fi adventure combining the best of military science fiction and fantasy. Fans of Star Wars, Dune, David Weber, and Steven Erikson will love this one.

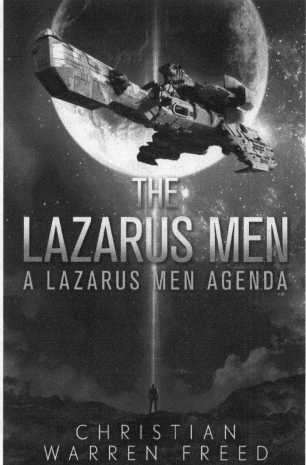

THE
LAZARUS MEN
A LAZARUS MEN AGENDA

CHRISTIAN
WARREN FREED

Welcome to the world of the Lazarus Men.

A thrilling sci-fi noir adventure combining the best mystery of the Maltese Falcon with the adventure of Total Recall and suspense of James Bond.

It is the 23rd century. Humankind has spread across the galaxy. The Earth Alliance rules weakly and is desperate for power. Hidden in the shadows are the Lazarus Men: a secret organization ruled with an iron fist by the enigmatic Mr. Shine. His agents are the worst humanity has to offer and they are everywhere.

Gerald LaPlant's life changes forever the day he accidentally witnesses a murder and discovers an alien artifact in his pocket. Forced to flee, he is chased across the stars by desperate men who want what he has and are willing to stop at nothing to get it. Along the way Gerald meets a host of villains and heroes, each with hidden agendas. If Gerald has any hope of surviving, he must rely on his wits and avoiding the one thing that could get him killed more than the rest: trust.

For he has the key to the galaxy's greatest treasure. Half want him dead. Half need him alive.

It's a race against time to see which wins.

THE CHILDREN OF NEVER
A WAR PRIESTS OF ANDRAK SAGA

CHRISTIAN WARREN FREED

The war priests of Andrak have protected the world from the encroaching darkness for generations. Stewards of the Purifying Flame, the priests stand upon their castle walls each year for 100 days. Along with the best fighters, soldiers, and adventurers from across the lands, they repulse the Omegri invasions.

But their strength wanes and evil spreads.

Lizette awakens to a nightmare, for her daughter has been stolen during the night. When she goes to the Baron to petition aid, she learns that similar incidents are occurring across the duchy. Her daughter was just the beginning. Baron Einos of Fent is left with no choice but to summon the war priests.

Brother Quinlan is a haunted man. Last survivor of Castle Bendris, he now serves Andrak. Despite his flaws, the Lord General recognizes Quinlan as one of the best he has. Sending him to Fent is his best chance for finding the missing children and restoring order. Quinlan begins a quest that will tax his strength and threaten the foundations of his soul.

The Grey Wanderer stalks the lands, and where he goes, bad things follow. The dead rise and the Omegri launch a plan to stop time and overrun the world. The duchy of Fent is just the beginning.

The follow up to the L Ron Hubbard Writers of the Future award winning short: The Purifying Flame, the Children of Never is an all new novel set in a world of raw imagination.

BIO

Christian W. Freed was born in Buffalo, N.Y. more years ago than he would like to remember. After spending more than 20 years in the active-duty US Army he has turned his talents to writing. Since retiring, he has gone on to publish more than 20 science fiction and fantasy novels as well as his combat memoirs from his time in Iraq and Afghanistan

His first book, Hammers in the Wind, has been the #1 free book on Kindle 4 times and he holds a fancy certificate from the L Ron Hubbard Writers of the Future Contest.

Passionate about history, he combines his knowledge of the past with modern military tactics to create an engaging, quasi-realistic world for the readers.

He graduated from Campbell University with a degree in history and a Masters of Arts degree in Digital Communications from the University of North Carolina at Chapel Hill. He currently lives outside of Raleigh, N.C. and devotes his time to writing, his family, and their two Bernese Mountain Dogs. If you drive by you might just find him on the porch with a cigar in one hand and a pen in the other.

Milton Keynes UK
Ingram Content Group UK Ltd.
UKHW042105230224
438358UK00002B/3